ANNEKE'S LEGACY

Barbara Angermeier Malcolm

Barbara Writes

Barbara Writes
Barbara Angermeier Malcolm

Cover designed by Getcovers.

eBook: ISBN 978-1-970552-07-2
Paperback: ISBN 978-1-970552-08-9

Printed in the United States of America

This book is dedicated to my children, David and Ann.
They inspire me to be brave and chase my dreams.

CONTENTS

CHAPTER 1

Lucia answered the buzzing phone on her desk with a terse "Vandersteeg," and her life changed forever. Her eyes strayed to the wind-tossed snowflakes dancing over her skyline view as she listened to the Dutch-accented voice on the other end.

"Ms. Lucia Vandersteeg?"

"Yes, this is she."

"The great-niece of Miss Anneke Boon?"

Her full attention caught by the question; she listened for a moment to the long-distance crackling on the line before she answered. "Grandniece, yes."

"Ma'am, I am Pietr Smit. I have been taking care of your relative's affairs for the past few years, and I'm sorry to be the one who has to tell you, but Miss Boon passed away last evening." Mr. Smit told Lucia that he was an attorney on Bonaire, the small Dutch colony island in the southern Caribbean where her great aunt had lived her whole long life, that Lucia was the sole surviving relative and she needed to come to the island soon to deal with Aunt Anneke's estate.

"Didn't she have an executor?" Looking over the piles of papers, files, and USB drives on her desk, Lucia didn't see herself finding time for a trip to the island soon.

"You are the executor, Ms. Vandersteeg. Nothing can be done without your saying so."

Impatience tightened Lucia's grip on the receiver. "Can't

someone take care of things? I can sign over authority to you, perhaps. You can email me reports."

Feeling that she had solved that problem, she picked up a file from her desk and started flipping through the pages inside. She heard a far-off throat being cleared.

"I can't, Ms. Vandersteeg, I'm sorry to tell you. Netherlands Antilles law is very firm on the subject of estates. The duly appointed executor must be on the island to sign the forms and disperse the holdings."

Her grip tightened again on the phone. "Mr., uh, Smit, is it?"

"Yes."

"Mr. Smit, I am an editor at a medium-sized publishing firm. I have manuscripts to edit and authors to nursemaid. I don't have time to fly off to the Caribbean to deal with a few broken down chairs and chipped dishes. Have a damned rummage sale and take yourself to dinner with the proceeds." She tucked the phone between her shoulder and her ear and applied her full attention to the papers in the file.

"I am very sorry, Ms. Vanstersteeg, but it's more than a matter of a few sticks of furniture and dishes. There is the plantation house with all its surroundings, the contents of said house, a vehicle, and Miss Boon's investments both on the island and elsewhere. Have you visited Bonaire?"

An image of long, dim halls and billowing white gauze drapes filled Lucia's mind, and she sat back in her chair, the file's contents forgotten. "When I was a small girl, I went there with my parents. They died in an accident when I was nine years old, and I lived with my mother's sister and her family from then on. Aunt Anneke was my father's great aunt; we lost contact. So, it has been over twenty years since I was there. Why?"

****

Ten days later, Lucia felt the soft Caribbean night air seep into the over-air-conditioned cabin of the airliner that had just landed her and a group of happy vacationers at Flamingo Airport on Bonaire. She had watched from her first-class seat once she boarded the red-eye flight as smiling face after smiling face got on and turned to find their seats in coach. She had her laptop close at hand and a glass of wine to sip as the jetliner took off into the night sky. Lucia had spent most of the flight bent over her computer, working on a manuscript that was due to be published later that year if only she could convince the reluctant author to consider her recommended changes. Most of her fellow passengers slept during the four-hour flight time, but Lucia only dozed.

Dawn was over an hour away when she stepped off the boarding steps onto the tarmac. Groggy passengers followed her toward the brightly lit, pink-painted building that looked exactly like an island airport should. Lucia was first in line at the immigration counter. She answered the agent's question about the purpose of her visit with, "I am here on business." And she glared at the friendly agent behind the counter when he commented that a woman as pretty as Lucia shouldn't forget to have a little fun, too.

It felt like it took forever for the baggage to be brought from the plane to the terminal, and then it appeared the customs agents were more interested in the mound of boxes accompanying a local man than the tourist's belongings. Most of the other passengers seemed to be scuba divers and were scooped up by resort vans or rental car agents groggily holding up clipboards with names scrawled in black magic marker on sheets of paper.

A blond man who looked to be in his thirties elbowed his way between two of the people holding signs. His khaki shorts and shirt made him look like he was heading out on safari. He appeared wide awake, and Lucia wondered if he'd even been to bed that night. After looking over the tired passengers making their way to their rides, he opened his arms and enveloped a tall, dark-haired woman.

She squealed and said, "Manning, I'm so glad to be here. I've been waiting to see you again ever since we met during Race Week in Antiqua."

His hand slid down her back to cup her bottom. "I've been looking forward to seeing you again too, baby."

It occurred to Lucia that the man, Manning, didn't remember the woman's first name. She wondered how long it had been since they'd met. As she watched, he kept his hand on her butt and, letting her deal with her own suitcase, led her to his Jeep as she chattered about her trip. On his way past her, he gave Lucia the once-over and winked at her. What a creep, she thought.

Lucia stood, arms folded across her chest and one toe tapping. Pietr Smit said he would be there to meet her, but none of the people at the airport appeared to be looking for her. By the time the local man with the excess of boxes pushed his overloaded cart out of the arrival area cursing the customs agents under his breath, all the taxis and resort vans had gone. She could see a few couples still leaning against their luggage in the area in front of the car rental kiosks. Well, what had happened to Mr. Smit, she wondered, and why hadn't he sent word that she would need to get her own transport? Just as she was about to turn to the Security office and ask the agent inside to call her a cab, a man she had noticed leaning against the door of a faded green pickup truck across from the arrival area straightened up and started toward her.

As he neared, he said, "Ms. Vandersteeg?"

Lucia looked him up and down. He appeared to be in his mid-thirties, about six feet tall, and in very good shape. His khaki shorts and chambray shirt were clean and well-worn.

"Yes. Mr. Smit?"

The man stopped, put a hand on his hip, and scratched his ear. "Ah, no, I'm not Mr. Smit. Piet had a water heater roll over his leg yesterday, and his ankle was broken. He can't drive. He asked me to pick you up." He flashed a grin at her that never reached his eyes. "This all your luggage?" He indicated her small suitcase and carry-on.

At her nod, he bent to pick them up, but she stopped him by stepping in front of the bags. "Who did you say you were?" She folded her arms across her chest.

"Now I am sorry, ma'am. I forgot my manners." He wiped his hand on his shorts and held it out to her. "My name is Burke. Winfried Burke, but everyone just calls me Burke."

Lucia felt her hand disappear into his large, warm, rough one. "How do you do, Mr. Burke?"

"Just Burke will do."

"Mr. Burke, I am not in the habit of riding off into the night with strange men. Do you have anything from Mr. Smit introducing you?"

Burke shook his head. "Lady, you are on an island that is twenty-four miles by seven miles. That isn't a lot of geography to get lost in or to hide in. We can drive by my mother's house if you want a character reference; she should be awake, but I doubt if Pietr is awake. I know they gave him some powerful painkillers." He waved a hand at his truck. "Now, I know that this isn't the vehicle you're probably used to riding in, but it'll get you to your auntie's house in good shape. I promise I'm not a kidnapper. Could we just go? Please? It's getting late, and I need to go to work."

Realizing she didn't have any options on this strange island, she gave in and nodded.

"Finally," Burke muttered as he leaned past her, picked up her bags and turned to carry them to his truck. He swung them over the side and into the bed, shoving aside a tangle of fishing poles that stuck up like a cluster of aerials behind the cab. He turned and saw her still standing on the airport side of the lane. "This is not a moat, princess, no crocodiles." He took two steps and opened the front door of the truck for her. "Your chariot."

Lucia stalked over and slid onto the seat. "Thank you, Mr. Burke."

He slammed the door, and she heard him as he walked around to his door. "Mr. Burke, Mr. Burke. I tell her to call me Burke, but no, she has to be all formal. Catch me doing Pietr a favor again soon. He'd better appreciate this." Burke pulled open the driver's door and flashed her a patently fake smile that looked more like a grimace.

Realizing how warm she was in her wool gabardine suit jacket, she slipped it off and put it on the seat between them under her purse. She was surprised to see him put on his seat belt before he drove away, and she scrambled to find hers.

The pair rode in silence. Burke glanced at her from time to time, noticing how nicely she filled out her soft white blouse, which was molded to her by the confining seat belt harness.

Lucia looked around with interest at the neat, colorful buildings and the quaint downtown. All the time they drove north, she could see the sky lightening to her right.

Once they reached the outskirts of town, Burke put his foot down and the truck fairly leaped forward.

"What's your hurry?" she said. "Are you that eager to be rid of me?"

He grinned at her. "Partly. Mostly, I'm late for work."

"What work do you do?"

"I'm a fisherman, and a fisherman needs to get an early start. Your great-aunt's home is far from the airport."

As they drove across Bonaire, the sun was rising on the right. Shadows lengthened across the road, and buildings appeared out of the predawn murk. Lights winked on in windows as people prepared to start their day. Lucia wished Burke would slow down so she could see things as more than just blurs flashing by.

"How much farther?" she asked.

"Plenty," was his terse reply, and she was pushed back into the seat when he pressed his foot harder on the accelerator.

Lucia's right hand crept up to the handhold over the door, and her left hand gripped her purse on the seat between them. "Can you slow down, please?" she said as she felt the rear tires slide on gravel on the pavement.

Lucia was glad when the sun's rays lit their way. Burke was driving so fast she thought they were overrunning the headlights on the narrow and twisting roads. At one point, he swerved to avoid a donkey that stepped out of the brush beside the road, and he glared at her when she gasped. It was on the tip of her tongue to ask him to slow down again when he took his foot off the pedal to navigate a sharp turn at the bottom of a hill.

She could see the glitter of water far below the edge of the road. "Are we that close to the ocean?" she asked, hoping her voice sounded calm and curious rather than nervous.

"Yes, this road is on a little cliff right next to the sea." He glanced at her and noticed that she had a death grip on her seat belt. "Don't worry, Ms. Vandersteeg, I've driven this road for years and never fallen off once." He drove a little further in silence. "By accident, that is."

She turned to face him, mouth open in surprise. "You mean you've driven off on purpose?"

He looked at her out of the corner of his eye and gave a

mirthless chuckle. "Of course not. I grew up around here, and you know what boys are like, don't you? My buddies and I were always jumping off one cliff or another into the sea. Daredevil stuff when we were kids."

"Oh." She turned to look out the window, enjoying the unfolding of the landscape with the sunrise. The road twisted and swooped between the drop-off on one side and the sheer walls that jutted skyward on the other. In places, the walls on the land side moved inland, and Lucia could see the cactus and scrub that covered the land. "It's not very lush, is it?" she said. "Not like a tropical island."

"That's because it isn't. It's a real desert island. We get maybe ten or fifteen inches of rain a year. Not much will grow with that little. And since volcanic eruptions didn't form the island, it doesn't have the rich soil for it either."

She looked at the tortured black rock of the walls and said, "So how did the island emerge?"

"Stop at the visitor center. It's just up the road from your aunt's house, and look at the exhibits. They tell all about the island, but as I understand it, Bonaire is made of an ancient coral reef that was pushed up; it didn't erupt up." He slowed his pickup truck and turned off onto a rusty-looking gravel road that slanted up a steep hill. Around a curve appeared a collection of orange tile roofs atop the ochre stucco walls of a single-story house that sprawled across the hilltop against the pale yellow of the lightening sky. Aloe plants the size of compact cars sent their pointed leaves skyward; many of them had tall blossom stems shooting straight up from the center with soft creamy white flowers clustered at the tip. The rising sun cleared the hill behind the house as Burke pulled up in front and brought the truck to a jolting stop.

"Here we are," he said as he leaped out, ran around to open Lucia's door, then pulled her cases from the back as if they were weightless, and set them on the gravel. "I opened the door before I went to get you. You'll find coffee in the cupboard and milk and such in the refrigerator. You can pay me back later." As he talked, he was moving around to the driver's door, getting in, and starting the engine. She heard the last words as he drove away down the drive.

CHAPTER 2

Lucia stood stunned, watching the only person she knew on the island drive away and leave her out in the middle of nowhere without a way to escape. She watched the plume of dust kicked up by Burke's truck until it dissipated in the still air. "Well, wasn't that nice?" she said. "Looks like I'm stuck here until he decides to come back."

She pulled up the handle of her suitcase and slung her carry-on strap over her shoulder and went inside. The single-story house, as she wandered through it, didn't match up with her memory. At the front of the house, the study and parlor on opposite sides of the hall were small, dim, and crammed with furnishings. Where were the long, wide hallways and the spacious rooms? Had she imagined them? Leaving her luggage just inside the front door, she investigated the kitchen at the back of the house. She poked her nose into the refrigerator to find a loaf of brown bread and a wedge of Gouda. The coffee Burke had promised was in the cupboard. It surprised her to see a modern drip coffeemaker on the counter with a box of coffee filters at its side. There was an adequate bathroom with a tub that looked like it was built for two and a louvered window that overlooked the sweep of hillside down to the sea.

"Wow. For an old lady, Aunt Anneke sure had a luxurious tub."

She checked out the two bedrooms that opened off the central hall, one of which was small and cozy. The other one, obviously the primary and the one Burke had decided she would sleep in, was much larger and had the same view out of its louvered windows as the bathroom.

A tall four-poster bed flanked by narrow slit windows covered with screening that let in a cooling breeze dominated the room. Its crisp white sheets begged Lucia to lie on them. Suddenly exhausted from her long overnight flight and the exciting ride through the predawn, she kicked off her shoes and peeled off her city clothes. She padded to the bathroom; the clay tiles were cool on her tired feet and splashed a bit of water on her face to clean off the travel dirt. After relocating her bags, rummaging for her toothbrush and brushing her teeth, she went happily back to the inviting bed and lay down to rest.

When Lucia awoke, the sun was high in the sky, and the white curtains at the louvered window were still and limp. She rolled over and stretched her arms over her head luxuriously. She raked her fingers through her dark blond hair and sat up, the sheet falling from her breasts. Not remembering where she had left her suitcase, she set out in search of it. The sun shone hotly out each window she passed, but the thick old walls of the house kept the light and heat out. The tiles felt nice and soft on her feet as she paced down the hall wearing only her panties. She found her suitcase on the floor just inside the front door, its top flung back and its contents looking stirred. "Great."

She stooped to close it before rolling it into the bedroom and froze at the sound of a footstep behind her. Not wanting to turn and see Burke staring at her nudity, she said, "Yes?"

To her relief, a female voice answered her. "I don't mean to sneak, miss. You want some coffee?"

Lucia fumbled in the mess of garments in the suitcase and found a shirt that she quickly shrugged into. Tugging the tails down over her bottom, she stood and turned to look behind her. Once her flying fingers had buttoned the last button on the shirt, she folded her arms across her chest. "And you are?" she asked, suspicion tugging down the corners of her lush peach lips.

The woman bobbed a small curtsy. "I'm Susanna, miss. I did for Miss Anneke, and I thought you might need me too."

"Thank you, Susanna. I'll just take my case into the bedroom, and I'd love some coffee." She zipped the case shut, righted it, and rolled it after her down the hall. Once inside the room with the door closed behind her, she pulled on a pair of cotton shorts and replaced the shirt with a tee shirt. She brushed her teeth, swiped a cool washcloth over her face, and ran a comb through her hair. She went barefoot and quickly found her way to the kitchen at the back of the house opposite the front door.

It was Susanna's turn to be startled when she turned at the sound of Lucia's step. The island woman indicated a tray with a sweep of her hand. "I was just going to bring your coffee, miss. You didn't need to chase it down."

Pulling out a chair from the well-scrubbed wooden table, Lucia took a seat, tucking a foot under her as she sat. "It's no trouble, besides this kitchen is homey and comfortable feeling. I was hoping you'd have a cup of coffee with me and tell me about my great aunt, the house, and the island."

Susanna stood for a moment, obviously debating whether having Lucia in the kitchen for coffee was proper, but then she shrugged. The house was Lucia's now, so Susanna supposed she was the one who set the rules. She carried two mugs to the table and poured coffee into each of them. "Would you like milk or sugar?"

Lucia shook her head. "I drink mine black, thanks."

Susanna watched as she took a sip and saw her eyes widen. "Your auntie liked her coffee strong as she got older."

"I would say so," Lucia said with a grimace. "Maybe I should have some milk and sugar in it after all." After stirring them into her coffee, Lucia propped her elbows on the table and held her mug in both hands beneath her nose. The rich smell of the fresh coffee dissolved the cobwebs from the lack of sleep the night before.

Susanna watched her with a mixture of interest and insecurity as to what would happen now that the old lady had died.

Lucia slowly sipped her coffee, her eyes unfocused, and a small smile played on her lips. When the mug was half empty, she blinked and focused on the woman across the table from her. "So, Susanna, what can you tell me about my great-aunt?"

Susanna was surprised. "What do you mean? She was your aunt. Surely, I can't tell you much about her."

Lucia set her mug down. "Actually, I only met Aunt Anneke once when I was a tiny girl. My parents brought me down here when I was about five years old. I remember running down a long dark hall, sitting in a room with white curtains blowing in the breeze, and a very proper old lady." She gazed off into the distance as if trying to dredge up more, then shook her head. "My father's business got more demanding after that, and then the summer before my ninth birthday, both my parents died in a boating accident."

Susanna reached out and softly touched Lucia's hand. "I'm sorry. It must have been hard."

For a split second, the pain of that long ago summer was visible in her stormy blue eyes. "Thanks, but it was a long time ago." Lucia smiled. "Since Aunt Anneke was my father's aunt, and I was sent to live with my mother's sister, after a few years I lost touch with her. That I had a relative living on Bonaire got kind of pushed into the back of my mind. I hadn't given her a thought for years when Pietr Smit called ten days ago. So, tell me about her."

Susanna sipped her coffee, set the mug down, and

smiled her own smile of memory, thinking about the old woman she had been employed by for years. "Miss Anneke was quite the woman. I guess when she was younger, she ruled this plantation with an iron fist. The elders say that was why she never married. I thought it was because she had her heart broken when she was young and never got over it."

"Susanna, you're a romantic," Lucia said.

"I suspect I am, Miss, but I liked Miss Anneke. She was always nice to me, treated me like a real person."

"Don't most people?"

A look like she had revealed too much slid across Susanna's face before she got control again. "When a girl makes poor judgments, sometimes people treat her differently. Miss Anneke said she had made her mistakes when she was young too and didn't hold grudges. It made it easy to work for her."

Lucia decided not to pursue questions of mistakes, Susanna's or Aunt Anneke's, and said, "Tell me about the plantation."

"The plantation called Karpata used to cover this whole end of the island," Susanna began. "Miss Anneke's father and grandfather were granted the land the house is on and a few more acres, but they bought the rest bit by bit until there was no more to buy. My grampy said the government stopped Mr. Boon from buying more, so he didn't own the whole island one day."

"Nice."

"Now all that's left is the one dock that Burke ties his fishing boat to and the old boathouse where he lives."

Those words jerked Lucia to attention. "Burke lives here?" she said. "Where?"

Susanna pointed toward the front of the house. "Down by the shore. If it hadn't been so dark when you got here this morning, you could have seen the roof of the boathouse just before you turned into the drive. Didn't Burke tell you he lives here?"

"No, he didn't. Actually, he didn't tell me much, just drove up here like he was trying out for Le Mans, dumped me out, and sped away hollering something about being late for fishing." She shook her head. "How can you be late for fishing? Aren't the fish just… out there?"

Susanna laughed at the quizzical look on the younger woman's face. "Burke has contracts with several resorts and restaurants to supply their fish every day. Fishing is his business, his livelihood."

Susanna was nearly unstoppable once she got started talking about Anneke and the history of the plantation. Lucia learned about the families who used to live in the row of huts off behind the garage and the ships and crews who docked at the shore and loaded the cargoes of salted hides and aloe. The two women laughed and talked until the light from the sun creeping down the hall from the front of the house reminded Susanna of her duties.

"Oh, Miss Lucia, I should not have been talking so long. You need to settle in, and you haven't had a bite to eat." She jumped up and stood frowning at Lucia. "What Miss Anneke would say if she knew, I could only imagine."

Lucia put out a hand to stop her from getting too upset. "It's no big deal. I rarely eat breakfast, and I can find my own lunch." She stood too. "Aunt Anneke will never find out you sat with me for an hour. I promise I won't tell." She went down the hall to her bedroom, picked out some clean clothes, and went into the bathroom for a shower. Even though it was cool in the house, she kept the water tepid. Her breath hissed through her teeth at the delightful torture as the cool water trailed down her heated skin. She washed her hair and luxuriated in the freedom of not having to hurry out of the shower and dress for work.

After a light lunch of a delicious salad made for her by Susanna, Lucia spent the afternoon exploring the house. She was surprised over and over by how small the rooms were, indeed by how small the entire house was compared to her fuzzy childhood memories.

In a desk in the study, she found a stack of ledgers and account books that looked as if they dated back to when her great-great-grandfather bought the land from the island government. When she opened the first one, she was glad she had insisted on hanging on to one part of her father's legacy and studied Dutch in college, even spending one summer in Utrecht working in a publisher's office to understand the difference between American and European practices. She barely noticed when Susanna came into the room in the late afternoon with a pitcher of iced tea for her. Lucia nodded her thanks and kept on reading.

The drawers of the desk in the study yielded the most current information about Anneke Boon and the up-to-date workings of the plantation. According to the legal papers and the map attached to them, it had been reduced to the small plot of land the house stood on, the strip of driveway, and a bit of shore where the boathouse stood with its attached docks. Digging further through the desk, she found a document that said Aunt Anneke could live in the house until her death and then the island government would pay the estate fair market value for the land and buildings and be incorporated into the national park that surrounded it.

One of the most recent letters was from a speculator named Jack Spencer. He'd tried to buy Karpata with an eye toward developing the land into a modern estate. His plan was to build a big house on the footprint of the boathouse and another on the foundation of the current plantation house. Clipped to his letter was a copy of one from Pietr Smit saying that the government had the right of first refusal on the property. She found follow-up letters from Spencer becoming increasingly insistent as time went on. He encouraged Aunt Anneke to overturn or disregard the agreement she had with the government and sell to him. In each letter, he upped the price he offered for the land. Each letter was accompanied by another one from Pietr Smit reiterating that Miss Boon was uninterested in developing the land no matter how much money he offered. The final letter from Smit carried just one word—NO. Lucia smiled to see that even Pietr, that polite and patient man, had his limits.

Another letter was from a man named Dax Manning, offering Anneke an opportunity to invest in the hunt for a sunken treasure ship. Mr. Manning claimed he knew of a shipwreck off the northern shore of the island, and he needed a little "seed money" to get the search off the ground. In the letter, he referred to the gold doubloon he sent along as evidence of his past treasure hunting success. Pietr sent a polite letter saying that Miss Boon was not interested in such a speculative investment, but she appreciated him thinking of her and thanked him for the doubloon. He posted that letter the day before Aunt Anneke died, so Lucia wondered if there was a gold doubloon hidden somewhere in the desk or study. Lucia also wondered if there could be two men named Manning on the island or if the letter writer was the man who winked at her at the airport when she arrived.

The sun was low on the horizon, and the light in the room had faded to a pale orange. She reached to turn on the lamp that stood on the edge of the desk when she heard a man's voice echo from the back of the house. A shiver ran up her spine at the thought that it might be Burke. Oh, get a grip, she thought. She had spent barely an hour in the man's company, and he hadn't seemed the least bit interested in her. He had dumped her out at the top of the driveway and left her there. She forced her gaze back to the desktop and the sprawl of papers across it. It was harder to force her concentration back when she kept being distracted by the murmur of voices, male and female, blending and dipping, that came from the rear of the house.

Lucia had started with the most recent ledger, the one kept by Aunt Anneke, and she'd learned more of her father's family history than she had ever known.

Susanna came to the door and cleared her throat. "Excuse me, Miss Lucia, but there is a telephone call for you."

Lucia put the book down, sliding a piece of paper in to keep her place. "A phone call for me? I wonder who would call me. I didn't give out the phone number to anyone in the States."

"It's the attorney, Pietr Smit, Miss."

"Oh right. Where's the phone?"

Susanna took Lucia to a small table in the front hall, where an old-fashioned rotary phone rested on a doily, the receiver lying alongside it.

"Hello?" she said.

"Oh, good, you made it," said the familiar voice. "I'm sorry that I couldn't pick you up at the airport this morning, but I hope Burke explained I broke my ankle the other day and can't drive."

"Yes, he said that you had an accident. I hope that the break isn't too bad and that you aren't in much pain."

He chuckled. "The break is bad enough, but I have pain pills that are doing a good job, and I should be up and about in a few weeks. In the meantime, there is Miss Anneke's car that you can use. Well, it's yours now, and I'm sure that Susanna and Burke will give you good directions to the market and town."

She sighed. "Oh, good. I hoped that there was a car that

I could use. The house is so far out in the country, and there don't seem to be any buses or taxis around. Susanna uses a scooter, but we need something bigger for grocery days. Where is the car?"

"I had the garage mechanic pick it up last week to go over it to make sure that it's safe for you to drive. It has been a few months since Miss Anneke drove it, and I wouldn't want you to get stuck out in the countryside."

"Thank you, Pietr," she said. "Do you think he will deliver it, or will I need to go into town to pick it up?"

Pietr cleared his throat. "Perhaps Burke will drive you to the garage."

"When he's not fishing."

"He fishes only in the early mornings. Later it's too hot for the fish."

"Yes, he let me know in no uncertain terms that picking me up this morning and bringing me all the way out here was a big inconvenience."

"He did? He told me just now that he was happy to do it. And his boat is docked at the coast, right at the end of your driveway at the plantation boathouse."

"Maybe I rubbed him the wrong way when I asked him to slow down. He drove so fast and recklessly."

"Well, yes, he drives like there is a devil on his tail. I'm sorry if he frightened you."   Lucia looked around for a chair to sit on and ended up sitting on the floor next to the telephone table. "He didn't frighten me, not exactly, but it was a hair-raising ride across an unfamiliar island in the dark."

"Burke lives in the apartment above the boathouse belonging to the plantation just across the shore road from you, so he knows the way. The docks have been there for hundreds of years, ever since there were sailing ships calling to collect the aloe and hides."

She pulled her knees up and rested her elbow on them. "So, I'm his landlord? Does he pay rent on the apartment, boathouse, and dock?"

"No, not exactly. Burke's father and grandfather had an agreement with Miss Anneke. They provided her with help to maintain the house and grounds for the use of the docks. Burke moved in when his father passed to carry on the help."

"Interesting. I wonder whether he would like to buy it. That would give me one less thing to deal with in settling the estate."

There was a longer pause, and his voice was not as confident. "If you recall, the government of Bonaire had an agreement with Miss Anneke. She donated the land for the park and could live there until her death. With her passing, the land reverts to the island government. That includes the property that the boathouse is on."

She sat up straight. "Oh, I remember you saying something about that. How long do I have before the government comes and kicks me out?"

"I don't think they're in a hurry, but they know you have just arrived. In a few days, we should sit down together, and we can plan how to handle things."

"So, I don't have the sale of the house and lot to rely on to help settle things. Will it be expensive to get things in order? I'm not a wealthy woman."

"But Miss Anneke was. She was a very savvy investor, and her holdings are one of the things we need to go over. I am afraid that I'll need to ask you to come to my office for our meeting. I won't be able to drive for quite a while, but I'll hobble to the office in a few days."

"In that case, I'll need the car. Please call the mechanic and ask if he can deliver it. I'll be glad to have wheels. I don't want to depend on Burke. The other question I have is about Susanna. Do her wages come from the investments? Do I need to pay her myself?"

"No, no, there is a fund for household expenses, and Susanna's wages are a part of that."

"Oh good, I would hate to have to tell her not to come back." The scuff of a shoe alerted Lucia that there were other interested ears in the house.

CHAPTER 3

At that latitude, night falls with a suddenness that can take your breath away. Dusk is short that far south, and night pulls its blue-black veil over the sky with haste, almost as if it had something to hide. That winter, the night wind was busy elsewhere. It left behind a few puffs to rattle the palm fronds a bit, but most of the time, the air lay still like a damp blanket over the island. In the silence, the noise of small waves tickling the shore sounded like an intruder. Men were urged out of bed to investigate by women sure that someone was in the house. He would find no one and then stand on the porch in the clinging night, smoke a cigarette to keep away the mosquitoes, and watch shooting stars fall into the sea.

The oppressive heat and humidity affected every facet of life on the small island. Known for its hospitality to residents and tourists alike, tempers shortened and tongues sharpened. Friends turned away from friends when they met on the street or in the market. Tourists trailed back onto their cruise ships tied up in the middle of town, having bought nothing in the craft market set up for their benefit near the dock, telling each other that the next island would be better.

Sam and Maxi had flown in a week earlier, planning to stay at least a month, and the entire season if their money stretched. They had checked with the booking agent for their bungalow to make sure it was available and had even paid a premium rental for the first month as an incentive for her to steer prospective renters away. They didn't care that there was no wind, and it was hotter than Hades. All they planned to do was scuba dive, lie in lounge chairs with rum punches in their hands, read, and nap.

****

Lucia had just broken up with her long-time boyfriend, Rob. He had been jealous and controlling, and she finally had enough. They met in college and had an instant connection. Lucia had few women friends and no guy friends in school, so Rob was fine until she got her job and had male co-workers. He quizzed her endlessly about it, what they said, what she said, until she wanted to scream. She put up with it for a while but had recently broken it off. The need to come to Bonaire to settle Aunt Anneke's estate seemed like a divine intervention. Just when she needed an escape, one presented itself.

****

The next morning, Lucia was up early, and she was hungry. She usually skipped breakfast at home, but on the island she awoke ravenous. She put on her robe and padded barefoot into the kitchen to make coffee. Not as strong as Aunt Anneke liked, but not weak either. While the coffee brewed, she toasted a slice of the good brown bread Burke had left for her and cut a piece of Gouda to have with it. She needed to go to the store to get some yogurt and fruit. The toast popped up just as the last flurry of gurgles signaled the end of the brew cycle. Good timing, she thought. She poured herself a mug of coffee and carried it and her cheese toast out the front door to look at the ocean while she ate.

Once she had dressed, she went into the study to explore the most daunting part of her inheritance. Piles of old ledgers were stacked on dark wood shelves, and invoices, bills, and other business papers stuffed the desk drawers. She supposed she'd have to go through it all one piece at a time. The desk sat in the middle of the room, facing the windows that looked out to the sea and positioned where the breeze could cool the room.

"I might as well get started," she said to herself, and

pulled out the desk chair.

She sat there all morning paging through ledgers that detailed decades of the plantation's business. Seeing bills of lading for shipments of hides and aloe from before the turn of the last century brought mental images of sailing ships and powerful men hauling bales of cargo onto them to her imagination. In the oldest ledgers, mention of the price paid for slaves to work on the plantation made Lucia sad and embarrassed to read that part of her family history. She wondered how many of the people she saw on the island were descendants of Karpata's slaves.

Lucia found some old black and white pictures of the plantation house and a group of people, all white. She went into the kitchen and asked Susanna about them.

"That's Miss Anneke when she was young, there." Susanna pointed at a woman in a light-colored dress, with her hair drawn up on top of her head. "Those people are the families of the other plantation owners. At one point there were six other plantations on the island, all at this end, and as those families died out or moved, the Boons bought them up before the government gathered the money. Every inch was planted in aloe, and there was a village of houses—well, more like huts really—for the slaves and then later the field workers to live in just behind the house here. Once slavery was over, it was too expensive to pay all the laborers, Miss Anneke said, and battle the rain gods to keep the crop alive. So, little by little, they sold off the plantation."

"That bit up by Playa Frans, her papa sold to the oil refinery folks for the tank farm and the biggest part Miss Anneke sold to the island government with the understanding that they keep it a national park and not let developers get their hands on it. Old Mr. Boon had sailing ships, a fleet of them, to take the crop to market." The housekeeper went back to her work.

Soon Susanna set a plate with a sandwich and a handful of chips at her elbow. "Sorry to interrupt, Miss Lucia, I thought you might be getting hungry."

"Is it lunchtime already?" Lucia looked around, having been lost in mental visions of days gone by.

"Yes, miss." Susanna pushed the plate closer to Lucia's hand. "You need to remember to eat. Miss Anneke forgot to eat when she was reading those ledgers, too. I think she was reliving the old days when she did."

"It's fascinating. I can imagine what it was like in those days from the notes in these books. I wish someone had written the names of the people on the backs of these pictures. In these books, there are names and places I've never heard of. Parties they hosted and people they loved. Although it distresses me to think they owned slaves." She put down the heavy ledger and pulled the plate closer. "Thanks for bringing me lunch."

Hours later, the male scent emanating from Burke caught her attention before she realized he was standing in the doorway. His voice was like warm honey when he said, "Susanna asked me to bring you a drink." He set a glass of lemonade on a coaster on the desk. Her fingers slid on the old leather binding of the ledger she was holding.

"Oh, I didn't hear you." Her hand smoothed her hair, and she sat up straighter. "How was your day?" she asked. "Was the fishing good?"

He laughed. "Afraid there won't be any fresh fish for you? I already gave Susanna a nice piece of snapper for your supper."

"No, I was just asking how your day went. I don't care about supper." It embarrassed Lucia when her stomach gave a loud rumble. She hadn't realized how hungry she had become.

****

Within a month, Burke was tired of the heat and calm.

The ocean had lain down, and though the water was clear, it just let the sun beat down and drove the fish into deeper water or into holes in the reef. He intended to invite Lucia to come with him someday. Burke thought she would enjoy some time on the water, and he also thought she was spending too much time with Pietr Smit in his office now that his broken ankle was mending. He was limping, used crutches to get around and, as far as Burke could see, he was playing it for all it was worth while he was around Lucia. Burke was not at all convinced that settling Miss Anneke's estate involved as many meetings and private conversations as Pietr and Lucia seemed to have. He asked Susanna if she knew what went on in those meetings that were held in the plantation house, but she just laughed at him.

"I think that you have too much interest in Miss Lucia, Burke. Maybe you had better pay attention to your work and a woman more your type." She arched her eyebrow at him and sashayed away, making sure he was aware of the generous arc of her hips.

He knew Lucia spent most afternoons swimming off the beach next to the boathouse, and he also knew that she tried to be back at Anneke's house before he came home from delivering his catch to his customers. Burke didn't know why she avoided him. He didn't think he had done anything to offend her, but then he was not very experienced with American women, unlike some men he knew. He thought it showed a lack of self-respect to hang around the resort bars and try to pick up a rich or lonely tourist woman and see how much money could be wrung out of her in a week. Even that casual attitude toward sex was distasteful to him. Not that he was a prude. He wasn't a virgin, not by a long shot, but he didn't feel comfortable with casual sex where the couple didn't even know each other's last names and had no real interest in each other as people. They were just interested in having a warm body to hold on to for a night or a notch in their belt for another conquest.

Burke had seen the American guy Manning cruising the waterfront looking for women. He drove the *Baca di Amor* water taxi a few days a week, and the rest of the time he sold himself for a meal or a tumble. For a while, a few months at most, Burke knew Manning had worked as a divemaster for one of the dive boats working out of the Plaza Resort, but he had heard that Manning was accused of flirting too much with a guest's wife and fired. Burke had spent a couple of evenings listening to Manning talk about his methods, and Burke found him disrespectful of women and too easily dishonest. Now it looked like Manning had hooked up with that Rasta fool Bunny, playing his errand boy. He had also heard from one of the other fishermen that Manning was running a shipwreck scam with one of the Venezuelans, named Santiago. Burke had met Santiago and thought he was an okay guy but was too willing to take the easy way to a goal. Burke believed in hard work and giving honest labor for honest pay, so he had little patience with sly men who worked the angles and preyed on the gullible.

Manning's scam couldn't be too complex, or Bunny wouldn't be of much help. Bunny was a good sort, but he had been smoking weed for too long and too often, and his grasp of reality was loose. Bunny spent a few days a week leading tours of the Arawak Indian inscriptions in the caves near Spelonk, and Burke would have liked to find the time to go on one. He bet that Bunny's commentary and the answers he gave would be worth the price for imagination and creativity alone. That day, Burke had quit fishing early. He was lucky enough to hook a dorado, so he came in, cleaned and filleted his catch, and delivered it to his client's restaurants.

****

Up on the slope above the drop-off to the sea on the north end of the island, Lucia Vandersteeg was learning just why her ancestors had built their house where and how they had. At first, it disappointed her that the plantation house was not a tall white edifice with columns and open, spacious rooms inside. But since the wind went away, she understood why they had built the squat single-story house with thick stucco walls. The low roof and wide eaves kept the windows shaded when the sun beat down in the middle of the day, the thick walls kept in the night's cool, and the windows caught what little air was moving.

Lucia would sit on the porch in the evening, watching the sun sink into the ocean and thinking about all the generations of Boons who had lived there before her. Over the last month, she'd read through many of the ledgers Aunt Anneke had meticulously kept in order during her years running the plantation. She had even downloaded the Rosetta Stone language app to brush up on her Dutch so she could read the earlier ones kept by her grandfather and great-grandfather.

Happy to be in the shade, she listened for what she thought of as the sunset breeze to blow. No matter how still the day had begun, when the sun had totally sunk below the horizon, a light wind blew from the sea. Usually. For the last week or so, there had barely been a puff to rustle the leaves of the flamboyant tree next to the porch. Lucia was glad that the position of the house captured and magnified even the tiniest breath of breeze.

She watched the ocean a quarter of a mile below, wondering if Burke had returned while she was in the house looking for more information on the history of her family. She knew that if he were in his little apartment over the boathouse, she wouldn't risk going down to the rocky beach for a swim.

Ever since arriving on the island four weeks ago and being so unceremoniously dumped here by Burke, she had tried to avoid him. It hadn't been easy in the beginning while Aunt Anneke's lawyer, Pietr Smit, was recovering from a broken ankle, which made him unable to show her around or help her settle her aunt's estate. That threw her into constant contact with Burke. Lucia understood Burke was the logical one to show her the island and give her advice since he had known Aunt Anneke all his life and lived in her boathouse, but he was too… too defensive about it and much too superior acting for her ever to feel relaxed in his company. He laughed at her because she expected what he called "big-city time" to apply to the island. It had taken her a while to adjust to island time.

Susanna had tried to help her, had taken her to the shops and the markets, trying to calm her when it took stops at four different food stores and two mini-marts to fill a short grocery list. In the beginning, Lucia had stormed out of the third grocery store to sit fuming in the car while Susanna went up and down each aisle, looking in shadows and corners to see if she could find what she was looking for. Many times, the item they sought was nowhere to be found on the entire island, so they had to adjust the menu or do without.

Lucia felt like they had struck gold the day they went to La Portuguesa, a fruit and vegetable market out on the south Nikiboko Road. Susanna smiled like the tiny store was a treat she had been keeping for a particularly frustrating market day. La Portuguesa had pineapples, oranges and mangoes, all the things they needed to make a huge bowl of fruit salad. Plus, plantains and carrots and chayote, vegetables to serve with the snapper filets Burke would bring home for supper.

Lucia always corrected herself, even in her mind when she thought things like Burke bringing things "home." She didn't want to get into the habit of thinking that Burke lived with her. Burke lived near her. It was a very sharp distinction, and one she intended to keep foremost in her mind.

****

That night Lucia lay awake, straining to hear a breeze. She had found a fan in the corner of the storage room off the kitchen, but something had chewed the plug off the cord, so it was of no use. She would have to see if Susanna knew an electrician who could fix it. She had opened all the windows when the sun went down, hoping to catch a breeze, but not a breath was stirring. Lucia left the bedroom and went out onto the porch to stare out at the ocean. The moon had risen and painted the tops of the little wavelets a bright white and made a trail across the water that pointed to her. She was tempted to walk the hundred yards down to the beach and slide into the water to cool off, but she was still nervous about being outside alone at night. Golden light shone from one of the boathouse apartment's windows, so she knew Burke was awake. It made her feel better knowing he was there. She wondered if he looked up at her house sometimes to see if she was home and awake.

Some letters of Aunt Anneke's she had found in the bottom of an old trunk were from a man who signed his letters Burke. The tone of the letters was intimate, almost love letters. In one of them, Burke was inviting Anneke to a party at his home. She wished she could have been there to see the dresses and the decorations. He had to be related to her Burke. She felt a blush rise in her cheeks at the thought of Burke being hers. He was not hers, and she didn't think she wanted him. Even though he was handsome and strong and a hard worker, everything she'd wanted in a man since she was a kid. When she was in college, she had refined her wants, narrowing the parameters so that fewer and fewer men fit in. She had dated men who fit into her professed frame, but none of them were right. She could see now that they were too involved with appearances and not living.

Burke lived. He had a lusty appreciation of life and seemed to accept it as it was. He didn't exhaust himself trying to shove the rest of the world into a mold. Burke lived his life and sidestepped the things that made him unhappy. Take fishing, for instance. Susanna had told her a few days back fish didn't bite in hot still weather like they were having, and yet every time she saw Burke he was smiling and cheerful. He didn't grouse like a lot of men she knew back home, didn't cast about for someone else to blame for things that were out of his control or for things that were in his control that he had screwed up. Pass the buck, pass the buck. That should be the motto of the new millennium, Lucia thought.

****

Burke hated it when the wind died for days, like it had this winter. The water lay down, and it looked like his boat, the *Miss Ana,* was suspended in the air above the sandy bottom. Being out on the water with the sun beating down and no wind was like sitting under a broiler. Even the fish seemed to feel the heat. They lay in the shade of the reefs and waited for their food to swim by. Very few were out on the prowl even in the early dawn, when he could almost guarantee fish to catch. Every day he went farther and farther offshore to find fish, hoping for dorado but settling for wahoo and snapper. His restaurant customers had complained, and not good-naturedly either.

Everyone's temper was short these days. Most nights when he stopped at Karl's after supper for a beer, there was a fight, or at least a shoving match. He had heard more profanity on the streets of Playa lately than he had heard in the last year. Husbands and wives whose marriages he knew were happy and stable were fighting in the middle of the market. What used to be boisterous groups of young men parading up and down the front street, ogling the girls and posing to show themselves off, had become street gangs. They shouted at each other and threatened tourists coming out of restaurants in the middle of town. Burke wanted to take them aside and warn them they were scaring away their own bread and butter, but he remembered being their age and hating that making his living depended on the whims of thoughtless tourists.

Burke had also taken to spending the evening in town. He was too eager to stroll up to Miss Anneke's old house to see what Lucia was doing, to see if she needed a little company. A few times he had seen her down on the little rocky beach next to the boathouse with her straw mat trying to get comfortable, then giving up and going in for a swim. He admired the long, lean shape of her knifing through the water and was tempted to go down and join her, but he knew somehow she would not appreciate the company. She was a hard one to figure out, Ms. Lucia Vandersteeg. Not at all like the other young American women he had met at Karl's Beach Bar over the years. Lucia had the same confident look of entitlement that all Americans wear, but she also had the cool Nordic look of her Dutch ancestors and the hint of a deep-down passion that he longed to ignite. But then he thought that igniting that woman's passions could be dangerous and nearly fatal.

He looked out the wide windows that faced the western horizon and spied Lucia's long, lean form slicing through the waves. With the sun in his eyes, she looked nude, and he spent an entertaining few minutes imagining being out in the water with her, but when she turned back toward shore, he could see the straps of her suit across her shoulders.

"Too bad," he said, chuckling at his response to the thought of Lucia naked. He shook himself and stepped away from the glass in case she should glance up and get angry at him again for spying on her. She seemed to get angry with him almost every time they met. Lately, he had been trying to time his visits to drop off fish so that he saw only Susanna, but he was successful less than half of the time. On an island this small, it was too much to hope that Lucia would find things to occupy her away from home. She had been on the island for over a month and was still very involved in learning the history of her family and dealing with the legal aspects of settling Miss Anneke's estate.

CHAPTER 4

After six weeks on the island, Lucia supposed she should be glad that Pietr Smit had recovered enough to hobble around with crutches. Now she had his help to navigate the shoals of Dutch bureaucracy rather than trying to do it all herself as she had when Pietr could not get around. Most of the people she tried to see didn't speak English, or couldn't be bothered to, so her trips to the government offices had been frustrating and unproductive.

She knew that she and Pietr made a striking couple, both of them were tall and slender and blonde, but she must have had some ancestors from warmer climates because her skin was gaining a warm caramel tan instead of turning bright red as Pietr's did. Lucia had bought a big hat to wear when she was outside, trying to keep her face from looking like an old wallet. She felt silly covering up to go out and sit in the sun, but she had seen enough of her aunt's friends growing up back home who had spent their youth sunbathing, and they looked like wrinkled leather. Lucia didn't want that to be her in twenty years.

Her hair had changed since she had arrived on the island, too. It was a lighter color, much lighter, and repeated dunking in salt water on her daily swims had softened it so that wisps of it slipped out of any attempt to contain it. She felt stronger, too. She was walking more, she supposed. It was more than a quarter mile down to the beach, and she went down there at least once a day for a swim. Since the wind had died, she had been going down there more often to sit in the shade and dip her overheated self in the cooling waves. She loved to take a mask, snorkel, and fins with her and lie motion-less on the nearly invisible water watching the daily life of the reef unfold below her. However, she learned a painful lesson shortly after arriving when she spent so much time watching that she got a bad sunburn all down her back and on the backs of her legs. Susanna had brewed strong tea and dabbed it onto the burns three or four times a day and had gone out into the yard to cut aloe leaves, split them, and gently rub the slimy juice on her burns. The combination of remedies eased the pain and stiffness of the burns. But the fever-like shakes of the first night convinced her to be more careful in the future.

She liked Pietr, she did, but he was so serious and so lit-eral. He would stop and think about whatever she said, and she could almost hear the gears turning, hear him trying to decide if she had been serious or was making a joke. It was tiring.

She enjoyed the verbal jousting she did with Burke more than anything else. He seemed to be on her wavelength, and he got her humor. He would dish that dry, underhanded snip-ing back at her just as fast as she shot it his way. What she didn't like was the way Burke seemed to take for granted that she liked him as more than a friend. She caught him eyeing her when he stopped up at the plantation house to drop off fish for supper, and she had even spotted him standing back from his windows, watching her swim in the early evening. He thought he was so smart, so crafty, but she had good eyes and wasn't afraid to use them. She kept an eye on his boathouse and had learned the sound of his boat motor so she could be reason-ably sure when he was away, so she could sit on the beach without being spied on. What if she lay there with her top off? What then? What if he was sitting up there looking down on her, thinking, well, thinking lustful thoughts? How would she handle that? She felt a flush of warmth rising from her middle at the thought of Burke up in his aerie, looking down on her with his gray eyes and long eyelashes. She would start making darned sure he wasn't home before she went down there the next time.

But it was so hot now that the wind had stopped blowing, and it made her think she might let that annoying man keep her from cooling off on her own beach. The next time she caught him ogling her, she would march right up to his apartment over the boathouse, her boathouse, and evict him. Sure, she was grateful to him. He'd taken such good care of her Aunt Anneke all these years, even though she hadn't known that Aunt Anneke was still alive. And she was grateful that he hadn't let the property decline so it wasn't worth anything, but the proprietary air he had around her and around her home was going to stop, and right now.

She stomped around the house, snorting and harrumphing like a British colonel in a farce of an old black and white movie. Lucia moved a pile of ledger books off the desk in the study, back onto the shelves in the second bedroom where she had found them. Then she rearranged the furniture in the study, trying to find a place to sit to catch a breeze. Finally, she gave up and went out onto the porch, where a ceiling fan moved the air a bit. She was bound and determined not to go down to the beach for a swim because she'd seen Burke come back half an hour ago and hadn't seen either his boat speed away or heard his truck pass by on his way back to town.

CHAPTER 5

Nora and Jack had been on the island for less than a month when she saw Manning in the bar at the Plaza Resort. They had gone there for dinner and were sitting in the bar afterwards listening to the jazz quartet play softly in the corner. Manning had the look of an adventurer, tanned and fit, wearing khaki shorts and a chambray shirt with the sleeves rolled up. He came into the room and paused in the doorway, where he removed his hat and sunglasses, shook out his golden blond curls, and waved at someone across the room. Nora noticed him immediately, his air of confidence and the crinkles in the corners of his blue eyes sending a little zing up her spine. She reached her foot over and stroked Jack's shin.

He looked up from trying to fish the olive out of the bottom of his martini and said, "What?"

A sensual smile curved her lips. "Oh, nothing."

He frowned at her, looked around the room, caught sight of Manning, and snorted. "That's a bit too rough for you, my dear. Better lower your sights." And then he went back to chasing the olive in his glass with a swizzle stick.

Nora pushed out her lower lip in a pout that she had seen Meg Ryan use in an old movie once. That pout had gotten a lot of mileage, Nora remembered. Too bad Jack was immune to womanly wiles; he was more of a shot and a beer guy deep down. He had made a lot of money in the dry-cleaning business in a few medium-sized cities in Indiana and a lot more money when he sold out to a giant conglomerate ten years ago.

Jack had a battery of lawyers and a crack investment banker who had done nothing but increase his money no matter how much he spent. Not that Jack wasn't ruthless. Jack was very ruthless. He liked to tell people he had gotten his fortune through a connection with organized crime, but Nora suspected he was too much of a bully to have ever been a part of that life. That Jack's last name was Spencer instead of something Italian also helped plant seeds of doubt.

Nora herself was not from the upper class. Hell, Nora's upbringing was barely middle class. Her parents were aging hippies holding on with a death grip to the carefree days of their youth. They lived in a cluster of yurts outside Des Moines, for God's sake, where her dad taught philosophy and Eastern religions to the sons and daughters of corn farmers and her mother scraped a living as an intuitive potter. That meant her pieces were attractive in an organic way but seldom actually useful. That Nora's life of capitalism and its many excesses was paid for by a man who represented all that Lucas and Beth despised disgusted them. Their daughter, Moonlight, had changed her name to Nora as soon as she left home and set about getting as far from her roots as possible.

She worked her way through junior college and then got a job with a law firm in Chicago as executive assistant to the firm's financial officer. Good old George had taken Nora under his wing and taught her the ins and outs of investing and accounting so that she got an excellent education on the job and had a pretty good head on her shoulders for money matters.

Jack had rented a villa in the Belnem neighborhood south of the airport right on the ocean, with a million-dollar view of Klein Bonaire, the little offshore island, and the sunset. There was a cement block wall around the property, mostly hidden by plants and topped with broken bottles cemented on to discourage acrobatic thieves. There was a small pool right on the edge of the seawall so that they could lie on lounges or float in the pool and look at the ocean waves. Nora liked to get up early each morning, slip into her swimming suit—not a bikini, a real live swimming suit—dive off the dock and go for a swim up the shore. She'd swim for a half hour, then put on the mask, snorkel and fins she left at the end of the dock and paddle around the dock pilings to see what fish and critters were there that day.

Jack didn't enjoy going into the ocean. He said, "Fish crap in there. Why would anybody want to swim in fish crap?" He preferred the pool.

Nora was just as happy that she had the ocean to herself. The longer she and Jack were together, the more of her life he controlled. She'd known when she agreed to quit her job and travel with Jack as his companion five years ago that she was risking him bullying her into the sort of woman he wanted.

****

Manning motored into Playa one fine November day a year ago, tied up to the dock, and stepped ashore into the sweetest deal of his life. Right next to where he had tied the *Tina Marie* was a sign that they were looking for water taxi drivers. He stopped and talked to the guy dozing in the boat, which was painted with cow spots, and found out there was nothing to the job. The company offered rides out to the little uninhabited island about a half mile offshore every hour, and there was a sandy beach to run up on to drop off and pick up passengers. It was literally a taxi. No need to cozy up to old ladies or learn endless spiels of boring island history. Manning told the guy, who introduced himself as Oxford, that he would be interested. All he had to do was find a dry place to sleep. Oxford looked over the *Tina Marie*, said his cousin at the boatyard might rent him a room over the workshop in return for parting out the boat. Since the only investment Manning had in the boat was less than a hundred bucks in gas and a few pounds of caulk, he thought that was a terrific idea.

He spent an hour wandering around the town, then after Oxford's shift was over, he and Oxford ran the boat down the shore to the boat launch where they met Cousin Emile with his boat trailer. It didn't take the three men long to winch the boat up onto the trailer and drive it across the island to Emile's boatyard. Using a forklift and a canvas belt, they wrestled the boat onto a wooden cradle behind the shed, where water spilled out of her bottom slowly for the next few weeks. The promised room above the workshop was adequate with a single bed, a row of hooks for clothes storage, a basin in one corner and a two-burner gas stove in the other corner with a shelf holding two plates, two mugs, a glass, a fry pan, a saucepan, and various silverware above it. Emile gave Manning a key to the workshop so that he could use the water closet and shower. The men shook hands, and the deal was sealed.

Emile was smart enough not to ask for boat papers, and Manning never mentioned them either. For transportation, Manning found a rusty bike frame in the junk behind the shop, scrubbed it, greased it, and bought new tubes and tires. He wrapped an old towel over the seat a few times and secured the whole thing with half a roll of duct tape. He wire-tied a plastic milk crate to the handlebars, and he was set.

Running tourists out to Klein Bonaire was not a hard job. It took Manning about fifteen minutes to get the hang of it. The worst part of the whole thing was the name of the boat, *Baca di Amor*, which Oxford told him meant Love Cow. He wasn't sure he believed that was what it meant, but he wasn't about to argue with someone who was paying him to drive a boat a half a mile, run up onto the sand, hand off a few tourists, boost a few on, and head back to the dock.

Most of the passengers tipped him, too. He learned to spot the ones most likely to tip and paid special attention to them. He was especially nice to the mamas, as he called them, those middle-aged dragons towing their sweet young daughters in their wakes. He knew that if he charmed the mamas, it made getting close to the daughters much easier. Of course, he didn't want to appear too respectable. Then, spending an evening with him would lose all the spark of danger and adventure that those young women most desperately wanted to take home from their vacation. He wanted to be "that guy I met on the island" for as many women as he could handle.

For a while, Manning was content to prowl for young

women to bed, but he came to realize that most young women have little money, so their tips were small. Middle-aged women, however, have money, and they proved to be a rich vein to mine. He learned to read the signs of when a wife was disenchanted with her husband, when a warm smile and a brief flirtation would earn him a surreptitious sweetener from the little woman after the big man had magnanimously handed over five bucks. Five bucks, buddy? Can you spare it? He was tempted to shout at the retreating back strutting down the street, but he kept his cool and kept quiet.

Sometimes the sweetener came with a breathless note, setting up a late-night meeting outside one of the resort hotels. He was quick to nod agreement to the shy, pleading, hopeful eyes and made sure that even if the encounter involved only a few soul kisses in the shade of a bougainvillea and a quick grope that the woman went home feeling like she had been rebellious and had an adventure.

Single, middle-aged women were even better. Some were dykes, of course, so they were immune to his charms, but many more single middle-aged women traveled alone as the months went by, so Manning's opportunities expanded. He was always careful to carry at least one condom in his wallet and a few in the glove box of the rusty blue Jeep he bought with his first month's pay. He was careful not to catch anything from the women he bedded. Most of the husbands looked like they wouldn't hesitate to have sex with just anyone, and he was sure most of the wives were infected.

Manning learned to scuba dive from another of Oxford's cousins, Stebby, so he worked on a dive boat too. He hauled tanks onboard, helped customers with gear assembly and got them into the water, and he swam at the back of the group to keep stragglers from straying. Stebby worked for Lora Divers at the Plaza Resort, the priciest one on the island, and he brought Manning on as boat crew while Manning went through scuba classes to get the certifications to lead dives. At first the job didn't pay much, but with his work on the Love Cow, it was enough to pay his rent now that he no longer lived over Emile's workshop, pay for food, and put a bit of gas in his Jeep. One bad thing about an island that small, he had to clean up his act a bit, stop siphoning gas from cars parked near him and scale back his petty larceny, because everybody knew everybody else and word spread like lightning. You screw someone in Playa and before nightfall, everyone in the village of Rincon on the north end of the island knew.

CHAPTER 6

The next time it was market day for Lucia, Susanna was ill, so Burke volunteered to go along. Even though Lucia said she could do the grocery shopping by herself, Burke insisted, saying he would never forgive himself if she got lost.

"Lost?" she said. "On an island this size? How can I get lost? It's not that complicated. I don't need a minder."

But Burke insisted and dusted the fish scales off the passenger seat in his truck and escorted Lucia in. He even sat patiently while she ran back into the house to get the shopping bags she had forgotten to pick up in the heat of the argument. She stared straight ahead as he drove them into Playa, enjoying the view of the ocean but not allowing herself to be drawn into conversation.

Her stubbornness amused Burke, and he redoubled his efforts to be charming and to get her to talk. For her part, Lucia couldn't help but admire Burke's strong hands and manly form next to her. His clean smell filled the truck cab and reminded her of how her aunt's garden had smelled after the rain. She had trouble concentrating on keeping her mad going when he pointed out the houses of the wealthy residents of Santa Barbara and shared stories of the problems there had been building them and getting the special fittings and furnishings the people wanted. It was all she could do not to pry for more details, and she knew he was doing it on purpose. She could see that he was laughing at her, and it only made her madder.

Once they got to the first grocery store, she couldn't convince him to stay out in the truck and let her shop. Lucia said, "I can do this myself. You don't have to come with me."

"I don't mind," Burke said. He insisted on pushing the cart and giving his opinion about every item she chose. "What are you going to do with two cans of tuna? Isn't the fish I bring enough for you?"

"I like tuna salad. Get over it."

Every single person in the store, whether they were working or shopping, knew Burke. He was hailed from every quarter, and he made certain to introduce her to every one of them. At first, she felt embarrassed and under a microscope, but then she decided to just go with the flow and smiled and shook hands, laughed at jokes and at the gentle teasing that was handed out mostly to Burke.

A pair of old ladies dressed in what looked like their Sunday best buttonholed him in the dairy aisle and spoke to him for a long time in rapid Papiamentu, the native Creole.

When they moved on, Lucia said, "What were they saying?"

He turned bright red. "Nothing. They asked me about my mother and how the fishing was going."

"Uh-huh. Sure."

He might not tell her what they were saying, but a blind woman couldn't miss the looks the women gave her. She would bet the farm that the two old biddies were telling Burke he should hitch his wagon to her star and see where it led.

****

That day was the thirty-seventh night in a row with no wind. At first, people laughed that the sun was dragging the wind with it as it made its way around the earth, but after a while, the joke wasn't funny anymore. The night wind was the only thing that made it bearable to sleep indoors. With no wind, the mosquitoes swarmed, clogging everyone's ears and biting every bit of exposed skin. People not lucky enough to have air conditioners in their bedrooms suffered because it was too hot to sleep under covers, so the all-over itching from too many mosquito bites woke people up in the middle of the night to curse and scratch. Sales of repellent skyrocketed, and every store was sold out of the old-fashioned mosquito coils.

Lucia stopped in every store she thought might carry bug spray, but had no luck until she got to the Sand Dollar mini mart. The clerk was restocking the shelf with cans of *Off!* and she bought all six. That earned her a dirty look from Nora Davidson, who came in as she was checking out, asking for repellent. The clerk told her she was out and motioned to the cluster of cans that Lucia was slipping into her shopping bag.

"I don't suppose you'd consider selling me one?" Nora said with one hand on a hip.

Lucia looked at the woman. She took in Nora's expensive clothing and ostentatious jewelry, her Manolo sandals, and shook her head. "Sorry," she said, "I have a sick baby at home."

Nora was so taken aback at having her offer refused, she didn't even react to the fact that cans of bug spray would do little to help a sick child feel better.

Lucia was a bit surprised at herself and her gut reaction to the woman. She was not in the habit of lying in the first place, and she was normally a generous person willing to share. "It must be the heat," she muttered as she slid in the clutch and prepared to back out of the parking place. Before she even moved, she turned off the car and got out. Next door to the Sand Dollar mini-mart was Lover's Ice Cream. She needed a cone, a two-scooper. It was hot, and what had happened to the trade winds?

****

After Burke cleaned this boat and took a shower, he got in his truck and went into Playa to do his grocery shopping and check his mail. He stopped at Karl's Beach Bar for a beer and spent a little time talking to Mairie, the bartender who had gone to school with his sister, so they caught up on the old neighborhood gossip.

Driving back home, he glanced at the parking lot in front of the Sand Dollar mini-mart and was surprised to see Miss Anneke's, or rather Lucia's, car parked out front. He slowed down and turned in, wondering what Lucia was doing at a tourist store. He knew Susanna had taken Lucia around the island and shown her where to shop. Burke was sure that Susanna would not forget to warn Lucia about prices in places aimed at tourists. No one discussed the practice, but it was foolish not to charge the tourists a little extra. They could afford it, and the island economy benefited.

He parked a couple of spaces away from Lucia's Toyota and got out. Burke craned to look past the rank of posters and handwritten signs in the Sand Dollar mini-mart windows, but he couldn't see Lucia in there. He stepped through the door to look in the back, but she wasn't there either. The young woman behind the counter gave him a smile, but he just waved at her and moved on. The next shop was Lover's Ice Cream, and that's where he found Lucia. She was sitting on one of the not very clean white plastic chairs, licking a double-decker ice cream cone. She didn't see him, so he smoothed his hair and tugged his shirt away from his sweaty back and went in.

The rush of cold air that hit him almost made him light-headed. He hadn't realized how hot he was until he walked into the icy shop. He made his way to the counter and ordered a single scoop of honey almond yogurt in a cup. When he had paid and got a napkin, he turned and pretended to be surprised to see Lucia.

"Miss Lucia," he said, "I didn't see you when I came in. May I sit with you?"

She smiled at him and nodded, too busy licking to speak. He thought she looked like an appealing child with her chocolate ice cream mustache. He didn't tell her about it for fear that she would be embarrassed and wipe it off.

She looked at his cup. "Only one scoop?" she said.

"Only one," he agreed. "And it's yogurt. Dairy doesn't agree with my stomach, not to be too blunt."

She shook her head. "Oh, too bad. I'd die without real ice cream. I'm addicted." She smiled at him as if she had confessed an addiction to cocaine. "As hard as I try, I can't leave it alone. I stopped next door to see if they had any bug spray and couldn't drive away without stopping for a cone. I'm a two-scoop girl, as you can see."

He slowly spooned up his sweet cold treat. "Mmm, this is so nice. It's too hot to resist, I agree. And were you successful in finding bug spray?"

She nodded with a mischievous look on her face. "I bought it all and made a rich American woman furious when I wouldn't share with her." She giggled. "I didn't like the way she looked at me, and she was wearing too-expensive shoes for Bonaire."

Burke didn't understand the shoes remark at all, but he was glad that Lucia seemed to enjoy sitting and talking to him. He just smiled and nodded and wondered if his stomach would tolerate a second scoop, so he had an excuse to sit there longer.

CHAPTER 7

Jack Spencer was a self-made man. He had started with one dry cleaning store in Evansville, Indiana, that he turned into eight locations in less than ten years. He was a smart investor and was lucky to have hired honest managers. As his income increased, so did his opinion of himself. He hung out with other *nouveau riche* people and shed the values and morals he had grown up with. He dressed like Dean Martin, and he acted like him, too.

For a while he was never seen without a drink in his hand, but then his liver gave out, so he quit drinking as much and took up smoking. That lasted only until he woke up with a hacking cough. Turned out, Jack was not the tough guy he always imagined he was, at least physically. He kept his Rat Pack wardrobe and love life and let the excesses of drinking and smoking go. Jack even watched his diet, but he didn't change his attitude toward life and especially toward women.

He considered them stupid second-class citizens. Some women he met quickly turned away when they realized the contempt he held them in, but others were happy to fall back into the old ways and trade their independence and self-respect for having all their bills paid and all decisions made for them. His treatment of them became too much, and they would rebel, but Jack smacked them around, and they either left or changed their ways.

Nora had been with Jack the longest of any of his women, mistresses, whatever you want to call them. She had worked as an assistant at his tax accountant's law firm. She came to his house on her way home one day to deliver his quarterly estimated tax forms, and he invited her to stay for a drink. Nora did, and within a month, she had moved in with him and quit her job. He teased her that he was not gaining a lover; he was sleeping with an employee.

She smarted back with a flip remark that she expected to get paid then, and he grabbed her arm in a tight grip and through clenched teeth said, "I'll be the one who decides when you get paid."

At that moment, Nora thought about leaving, but in the next breath, Jack was smoothing his hand down her back to her bottom and breathing in her ear how she turned him on. That night at supper, there was a jeweler's box at her place with a diamond bracelet in it.

"What is this for?" she asked.

"A welcome home present," he said.

All the same, she suspected it was an apology for his behavior earlier.

Through the years, whenever Nora acted or spoke more independently than Jack thought necessary, he would clamp down quickly and let her know she had crossed the line. After a while, Nora lost her need to rebel and forgot all about getting away, almost as if she needed to be kept in check.

They came to Bonaire a month ago because Jack had read something about the island in a magazine or heard about it from one of his cronies as a place with casinos. There were casinos on the island, it was true, but they didn't open until eight in the evening. They weren't hardcore, high-rolling casinos like Vegas or the Bahamas, or even Aruba. Bonaire's casinos were more like casinos lite.

It was late when Jack came back to the villa from the casino. Nora had stayed home, saying she was not feeling well, but she really needed a night off from being Jack's arm candy. Jack insisted that she not go to bed before he got home on the nights that she didn't go with him, and she was certain that he stayed out later and later, looking for a reason to yell at her. She was determined not to give him any reason. She dozed as soon as he left, even setting an alarm so she wouldn't sleep too long if she was extra tired, so she would sit quietly reading or on the patio watching the stars and listening to the waves when he rolled in.

Most of the time, she went along to the casino. At least at the casino, there were other people to look at and maybe to talk to. She would stand beside Jack's chair as he played blackjack, his favorite game of course, making sure he had a fresh drink at hand, but as the evening got later, she would lean over and whisper, "My feet hurt." He would flap his hand at her as if she were a pesky fly. That was her signal that she was free to find a seat. Most nights there was at least one other wife or girlfriend in the same predicament, so the women would sit together drinking coffee or soda waiting for their own personal high roller to be ready to leave.

Even at the Plaza Casino, the fanciest casino in the swankiest resort on the island, Nora felt overdressed. She had asked Jack, begged really, if she could buy more appropriate clothes to wear.

He had said, "Hell no. I'm not paying for you to run around here looking like I can't afford to dress you nice. You got plenty of nice things. Wear them."

Nora knew very well that as soon as Jack started talking like an old black and white movie gangster, the discussion was over, and she had lost.

The big grin on Jack's face when he got home that night surprised her.

"I met this Limey guy at the casino, a friend of a friend, you know how it goes."

Jack pulled her up out of her seat by her upper arm and dragged her along with him into the bedroom.

"Anyway, this guy Charles something, he and his missus live here. They been on the island a couple of years."

He shoved her onto the bed and started undressing. She slid back to lean on the pillow, figuring this was going to be a long story.

"See, they've lived here long enough to know everybody and be all connected, juiced you understand."

Nora could hear that Jack had had too much to drink. She was tempted to comment that he seemed a bit juiced himself. She knew that making a remark like that would earn her one of Jack's fierce grips on her arm and keep her out of the public eye for days until the bruises faded, so she said nothing, only nodded.

"I figured that somebody like him would be connected to any action on an island this small, so I wrangled an introduction tonight at the Plaza Casino."

Jack was struggling out of his shirt as he spoke, but the synthetic fabric was sticking to his sweaty skin, so it looked like he was trying to escape from a trap. It was all Nora could do not to burst out laughing. As it was, she had to fake a coughing fit as he struggled. She couldn't ask if he needed help, either. He would interpret that as a commentary that he couldn't undress himself and be mad too, so she just sat there and watched him struggle. Finally, he emerged from the bottom of the shirt and pulled it off his arms. His hair was all tousled, and his face was flushed from the effort of fighting his way out, but Nora kept her face still and didn't even smile at him.

"I met this Charles guy and his friend, um, well, anyway, Charles is having a big party tomorrow night for some climbing tologists or some damned thing. Weather scientists of some kind, he said."

Jack overbalanced onto the foot of the bed as he tried to take off his slacks and keep looking at her. He lay on his back kicking his foot to try to get the slacks off, and they were flapping back and forth like a pennant in a strong wind. He kept talking while holding the end of his thigh and frowned while grunting and working his leg up and down to try to dislodge the fabric.

Nora could feel her effort to suppress her laughter shaking the bed, but Jack's antics were shaking the bed enough that he didn't notice.

"So, we're going to a cocktail party at Charles's tomorrow night. His missus will call you. I forget her name."

He finally kicked his slacks off and turned to her, grinning like he expected praise for the accomplishment.

"Fine." Nora slid her legs over the side of the bed. "Be right back," she said.

Jack hummed his agreement.

When she got back from the bathroom, she laughed to see that Jack was sound asleep, lying just where he had been across the foot of the bed. Nora turned out the lights, leaving a night light on in the bath, then she slid into bed and said, "Goodnight, Jack."

Jack hummed again, turned over and fell off the end of the bed.

CHAPTER 8

Lucia and Pietr spent a couple of days going through Aunt Anneke's papers. Pietr was still on pain meds for his broken ankle, so he had limited endurance and concentration for the work. Aunt Anneke's will was a maze of clauses and bequests that made Lucia's head spin.

"Who are all these people?" she asked.

Pietr blinked at her, thrown by the break in his focus. "They're old friends, past servants, and worthy organizations that Miss Boon felt needed her support. With the past servants, she paid their rent and made sure they had enough money to pay their bills when they could no longer work."

"I notice the Historical Society isn't on the list."

"No, Miss Boon didn't have patience for their grasping at her things before she was even dead. They bedeviled her, trying to get her to promise she would leave her house and everything in it to them for a museum. She told them time and time again that the government had first claim on the land and the house, but they were persistent." Pietr gathered a pile of papers and tapped them on his desk to line them up. "I wouldn't be surprised if you got a visit from one or more of those ladies hoping that you would take pity on them and donate the estate to them."

"I'll watch out for them." Lucia closed the notebook she had started so that she could keep all the volumes of information straight. "Why don't we call it a day? My mind is whirling, and I'm sure yours is, too. Thanks for all you're doing, Pietr."

She slid the notebook into the tote she'd begun to keep all the estate paperwork in and got up to walk to the door.

"Uh, Lucia," Pietr cleared his throat, and his cheeks were flushed. "A couple of my clients are having a cocktail party tonight for some visiting scientists, and I was wondering if you'd be interested in going with me." When she hesitated, he said, "I know it's late notice, but I thought you might enjoy meeting more of the people on the island. They're British and have been here for a while. I'm sure they'd like to get to know you."

"I don't know. Would they mind if you brought me?"

"Not at all. Amelia and Charles have been my clients since they moved to Bonaire. I'm sure they would love to welcome you. Please say yes, Lucia."

She looked at the pleading eyes and agreed. "Yes, I'll come, but you have to let me drive. I don't want you driving out to my house in the dark with a broken ankle and on pain meds. That's a recipe for disaster."

He protested he could perfectly drive them to and from the party, but she insisted, and he gave in. They talked about what to wear and what time Lucia would pick him up.

The party was in full swing when Lucia and Pietr arrived. They made a striking couple, both of them tall, lean, and blonde.

Pietr wasted no time in introducing Lucia to their hosts. "Charles and Amelia, I'd like you to meet Lucia Vandersteeg. Lucia, these are our hosts, Charles and Amelia Eastman."

They exchanged handshakes and how-do-you-dos, and Amelia gestured them toward the table laden with glasses of rum punch and trays of appetizers. As they each picked up a glass, Lucia was surprised to see Burke on the other side of the table.

"Hello, Burke," Pietr said. "It's good to see you this evening. Are you friends with the Eastmans?"

Burke smiled back at them. "Hello, Pietr, Lucia. I'm Amelia's fish connection. She's been my customer since before I was successful, and I always keep a little delicacy aside for her." He pointed to the tray of crostini heaped with ceviche. "There's some of my day's catch right there."

"Oh, I love ceviche," Lucia said, and she reached for one. She took a bite, chewed, and swallowed. "So good. So fresh. Delicious."

"How's your ankle, Pietr?" Burke asked.

Pietr leaned heavily on his cane. "I'm really not supposed to be standing so much. Knowing I would be at the party, I skipped a pain pill, and I'm feeling it."

"Have another rum punch. That should be a kind of painkiller." Burke raised his glass to them. "I'll leave you two to circulate. Good to see you." He walked away into the crowd.

She turned to look at Pietr. "If you're in that much pain, it's a good thing I drove tonight." Lucia watched Burke leave. "Bonaire sure is a small island. I never expected to see Burke at this party."

"Burke's family was one of the first European families to settle on Bonaire. His grandfather and Miss Boon were great friends. Rumor has it they had an unhappy love affair, which is why Miss Boon never married." Pietr shook his head. "I don't know if that's true. Did you find any love letters yet?" He smiled at her.

Lucia laughed. "Sort of. I've found a few letters signed 'Burke,' which sound like he's sweet on her. I figure he must be Burke's grandfather. Most of the papers are bills of lading for shipments of hides and aloe and enough ledgers to stack nearly to the ceiling. I'll let you know if I find anything romantic."

As they made their way around the room talking to Pietr's clients and friends, Lucia couldn't help noticing a crowd of people around a man with curly, sun-bleached hair fingering a gold necklace and talking about shipwrecks. The guy talking caught Lucia's eye and gave her a wink.

"Who's that?" she asked Pietr. "He winked at me in the airport the morning I arrived."

Pietr looked over and said, "Oh, that's Dax Manning. He drives the *Baca di Amor* water taxi and tells everyone who will listen about shipwrecks and treasure that he's found or dived on. I don't think he's very trustworthy. I'd steer clear of him if I were you."

"I found a letter from him earlier asking Aunt Anneke to invest in his treasure scheme and said he sent a gold doubloon too. You sent a letter back declining the opportunity for her. I wonder what happened to the doubloon. Did you send it back?"

"No, I don't think so. That was a day or two before Miss Boon passed away. I had too much to do, like finding and calling you, right then to think of returning it. It's probably around in her study somewhere." Pietr took Lucia's arm and, limping, led her to another group of people to introduce her to them.

****

Jack being Jack, he had chatted up everyone he met on the island until he found the expat community and wormed his way into an invitation to one of their parties. Nora was happy to be going to a party and eager to meet some residents of the island, but Charles Eastman and his wife Amelia were far out of Jack's regular circle. They were British, very, very British. Everyone at the party was proper and polite, and most of them were climatologists on the island for a conference, so there was a speaker who talked endlessly about global climate change and coral bleaching and all sorts of scientific stuff.

None of it was of any interest to Jack, and he didn't hesitate to let the entire room know. Nora was watching Amelia's face, and she could clearly see that Amelia didn't want to have anything to do with Jack ever again. Nora was disappointed as she admired Amelia's art collection and had begun to talk to her about it when Jack came up and pulled her away to stand beside him while he told the scientists how smart he was.

When Pietr and Lucia introduced themselves to the climatologists, Pietr told them she was on the island to settle her aunt's estate. Jack stood with the scientists and was quick to try to talk her into selling Aunt Anneke's property to him.

"I wrote your aunt a few letters asking her to talk to me about me buying her place and developing it, but all I got was form letters from her lawyer," Jack said.

Lucia told him that the will stated that the government

would buy it and add it to the national park, but Jack had other ideas he wasn't shy about sharing.

He said, "You'll be missing out on a lot of money if you don't sell to me. I can guarantee you a profit of a few hundred grand over and above the selling price. Waterfront property in a place like this is over the moon." He reached out and gripped Lucia's arm. "I tell you, I can make money for you. More money than you'd ever imagine. Let's get together and see if we can't make a deal."

"I'm sorry, Mr. Spencer…"

"Call me Jack."

"Okay. Jack, I'm sorry, but I'm bound by the terms of Aunt Anneke's will to sell the property to the island government. I'll say it again; there's nothing I can do to change it."

Lucia recognized the woman standing next to Jack Spencer as the rich woman who wanted to buy one of her cans of bug spray. She linked arms with Pietr and pulled him away from the group when Jack wouldn't stop trying to convince her to sell.

That was the night Jack met Manning.

Manning spent the evening entertaining many of the guests with stories of underwater shipwrecks and treasure. He wore a Spanish doubloon on a chain around his neck that he rubbed as he talked, like he was rubbing a genie's lamp. He attracted middle-aged businessmen like a flame attracts moths. Nora could see the gleam of adventure in every one of the men's eyes as they stood around Manning listening to his tales of Spanish galleons and treasure lost under the sea.

****

As soon as he saw Jack Spencer, Manning knew he had his next pigeon. Jack's eyes kept flicking to the Spanish doubloon he wore around his neck, and Jack kept inching closer to his side. Whenever someone went to get a fresh drink or moved away to speak to a friend, Jack shifted into the vacated spot. Manning paid little attention to Jack, didn't always answer his questions, and appeared more interested in the climatologists and their global climate change talk. But Manning's radar had homed in on Jack from the beginning. With no one needing to tell him, he knew Jack was a self-made man and that he thought he was smarter and sharper than most people in any room. Just the sort of patsy Manning lived to find. This guy would be too egotistical, too greedy to think too much or too long about sinking money into a venture with so many variables. It would be easy to string him along. A few apologetic looks at first, saying that he didn't want to offer his new friend such a high-risk investment. Then he would let the pigeon trap himself. Let Jack Spencer convince Manning to let him invest, insist that Manning accept his money.

He also wanted to get to know the tall blonde that he had winked at. She was gorgeous and just the kind of woman he was attracted to. She seemed to be with that Dutch attorney guy, Smit, but Manning was sure that he could pry her away from his side and claim her as his own.

Lucia felt a hand slide under her elbow, and a man loomed over her shoulder.

"Hey, we haven't met. I'm Manning. Dax Manning. You're new."

She looked down and moved her arm away from his hand. "I'm Lucia Vandersteeg. Yes, I'm new on the island, and no, we haven't met. What do you do, Mr. Manning?"

"Everyone just calls me Manning. I'm a treasure hunter, Lucia. Haven't you ever wanted to go find riches? I search for them underwater." He touched his necklace, which Lucia could now see was a gold doubloon. "I find it too."

"Interesting. I've never thought that the Spanish treasure fleet sailed this far south, but then I haven't studied it. I'm sure you have."

He reached out to touch her hand. "And what do you do on Bonaire, Lucia?"

"I'm here for a short time to settle my late aunt's estate."

At the word "estate," Manning's eyes lit up, and he took a half step closer to her. "That must be a lot of work. If there's anything I can do to help, just call me."

Pietr stepped between Lucia and Manning. "That won't be necessary. I can provide all the help that Miss Vandersteeg needs."

"Oh really? How lucky for her." He turned to Lucia again. "Like I said, get in touch if there's anything I can do for you." He emphasized the word "anything," then sketched a salute and walked away, interested men following him like rats followed the Pied Piper.

****

By the time the evening was ending, Jack had wormed his way through the crowd and was standing next to Manning, talking earnestly to him. On the way home he told Nora that he had invited Manning over for lunch the next day and she should tell Yana the maid to make a man's lunch "not one of those sissy pasta salad lunches you women eat," and then to find something to occupy herself for the rest of the day because he and Manning had business to talk over.

Nora was smart enough not to ask if that meant Jack was planning to sink money into underwater treasure hunting. She didn't want to have more bruises to cover up the next day, so she didn't ask.

The next morning when Yana came to work, Nora sat down with her and the two women devised a menu for real men (they both laughed over that) of sliced beef sandwiches with fried onions, sliced tomatoes with fig balsamic vinai-grette, and chocolate cake for dessert, served with beer of course.

Nora called Amelia Eastman a bit shyly, asking if she would meet her for lunch to thank her for being so welcoming the night before. Nora was relieved and a bit flattered when Amelia said she'd be delighted. They agreed to meet at *Fishes From Heaven*, one of the most popular restaurants in Playa, on the waterfront in the middle of town at twelve thirty.

****

Manning knew he would have to get in touch with Santiago right away to get the fake shipwreck site set up. It had to be somewhere close enough to shore so that Jack could drive out and see the boat on the site. But also, where it was too dangerous for an amateur, so Jack wouldn't insist on diving there. Santiago said he found an old wooden freighter wreck just outside his home harbor and he could haul up some of the railing and a timber or two, which he would bring over, and Manning could show to the pigeon as proof of the wreck. They could even sink the stuff in the offshore spot they chose so that the mark could watch from shore, with binoculars even, to see it emerge from the bottom encrusted with barnacles and meet the boat at the dock to see it and touch it for himself. As a plan, it was perfect. What could go wrong?

****

It was too hot to sleep. Lucia got up, sprayed bug spray on her arms and legs, and went out onto the front porch hoping for a breath of a breeze from the west and the ocean. The late-day heat radiated from the wall of the house, making her feel even hotter. "Dammit." She had forgotten to look for a fan when she was out shopping or to find a hardware store for a replacement plug. She needed to ask Susanna about that the next day.

A thread of music came to her through the air. It sounded like *Stardust*. She looked down at the boathouse and saw two figures silhouetted in the window. It had to be Burke and a woman. Then she heard laughter, and the figures merged into one. She didn't know why she was surprised that Burke had a girlfriend. He was good-looking, had a decent job, and had a charming smile.

The heat forgotten, Lucia watched the couple move together, then apart, then sway. She realized they were dancing. It had been a long time since she had gone dancing, especially dancing with a man. Rock and roll dancing was one thing, but that cheek-to-cheek slow dancing was something altogether different.

It was too hot to be that close to another body, Lucia

thought. She felt the heat from the stucco wall behind her and stood up and walked to the edge of the porch, hoping for a breeze. It was cooler away from the house, and she could see the couple more clearly from this height. Feeling like a peeping tom, she still could not tear her eyes away.

Why did she feel like she was being betrayed? From the first day she arrived on the island, Burke had been nothing but a thorn in her side. He had dumped her unceremoniously on the doorstep along with her luggage and sped away to go fishing. He had teased her about hoping that he would bring her fish. He had insisted on escorting her to the grocery stores and to the vegetable and fruit markets when she told him she wanted to go alone. She had even gotten the feeling that Burke had stopped for ice cream the other day because he saw her car.

Her car, Aunt Anneke's car, she needed to get in touch with Pietr Smit and get some legalities ironed out. She had been on the island for over two months and still had not signed a single piece of legal paper. She was here to settle the estate, wasn't she? So why was Pietr dragging his feet? Or should she say foot since he had broken an ankle and was using crutches?

She leaned against the porch support and looked out to see the moon just set below the horizon. The light went out in Burke's window, and she didn't see the woman leave. Oh well, Burke was a grown man, and she had no right to lay claim to him. Headlights came up the coast road headed to Rincon, she guessed. She heard loud thumping bass from the car and figured it was a young man headed home after a shift at a restaurant or resort. Mosquitoes were swarming around her, so she went back into the house. It was no cooler in her bedroom, and the curtains hung limp at the window. It was a long time before she fell asleep.

CHAPTER 9

Nora parked around the corner from *Fishes From Heaven* on a tiny alley of a street linking the main road with the oceanfront street. She walked toward the ocean, reveling in the postcard view afforded by the space between the houses at the corner. They cast a dark shade that made the bright sunlit water and the small island a half mile offshore look even more appealing. Turning left, she dodged around a couple of cars parked up on the sidewalk, then slowed as she reached the restaurant. She was feeling presumptuous for having called a relative stranger and nearly begged her to have lunch with her, insisting that it had to be today. Even if Amelia had not heard it, Nora was very aware of the tight pleading in her voice on the phone when she had invited Amelia to lunch.

Amelia's calm British voice had seemed so soothing when she had said, "Of course, I'd love to have lunch with you, Nora," almost as if she knew how much Nora needed to have someone to talk to. Someone normal, almost like an actual girlfriend, something she hadn't had in too many years to count. She hadn't had a close friend since she had moved in with Jack. There were days when she wondered what perverse impulse had led her to agree to move in with him. Jack was not the type of man who appealed to her. He was not very tall, and he was twice her age. His wardrobe looked like it had come from Dean Martin's garage sale, and he acted like he had been caught in a time warp and been transported from the nineteen seventies to the present. She was certain that he had to send away to Asia or someplace like that for his Sansabelt slacks and Banlon shirts.

The one time she had tried to convince him it was not against the law to wear natural fibers and tried to wheedle him into some khakis and a linen shirt he had been so angry she had been forced to wear long sleeves for two weeks until his finger marks faded from her upper arms. He would grab her and squeeze so that it felt like he could rip off her arm with a flick of his wrist. Then he would lower his voice to a whisper and, through clenched teeth, tell her in no uncertain terms exactly what was wrong with what she had done or said.

Nora looked down at her clothes—a bright Indian-patterned broomstick skirt, a navy tee shirt and some gold thong sandals—hoping that she was neither over nor underdressed for the restaurant. She looked up to see Amelia waiting at the entrance, and she was smiling.

She looks like she's happy to see me, Nora thought. I wonder why. But she wasn't in the mood to argue with finding a friend, so she smiled and waved, and climbed the three steps up from the street into the open-air restaurant. After they were seated at a table along the open front of the restaurant, Amelia ordered a bottle of white wine.

"I know you'll enjoy this, my dear, and it's my treat," she said when Nora protested she wasn't sure wine was wise.

Nora thanked Amelia for meeting her.

"Oh, don't thank me, Nora." Amelia smiled and patted her arm. "I should thank you. Charles is always insufferable after a party. He keeps wanting to go over how very charming it all was, and then I must spend at least half the day telling him he is the personification of an excellent host."

Nora had trouble thinking of a response. "That sounds… frustrating."

"Oh, it isn't frustrating. It's tedious, but Charles is seldom frustrating. Since he retired from business, he has taken up a couple of hobbies that consume his time and interest, so there are days I feel I need to make an appointment to see him." She paused while the waiter poured her a sip of wine. She nodded her approval, he poured them each a glass, and he nestled the bottle in a bucket of ice that he set on a tripod next to their table. "Is Jack like that?"

Nora avoided answering right away by taking a sip of her wine. Then she said, "Jack isn't like that. He is only interested in making himself look like a big shot and, and…" her voice got softer and high pitched, "making me look small."

Amelia didn't even think and reached across the table to rest her hand on Nora's.

The small kind gesture broke through Nora's self-control like nothing else would have. She began to have trouble breathing, to gasp with agonized inhalations, trying to keep some semblance of control over her emotions.

"Oh, oh," Nora said. "I didn't mean…"

Her voice failed her. Certain that saying one more word would open the floodgates and send her wailing and weeping to the tile floor, she blindly reached for her wineglass and brought it trembling to her mouth.

Amelia removed her hand and picked up her own wine and took a sip. She turned her gaze to the horizon. "Look at the beautiful sailboat," she said quietly to Nora. "It looks like a flying dove, doesn't it?"

Nora turned her face toward the west, her lips white from the strain of holding in her emotions. "Yes," she said, her voice squeezed from her paralyzed throat. "It's beautiful."

Amelia replied softly, "It almost makes one weep," giving tacit permission for Nora to cry.

That small comment, that sympathetic validation of her feelings, gave Nora the strength to regain her composure. She dabbed under her eyes with the corner of her napkin, cleared her throat, and took another sip of wine. Nora caught sight of the hovering waiter. "We should order." Her hand was trembling so hard when she reached for the menu that, embarrassed, she dropped her hand back in her lap.

"Shall I order for both of us?" Amelia asked.

Nora nodded, thinking that it had been years since someone had understood how she was feeling and hadn't criticized her for it. It was a relief.

It took nearly all of Amelia's self-control, but she let Nora get command of her emotions, sipping her wine and gazing out at the boats passing by. She decided that their first meeting was too soon to snipe at the way Jack treated Nora. Besides, until she had earned Nora's trust, taking potshots at Jack would probably force Nora to defend him, and that was the total opposite of Amelia's intent.

Soon enough, Nora's chin came up, and she had even mustered up a watery smile. "This is a beautiful spot," she said.

"Yes," said Amelia. "It's one of my favorite restaurants on the island, at least for the view. The food is not quite as good as it was when the previous owners were here, but I like the décor better, I think."

"What was it like before?"

"Oh, tacky tropical, I think you'd call it."

Nora giggled and put her fingers over her mouth so only her twinkling eyes were visible.

Amelia continued. "They had dusty old fishing net stretched across the ceiling, glass net floats and garish tin fish hanging from it. There were many bamboo, tin, and seashell fish sculptures arrayed all over on the tops of the walls and on the tables, which are small enough as they are. It was just too much, too busy. And everything—walls, tables, everything—was dark, stained or painted. I find this new white and streamlined look very restful. Plus, I think it makes the view the feature rather than all the kitsch."

Nora looked at her as if she had discovered a treasure under an old bucket. She had never imagined Amelia, proper British Amelia, to have such a wicked sense of humor. Laughing had removed the last of Nora's sadness for the moment, so the women enjoyed a long lunch, getting to know each other a bit. For Nora, it had been years since she'd had a girlfriend to talk to and laugh with, so this freedom to speak her mind was like a vacation. She'd forgotten what it felt like to say what she wanted without having to stop and think first.

For her part, Amelia was happy to see the change in the younger woman, to see her shoulders relax and the caution leave her eyes, if only for the duration of this lunch.

After they had finished their meal, they crossed the street and sat on a bench overlooking the ocean. The line of sailboats moored there intrigued Nora when Amelia told her they were transient boats sailed by people who were working their way around the Caribbean for the winter or people for whom the boat was their home. The idea of all that freedom from being tied to land was a new and interesting one for Nora.

As they sat there enjoying the view, Lucia walked by and, recognizing Amelia, stopped to say hello. "Thank you again for welcoming me to your party," Lucia said to Amelia. "I know I wasn't invited, but I was afraid that Pietr would crash his car with that broken ankle and still being on painkillers."

"That's quite all right, my dear," Amelia said. "You're always welcome. Pietr was lucky to have you drive him." She turned to Nora. "Have you met Nora Davidson? She and her partner, Jack Spencer, were at the party too."

Lucia blushed, recognizing Nora as the woman she wouldn't share her bug spray with. "Hi. I saw you at the party, but we haven't been introduced." She held out her hand. "How do you do? Have you been on Bonaire long?"

Nora shook hands with Lucia. "Not too long, a few months, but I like it. What about you?"

"I've been here a couple of months working to settle my great-aunt's estate. In fact, I'm on the way to Aunt Anneke's attorney, Pietr's office, to do more estate paperwork. The government doesn't seem to be in any rush to step forward and buy the land and buildings from the estate. We're trying to hurry them along." She started to walk on. "It was nice meeting you, Nora, and seeing you again, Amelia. I hope we'll run into each other another time."

Nora and Amelia sat on that bench for a long time just gazing out to the horizon talking about places where Amelia had lived, about dreams they each had achieved and those they had not, deep things and shallow things, some neither had told to anyone else. Nora wondered aloud why she found it so easy to say things to Amelia.

"Because I'm a relative stranger. It's the same reason I feel comfortable saying some things I've said to you. We don't know each other well enough to make judgments about each other. We are building a relationship, a friendship, so we are piling up our history for each other."

"What an interesting idea," Nora said. "You believe we're speed-building a friendship?"

Amelia nodded.

Nora looked puzzled. "Why?" she said.

Amelia looked away from her to the small uninhabited island offshore from where they sat. She dropped her gaze to the tiny waves lapping at the rocks at the base of the seawall in front of the bench they occupied. Finally, she looked back at Nora, looked her straight in the eyes. "Because I think you need a friend."

The bald truth of the statement struck Nora dumb. She did need a friend, had needed one for a long time, but Jack didn't want her to have a friend. He wanted all her thoughts to be about him. "Why? What makes you say that?" She had to ask.

Amelia cleared her throat and took a deep breath. "Because I saw the way Jack treated you last night, and I feel you need someone on your side, someone to talk to, someone to tell you that you deserve better. I presume you are not in contact with your mother."

"No, my mother got angry with me when I quit my job to move in with Jack and shut me out." Tears rose in her eyes, and Amelia saw the effort to control them, to suck them back in.

"Well," Amelia reached over and laid a cool hand on Nora's forearm, "consider me your mother substitute on the island. I give you permission to call me at any hour, day or night, to talk or cry or laugh." She dug in her clutch purse and pulled out a card. "Here's my home number, which you already have, but also my cell phone number."

"There are cell phones on the island?" Nora sounded amazed.

"Oh, my dear, cell phones are everywhere. You can buy a cheap one at Sand Dollar Mini Mart and add minutes so you can be like everyone you see on television and talk on the phone while you drive. Which I think is totally dangerous, don't you agree? At any rate, you can even call the States. Although it's expensive, it is less expensive than the international phones you see outside resorts. Those things cost the earth per minute. Just terrible."

Nora took the offered card in her trembling hand. "Thank you, Amelia." She tucked the card into her purse. "I will call, I promise. Do you know what time it is?"

"Three-thirty," Amelia told her. "Why? Do you have a curfew?"

Nora gave a low chuckle. "No, Jack told me not to come back to the villa until after four o'clock. He's having lunch with that Manning guy. They're talking about some sort of business deal, I suppose, and he doesn't want me around. Do you know anything about Manning?"

Amelia snorted. "Jack is smart to want you out of the way. Manning is a terrible flirt and a real bounder. I couldn't believe it when Charles invited him to our party. Manning's responsible for quite a few marriages breaking up. He's a real hound, always available to soothe a woman's feelings when she's angry with her husband. Then she thinks Manning loves her, but if she leaves home, he wants nothing to do with her. Better stay away from him." She smiled. "Maybe Manning and Jack deserve each other."

Nora shrugged. "Maybe."

The women kissed each other on the cheek and parted ways, promising to keep in close touch.

****

On her way out of town, Nora stopped at a gallery to kill time until four o'clock. Maybe I'll take up painting, thought

Nora, standing in the mildew-y smelling blast from the Oleander Gallery's overworked air conditioner. I couldn't be any worse than this guy. She bent forward and squinted at the artist's signature smeared in the lower right corner of the framed canvas. Daniel Winters, it read, written in what looked like a child's handwriting. Was Daniel Winters someone influential's nephew, acclaimed as the family prodigy, and given a show in return for a juicy donation? Nora shook her head and glanced around, looking for a sheet describing the art. There it was, a haphazard pile of poorly copied pages flung in a cut-down corrugated carton. Very chic, she thought derisively as she stooped to pick one up. She frowned at the grainy black-and-white photo of the artist placed at a slight angle atop the sheet of text describing him and his works. She had met this man at one of Jack's influence-currying cocktail parties. The man in the picture had been convinced that Nora herself was on the appetizer menu. It had taken the better part of a Mai Tai poured down the front of his slacks to convince him otherwise.

****

Amelia stopped in at a gallery on her way home, too. She needed a gift for her daughter-in-law Elke's birthday next month. Instead of the Oleander Gallery on a side street in Playa, she went to the Windward Gallery in Antriol across the island. Amelia stood in the gallery, staring at the framed and matted photos. She didn't go to the galleries on the island often. Most of the art was patently made for sale to tourists. Tourists who most often left their good sense and good taste, too, at home. What seemed to sell best were naïve paintings of colorful flowers, palm trees, and romantic depictions of island life. Too many of them to count made their way onto cruise ships and airplanes to hang in middle-class living rooms as a reminder of a few days' holiday in the tropics. But these photos were different. Juan Porto, whoever he was, had used light like a paintbrush and his camera lens as his canvas. What might have been a trite picture of a lone flamingo at sunset in less imaginative hands had become, through Juan's eye, an abstract shape emerging from flame-colored water. No sky, no trees, just barely ruffled water and that distinctive silhouette. This would be a perfect gift for Elke. Amelia leaned closer. Damn. *Not for sale.* She would have to keep looking.

Amelia's drive back home across the island gave her time to think about the young woman she had just left. Nora seemed mature and confident, yet she had let herself be coerced by Jack Spencer to be his ornament, his property, for years. What could be lacking in her that kept her from running away from the little martinet?

CHAPTER 10

Lucia sat in the plantation house's study sorting papers. Stacks and stacks of papers. Aunt Anneke must have kept every bill, receipt, and letter she'd ever received. There was a letter from the Historical Society pleading with Aunt Anneke to donate her house and everything in it to them. Lucia thought that was pretty bold and a big ask.

She started finding personal letters more often. Some were invitations to tea or supper; others were for more elaborate parties held in other plantation homes. They were fun to read and made it easy to imagine life when Aunt Anneke was a young woman. Many were signed Burke. Those letters were courtly, bordering on romantic. Lucia was sure that he was Burke's grandfather and that he and her great-aunt had been in love.

Susanna had brought her a thermos of tea, and Lucia could hear the housekeeper moving around the house, sweeping the tile floors and cleaning the bathroom. When Lucia heard Susanna in the kitchen, her stomach rumbled because it was almost lunchtime. How can I be so hungry when all I've done is sit and move paper from one pile to another? she thought.

Another voice came from down the hall, a deeper voice, and Susanna laughed with him. Burke was in the kitchen. Lucia hadn't heard him drive up, but he must be dropping off fish for supper. Lucia listened to the easy exchange between her housekeeper and her neighbor. Of course they were easy together, they had known each other their whole lives. Burke was more relaxed with Susanna. He was tense and prickly with her. Lucia was easy with Pietr. She and he could work together all day and not hiss and spit at each other like two cats, like she and Burke did.

"Are you making any progress?"

She jumped and nearly spilled her tea. "You surprised me," she said.

"Sorry."

"I hope I'm making progress, god, I hope so. Every time I think I'm nearing the end, there's another box of papers or a drawer full of ledger books. It might be manageable if things were in some kind of order, but it seems like Aunt Anneke just shoved them away anywhere."

Burke's grin shone in the dimness of the doorway. "Isn't Pietr here helping today?"

She shook her head. "No, he's in court today, so I'm on my own with the latest avalanche of paper. Do you want to help?" she said with a smile.

He put his hands out. "Oh, no, no, I'm no good at paper-work. My sister-in-law keeps the books for my business. Other-wise, I'd be in trouble."

Lucia looked at the piles on every surface in the room. "Maybe I should have your sister-in-law help me, too."

Burke turned to leave. "Let me know if you want me to ask her."

Sister-in-law. Did that mean Burke was married? What if he were still married? Lucia sat in the quiet after Burke left, wondering about his sister-in-law. That must be his brother's wife. She nodded her head. Yes, that had to be. Or maybe Burke married young and got a divorce. Maybe he married his high school sweetheart, and she died. Susanna would surely have told her if Burke had been married and lost his wife. That was a story that was too good to keep secret. Unless Burke had asked her to keep it a secret, but why shouldn't Lucia know? It wasn't as if they were having a romance.

Pietr was more her type. They even looked somewhat alike. The thought struck Lucia. They looked like brother and sister, not the best basis for a relationship. But Lucia wasn't sure she was in the market for a relationship. She could tell that Pietr was falling for her. He touched her when he spoke to her about the estate and asked her to have supper with him whenever they worked together. She accepted occasionally. Was she playing hard to get?

"Lunch is ready, Miss." Susanna's voice from the doorway startled her, and she dropped the file she was holding. Susanna stepped into the room and bent down to pick up the papers. "I'm sorry, Miss, I didn't mean to make you jump. I thought you heard me coming down the hall."

Lucia laughed. "No, I didn't hear you. I must have been concentrating." Lucia bent down and gathered up the pages and stuffed them and the ones that Susanna handed her into the file and put it on the desk. "I'm starving. I'll go wash up and be right there."

Lucia had gotten into the habit of eating lunch with Susanna in the kitchen. Today's lunch was an open-faced ham and Gouda sandwich on whole wheat bread with pickles and fruit salad. Lucia poured them both glasses of sun tea.

As they sat eating and chatting, Lucia brought the talk around to Burke. "Susanna, is Burke married?" she asked.

Susanna looked up, startled. "No, Miss, Burke isn't married."

"Has he ever been married?"

Susanna shook her head. "Not that I have ever known. Why?"

Lucia took a drink. "Well, he said this morning that his sister-in-law does the books for his fishing business and the only way you get a sister-in-law is through marriage."

Susanna waved her hand. "Burke's brother Edward's wife Louise does his accounts. No, Burke is not married. Why? You thinking of getting in line?" She said with a sly smile.

Lucia could feel her cheeks color. "No, no, I was just curious, and don't tell him I asked."

"Are you curious about Mr. Pietr Smit too? Because he has been married and is divorced. He married a local girl right after he came to Bonaire, but she left him after a year and one child, a boy also named Pietr. I guess he wasn't exciting enough for her. She thought that being the wife of an attorney who works with the expats would get them invited to all the parties, but Mr. Smit doesn't mix business with pleasure and if he's invited, usually turns them down. At least that was what Therese said."

Lucia looked at her. "Who is Therese? The local gossip?"

"No, ma'am, she is the ex-Mrs. Smit and also my cousin. It was her water heater that rolled over Mr. Smit's foot and broke his ankle."

"Oh." Lucia finished her lunch in silence.

After lunch, Lucia changed into nicer clothes and drove to the post office. It was inconvenient not to have home delivery, but she found the long drive relaxing and the Keystone Kops aura of the postal service amusing. People were forever getting mail and packages that belonged to someone else. She had learned the hard way to go through the stack of mail before driving back home so that she could return anything misdelivered. While she waited her turn, Manning cut the line to stand behind her.

"Hey, pretty lady, didn't we meet at that boring party the other night?" he said, leaning over her shoulder.

Lucia gave him the coldest look she could muster. "Yes, we did." She jerked her thumb over her shoulder. "The line's back there."

Manning looked back at the disgruntled faces behind him. "Aw, they don't mind. I want to get better acquainted. Why don't you let me take you on a boat ride one of these days?"

She snorted. "On the Love Cow? No thanks. Besides, I've got a lot of work to do and then head back home to my job."

"I can use my friend's boat. We could have a little moonlight cruise, watch the sunset, have a few drinks, maybe a little snuggle. What do you say? It'd be fun."

"Next," the clerk said in a loud voice.

Lucia realized it was her turn. "Sorry. Gotta get my mail and get back to organizing the estate papers. Thanks for the offer, but I think I'll pass."

Today's mail contained three letters from developers trying to tempt her to sell the land, especially the part where the boathouse and docks were. One was another letter from Jack Spencer telling her he'd preserve the "historic look" of the development he had planned if only she'd consider his offer. She knew that Pietr had gotten letters and emails about it too, but she refused to consider the offers. She intended to honor Aunt Anneke's agreement, especially since the plantation house was at the edge of the national park and would be an inconvenient place for a vacation home. It made more sense to her to have the last plantation house on the island become a museum or the headquarters of the Historical Society.

CHAPTER 11

When Manning drove up to Jack's villa in Belnem, the upper middle class waterfront neighborhood just south of the airport, to have lunch, he was ready for anything. He took a shower right before he left home so that he had the look of just getting out of the water when he got there. Naturally blonde and made even blonder by hours spent on dive boats and driving *Baca di Amor,* he was tanned to a warm caramel color. He looked like the quintessential golden boy adventurer. His icy blue eyes looked even bluer, set deep in his tanned face behind his polarized sunglasses. His habit of squinting as if he were looking into the glaring sun intensified his gaze. He checked in the rearview mirror to make certain that his Spanish gold doubloon replica was right side up and visible under his shirt. Manning didn't find the doubloon on a shipwreck. He bought it solely to fool prospective investors that he hoped to sucker into financing his fictitious treasure hunt. He thought Jack was a prime candidate to be his first investor.

A guy like Jack, with a lot of money and who thinks he's a big shot, was the perfect target for a get-rich-quick scheme where he didn't have to do any of the work. The patsy could walk around all cocky, telling people he was a treasure hunter, pretending that he was someone like Mel Fisher, who found a Spanish galleon off the Florida Keys. The guy could wear a doubloon on a gold chain and be unbearably, insufferably egotistical about the whole thing.

Manning had spent years working the angles, ferreting out the people who could do him the most good for the least effort on his part. He knew when it was time to pull up his anchor and sail away. Manning made it a point not to drink too much, so he was always in control of his tongue. It wouldn't do him any good to get half in the bag and run off at the mouth about some scheme and have the listener warn the pigeon or, worse yet, be the pigeon. He looked at his hair, messed it up a bit, and went to knock on the door.

A pretty island girl opened it and greeted him by name. "Mr. Manning, Mr. Spencer is on the patio. Come this way, please."

He followed the enticing sway of her hips across the house to the wide shaded patio that stretched across the entire oceanfront side of the villa.

As she stepped onto the patio, the young woman said, "Mr. Spencer, sir, Mr. Manning." She sketched a little bow and went back to the kitchen.

Manning strode across to Jack with his hand extended. "Thanks for the lunch invitation. I'm glad to talk to you without all those other ears."

Jack's face lit up at those words. He had spent the morning in a stew of indecision and fear that one of the other eager listeners from the night before had moved before he could and bought the last shares. His strong and overly enthusiastic handshake told Manning all he needed to know about how today's lunch meeting would end.

Jack motioned to a glass pitcher resting on a towel on the patio table. "Drink?" When Manning hesitated, he said, "It's tea with some sort of fruit juice in it. Yana makes it, and I like it during the day. If you'd rather have a beer, I'll get you one." He started to rise.

Manning shook his head. "No thanks, I'll wait until later for a beer. After last night, tea will be fine."

The two men sat in the shade, drinking tea and watching the ocean. With a little prodding, Jack encouraged Manning to tell more tales of finding shipwrecks and the treasures they hold. Manning was glad he had done his homework.

As Manning talked, Jack couldn't keep his eyes off the

gold doubloon around Manning's neck. His fingers itched to touch it, to feel the centuries-old gold and touch the aura of the conquistadors and buccaneers who sailed the Spanish Main, swords strapped to their sides and white sails billowing overhead. A dreamy smile spread over his lips, and he sat back in his chair as if he were in a hypnotic trance.

Manning kept talking, recognizing the effect his words were having on Jack. When Yana came out to say that lunch was ready, Jack startled as if awakening from a sound sleep, and he rubbed the back of his hand over his mouth as if afraid he had been drooling.

Over a meal of roast beef sandwiches, sliced tomatoes and cucumbers, and potato chips, the men got down to the meat of the meeting. Jack broached the subject of investing in a share in the treasure hunt. Manning sounded cautiously optimistic, almost trying to dissuade Jack from risking his money.

That one thing alone showed how good Manning was at luring someone into his scams. If he had been too enthusiastic, too eager to relieve Jack of some of his money, Jack might have become cautious. Might have stopped to think, might have done a bit of research into Manning's claims of past treasure hunting success. But he didn't. Manning said all the right things that made Jack insistent, made Jack convince Manning to let him invest his money in the search.

"I don't know, Jack," Manning said. "I would hate for you to lose your money. Maybe you should wait to see if we find something." He shook his head. "I'm sure that what Santiago and I found is a Spanish treasure galleon. I've done some research in the archives in Seville, and I have retained an archivist who reads Old Spanish to search the records for me."

His words only inflamed Jack's desire to invest.

"Let me be a part of this, Manning. I can afford to help. Maybe you can hire a better researcher, or maybe you and Santiago will need some equipment. I can afford to risk a share's worth."

The pleading look in Jack's eyes was like champagne to

Manning. He felt drunk with the power he had to excite a man to part with big chunks of his money on his word alone. It was a heady feeling. By the time they had finished the meal, and were relaxing with beers after lunch, Jack was bemoaning the fact that it was Saturday and his bank in the States was closed.

Manning worked hard to be casual about it, saying he had to get the paperwork in order for Jack to sign first, that he wouldn't feel right taking Jack's money without all the legal papers signed and sealed.

The last bit of tension drained from Jack's body at those words. That Manning was concerned about having the legal forms satisfied before taking his money. That Manning had absolutely refused to hurry the transaction made Jack feel like he was making a good investment. With his new best friend, Manning.

****

Nora drove by the villa just past four o'clock to make sure that Manning had left. She was reasonably sure that none of the vehicles parked along there were his, no topless blue Jeep with a rust fringe around the entire body to be seen. Nora wondered how Manning had gotten his reputation as a ladies' man. She thought he was good looking enough if you didn't look too closely and he had an air of rakish adventure about him, but now that Amelia had warned her about his dishonesty, she knew she was in no danger of falling prey to his charms.

Jack was in a great mood when she got in. "Hey, baby," he said from the patio. "Hop into a bikini and come on out here. I have a pitcher of rum drinks we can share."

In the past, she would have been happy that he was so happy, glad that his day had gone well. But since the party last night and especially after having lunch with Amelia today, she felt like she was awakening from a long coma. It took a lot of control to smile and wave, call "be right back" and go do as he asked.

Nora could feel the pull of habit coaxing her to slide back

into her rut and just go with the flow. But she was determined to put a little starch in her backbone day by day so she could turn herself back into the independent and confident woman she knew she could be. She took her time, but not too much time, so Jack got mad, changing out of her tee shirt and skirt. Nora put on her red and gold bikini, Jack's favorite, and she brushed her dark hair up into a ponytail. She put a dab of perfume behind each ear, slid her feet into red leather sandals, and went out onto the patio through the bedroom's French doors.

"I was just about to come get you," Jack said with a roguish twinkle in his eye that made him look a bit like a caricature of Santa Claus, and not in a good way.

Nora dredged up a smile. "I wanted to make myself pretty for you." She walked over and sat on the end of his lounge chair. "How was your lunch, Jack?"

He reached over and slapped her thigh hard enough to leave a handprint on her skin. "Just dandy." He crossed his arms over his furry chest and looked very self-satisfied.

She saw him sitting there looking like the cat that ate the canary and knew that Manning had gotten whatever he wanted when he came for lunch.

"So, what did you let Manning con you into, Jack?" Her words knocked the smile off his face. He went pale under his tan, and he sat upright on the lounge chair.

"What do you mean, what did he con me into?" He reached as if to grab hold of her arm to squeeze it like he usually did when displeased with her, but she brought her hand up and fended him off.

"Don't do that, Jack. I won't let you try to hurt me like that anymore."

Instead of reacting, Jack leaned to pick up and light a cigarette. He slammed the lighter down onto the glass tabletop. "Well, you are sure full of yourself today. I suppose you learned that from Miss Hotsy Totsy Amelia, huh?"

She shook her head. "No, Jack, I just got tired of being your doormat." She stood and poured them both a drink, and then she sat back down on the foot of Jack's lounge chair. "So, tell me." She reached and caressed his foot. "What deal did you and Manning cook up at lunch today?"

Five years of living with him had taught Nora that Jack was putty in her hands if she rubbed his feet. She planned to do a lot of foot rubbing in the next few weeks to get what she wanted.

Jack couldn't resist telling her about Manning's treasure-laden shipwreck find, that he and Santiago were allowing a few select investors to buy in. And that day at lunch, he had convinced Manning that he was the man they had been looking for. Jack was excited that he had been invited to join the consortium so he could invest in the project.

"Have you seen the operation?" Nora asked.

"No, not yet. First, I have to have my bank wire ten thousand dollars in earnest money into Manning's account. Then I get to go out on the boat to the site, and they will show me more of the things they have already brought up."

"More? Have you seen any of it?"

"Just a little, and none of the treasure."

Nora was surprised. "What did he show you?"

Jack squirmed a bit and didn't speak.

"Oh, come on, Jack, what did he show you?"

Jack looked around as if checking for eavesdroppers. "I gave my word I wouldn't tell anyone."

"Jack. Who am I going to tell? The fish? The lizards? Come on, tell. I won't say a word. Cross my heart." She solemnly did just that.

Jack relented, took his refilled glass, settled back on the cushions of his lounge, and prepared to fill Nora in on his deal with Manning. "Okay," he said, and he rubbed his hands together.

I never knew people actually did that, thought Nora.

Jack when on. "Manning and this spic guy, Santiago…"

"You mean Hispanic, right? Or Venezuelan?"

He flapped his hand at her. "Yeah, yeah, whatever. Anyway, Santiago's a fisherman, and he got a line caught on something, so he talked to his pal Manning and took him out there to scuba dive to see if he, Manning that is, could retrieve his fishing tackle. Manning says that when he got down there, he couldn't believe his eyes. There was a shipwreck, and not some modern one either, an old one, a real old one, just rotting away down there. Manning says he fanned away some of the sand and saw something that looked like a cannon stuck in the reef. He unhooked Santiago's fishing gear from where it was stuck and went up to talk about what was down there." Jack's face was flushed, and he sounded like a kid.

Nora had never seen him so excited about something, so jubilant.

"Hey," he said, looking at his empty wrist, "what time is it?"

She leaned back to look at the kitchen clock. "Six thirty. Why?"

He reached out to smack her leg again, but she moved it just in time. He looked surprised. "Because I told Charles and his missus…"

"Amelia."

"Yeah, whatever, that we would come to some gallery opening that Amelia is all hot over. Ya know, schmooze with the island's big shots." He scooted off the chair and started into the bedroom. "You coming?"

She smiled and lifted her nearly empty glass. "All I have to do is change again. I'll finish my drink, dress, and be ready before you."

"Will not," he said with a shadow of his old kidlike smile.

"Will too." She smiled into her glass. Isn't that just like Jack? she thought. Just when I'm ready to chuck him, he turns back into a nice guy. She drained her glass, set it onto the table alongside the chair with a click, and followed Jack into the bedroom.

She was right. Nora was ready before Jack was even out of the shower, so she went back onto the patio to enjoy the last of the sunny afternoon. Even in the shade of the palms, it was warm because, like it had done so many other days since they had arrived, the trade winds that cooled the day died as the sun went down. She heard the phone ring, and Jack picked up the extension in the bedroom. From the tone of his voice, she could tell who was on the other end. She shook her head and refilled her glass with rum punch from the nearly empty pitcher. She turned to face the sea and concentrated on the restful blue of the barely moving water. Palm fronds clattered overhead as Nora waited for Jack to come out of the house. She knew he was on the phone with Manning.

A faint scratching behind her caught the breath in her throat and she whirled to see if someone was creeping up on her. No one was behind her. What had she heard? Her eyes caught a slight movement on the trunk of the nearest palm. A green and rust lizard slid up it, looking for supper, an opponent, or a mate.

When she had finished her drink and Jack still was not off the phone, she stood and walked around the villa. Nora stood looking through the pickets of the back gate. The pickets themselves were in good repair, excellent shape for wood in the tropics actually, but the flimsy gate represented much more. On her side was cool clay tile, laid with precision and well-scrubbed every day. Outside the gate was another story. Weeds and flowering vines grew rampant in the vacant lot, trash blew and heaped against the rusting wire fence. Fronds and tiny brown cones, detritus from the palms and pines that grew there, piled up to be sorted through and rearranged by the wild donkeys that roamed the island. Nora looked at her manicured nails, her perfect makeup, her styled and sprayed hair, and her rigidly chosen outfit and thought she looked like she was on the correct side of the gate. But the flamboyant mess outside the gate drew her eyes, and she couldn't help wishing she belonged there.

She was glad that they were going out so that Jack would have someone else to absorb some of his energy. Standing next to him was like standing next to a static electricity generator. Nora felt like her hair was standing on end when she stood beside him.

Tonight, Jack's enthusiasm for his new endeavor bled out his foot on the accelerator, rocketing them into town to the gallery showing. She always had the feeling that it was darker and that cars coming toward them were driving faster on the narrow unlit island roads.

Charles Eastman was outside the gallery door as they pulled up. Jack yelped his glee at seeing Charles. He parked haphazardly in the end spot of the parking lot across the street, half in the driveway, and leaped out to stride over to greet his new friend, leaving Nora to find her own way.

By the time she got to the doorway, Charles and Jack had disappeared into the crowded gallery. She made her way in, excusing herself, and picking up a glass of halfway decent red wine from a waiter. Not seeing anyone she knew, she picked up an exhibit catalog and looked at the art. None of the art looked very professional to her. In fact, it all looked like a bunch of fourth graders did it. Looking at the catalog sheet in her hand, she saw it was all the work of one man called Niki Turin who, according to his probably self-written bio, was an "untutored artistic genius." A snort of laughter escaped Nora, and she looked around to see if anyone had noticed. No one had. She was safe. It looked as though the artist had been dizzy when he painted the turtle. Concentric rings of color formed the shell like the brightly colored layers of candy in a jawbreaker, the head and feet looked almost real, and the background was a cloudy tan that looked like muddy water swirling down a drain.

She wasn't a very knowledgeable art connoisseur, but Jack had dragged her to enough of these gallery things that she knew the noises to make, so she appeared to have an opinion or care about art. She didn't. As far as she could tell, Niki Turin, tonight's featured artist, should have kept his job as an accountant or a phone installer or whatever he had been because she thought his artistic career was dead in the water.

She finally found Amelia talking to the young American woman she had met at the party last week. Lucia was her name, Nora thought. Moving through the crush, Nora was happy to see a familiar face. A blond young man with a crutch came up to Lucia and pulled her away. She waved goodbye to Amelia and Nora as they disappeared into the crowd.

Amelia said, "Have you seen enough art?" Amelia hooked air quotes around the word art.

Nora gave a sigh of relief. "Oh good. I thought I was the only one who thought the work wasn't very good."

Amelia grasped her elbow and steered them right out the door. "Not very good doesn't cover it," she said. "Niki Turin is a very nice man whose mother and wife have convinced him he is Bonaire's answer to Gauguin. He is not. And if Linda Michaels had not owed him a favor for fixing her refrigerator last fall, he would not be having a one-man gallery showing at all. She's afraid that this will tarnish the reputation of her gallery with the art buyers on the island." Amelia shook her head. "I told her after tonight to sneak in a few paintings by decent artists every day, and by the time the month is out, old Niki's daubs will be crowded right into the back room where they belong."

"The poor man. I hope he doesn't hear anyone speaking about his work like that. It would hurt his feelings terribly."

Amelia snorted. "Niki doesn't have feelings. He's an egocentric wanker who only hears what pleases him. Pay him no mind."

Nora stifled a giggle. "I'm not even sure what a wanker is, but it doesn't sound good."

"I'll tell you what a wanker is one day when I've had a lot of much better red wine, and you are probably right about what you think it means."

The women stood on the walkway outside the gallery and chatted in the soft Caribbean night air, happy to be out of the stifling crush of the gallerygoers. Eventually Jack and

Charles came out to join them, and the couples strolled a few blocks down the main street of Playa to *Chez Rendezvous*, which was famous for its shrimp bisque.

****

On the way back to their villa after the gallery show and supper, Nora and Jack argued. Jack had spent the whole evening standing around talking to Charles and a bunch of other men about his investment in Manning's treasure hunt.

Nora saw the look that passed among the listening men when Jack first mentioned having put money into the scheme. She could tell that none of them thought it was a good idea, but not one of them said a word. They let Jack rattle on and on and on about the world-class heap of treasure they were going to find and that the rest of them would be sorry they had passed up the opportunity.

Nora had wracked her brain to figure out a way to tell Jack that maybe he should reconsider his investment, maybe Manning was not the partner he wanted, but she finally just said it. Of course, Jack blew up at her words. For once she didn't back down, didn't let him shout her into submission.

By the time they got to the villa, both were so angry they stopped speaking. It was a good thing they had a king-sized bed because they each clung to their own sides, making sure not to touch the other.

CHAPTER 12

Manning woke with a smile on his face and whistled while he shaved. He showered while the water perked in the ancient Mr. Coffee. The water dripped through so slowly that the resulting brew was black as mud and tasted like tar. An ex-girlfriend suggested he use it to strip the rust off his beloved Jeep. He told her he liked his coffee just like his women, hot, dark, and strong. Then he laughed. Very few women who heard him say that ever laughed or stuck around long enough to try to change him.

After dressing in his usual khaki cargo shorts and washed-out aloha shirt, he headed into town on the shore road. He slowed down when he got to the Town Pier and scanned the row of bleary-eyed men huddled under the roof around a brazier with a battered coffeepot on its grate. Manning beeped the horn, and Bunny detached himself from the group, his jaw wagging as usual, his enthusiastic wave barely acknowledged by the Venezuelans.

"I didn't know you spoke Spanish," Manning said when Bunny settled in the passenger seat.

"I don't, mon." Bunny turned his ganja-red eyes to face Manning. "It is the spiritual connection of the downtrodden we understand. The brotherhood of the spliff, mon." He dug in the pocket of his shorts and pulled out a joint just as they drove past the Customs office.

"Put that away, for God's sake," Manning said. "You want to give those tight asses an excuse to arrest us before we've made our score?" He pushed Bunny's hand down and held it until the younger man stopped trying to put the joint in his mouth.

"I hear you, mon. I put it away now. Don' get all in a ruckus."

Manning glared out the scratched and spotted windshield. "How unlucky could I be to get myself a helper like you?"

****

Gray skies hung over the island. No wind stirred the palm fronds or blew away the sticky humidity. Everything was a struggle in the still air; tempers frayed. Jack closed himself in his office and moodily checked his emails and tracked his investments online while waiting for someone, anyone, to bring him coffee. Nora made herself a cup of tea with an herbal tea bag she found in the kitchen and stood sipping it as she watched the little tendrils of humidity rise in the first shafts of sunlight that peeped through the clouds.

****

Lucia stood on the main street of Playa looking around for a shop where she might find some long-sleeved men's shirts to wear when she had too much sun. She was glad that she was tanning instead of burning, but remembered her aunt's friends who had tanned in their youth and now looked like old leather. She didn't want that to happen to her. This had been the wrong day to come to town. Wandering cruise ship tourists clogged the street and shops, so she thought she might just turn around and go back home when a hand gripped her elbow.

"Hey, pretty lady, are you lost?"

She turned to see Dax Manning at her shoulder, holding her arm and smiling at her. "Oh, hi, Manning. No, I'm not lost. I'm trying to decide whether I want to buck the crowds and do some shopping or turn around and head home."

"It's a hot one today," he said. "Why don't I buy you a drink instead?"

"Okay. I guess I could stand a drink."

Keeping hold of her arm, he steered her through the

breezeway of the Pink Mall across to Karl's Bar on the waterfront. "What'll you have?"

"Something cold," she said. "How about a Coke?"

"A Coke? Don't you want rum in it? Have a Cuba Libre?"

"It's too early in the day for a drink like that. I'll just have a Coke."

He gestured to the crowd of tourists clustered around the bar and tables. "They don't think it's too early for a drink. Come on, live a little." He leaned down close, his forehead almost touching hers.

She took a step back. "No, maybe I won't have a drink. I think I'll just go home. Thanks anyway."

He reached and took her arm again. "You can't be serious. I offer you a simple drink and you run away? All I'm offering is a drink, not a roll in the hay." Manning pulled her closer. "Although I could arrange that if you're interested."

Lucia eased her arm out of his grasp. "I'm not very thirsty, and I have a lot of estate work to do. Thanks for the offer, but I'll be going."

His hand rose in the air, and for a minute Lucia thought he meant to hit her. "All right, all right." He turned away. "I'll see you around." He stomped off and disappeared into the crowd.

Walking back to her car, she passed a store that looked like a place where the locals shopped. It had racks of underwear and regular-looking shirts and pants. She went in and was pleased to find just what she was looking for. The store clerk helped her pick out two lightweight cotton men's shirts to wear over her swimsuit to keep the sun off when she'd had too much. She didn't give Manning another thought.

CHAPTER 13

Golden light shone from one of the boathouse windows, so she knew Burke was awake. That made her feel better knowing that he was there. She wondered if he looked up at her house sometimes to see if she was home and awake.

She decided to go cool off in the ocean. A quick trip to the bedroom to slip into her swimsuit, shorts and shoes, and she was striding off toward the beach. When she reached the side of the road between the plantation house and boathouse, a cloud covered the moon, and suddenly the path was not as clear. Her footsteps slowed, and she felt as if her next step would plunge her off a cliff. Even though she knew there was no cliff between the house and the shore, just a one-lane road, she couldn't help being frightened, as if she had been transported to a foreign place. She was in a foreign place, not the place she grew up in. Cursing herself for not thinking of bringing a flashlight, she stood still and waited for the cloud to drift by.

While she stood there, she heard tiny scratching in the cactus scrub alongside the gravel drive. Her heart sped up, but she took deep breaths and worked to convince herself that it was just lizards going about their business and none of the lizards on the island were big enough to hurt her. Soon enough the moonlight was back, and her path was shining white, so she kept going, carefully crossing the road because even this late at night sometimes there were vehicles filled with divers coming up the coast.

She went down the steps behind the boathouse, careful not to twist an ankle on the rocky stairs, and crunched across the coral beach. She stopped next to a boulder at the water's edge, slid out of her shorts and sandals, put them on the boulder, and tiptoed carefully into the water. A groan escaped her as the cool water slid over her overheated flesh. The temperature change was so great it made her teeth chatter for a moment, but once she had dived under and come back up, the water felt great. She struck out for the moon, swimming away from shore, laughing at the thought that she could swim far enough to catch the light and pull herself onto the cool white disk in the sky.

Lucia had not noticed when Burke's lights went out, but when she turned back toward the shore, there were no more golden squares to be seen. She swam carefully back, watching for dark shapes that were patches of reef, sticking to the white places in between so that she wouldn't scrape herself. When she reached the shallows, she stood up and slicked her hair back before making her way to shore. As she neared the boulder where she had left her clothes, a voice came out of the darkness.

"Did you remember a towel?"

A small shriek escaped her lips before her conscious mind registered who had spoken. "Oh my God, Burke, you scared me half to death."

"I'm sorry," he said. "I didn't mean to frighten you, but I saw you swimming and thought I'd come out and join you. Then I thought if I swam out to you, you might think I was a shark." He laughed, a low, sexy laugh.

Lucia looked at him standing in the moonlight, his fists on his hips and his head thrown back. At first, she thought he was nude, but then she realized he wore a racer's swimsuit rather than the baggy shorts that most men favored. She thought she would like to see him in the daylight.

Burke started walking toward her and as he got closer, she could smell the clean scent of him, a mix of spices and soap and something else she thought might just be his own scent, a distillation of all the exotic places his ancestors came from and all the experiences of his life. She was surprised to feel disappointed when he walked past her into the sea. What had she thought he had come down here to do? Ravish her?

When he was about hip-deep in the warm salt water, he turned and said, "Are you coming?"

"What?" It mortified her thinking he read her thoughts.

"Are you coming in swimming?" He waited for her response, but none came. "To cool off, remember?"

She shook herself back to awareness. "Oh. Yes, to cool off. Yes." She pushed herself away from the boulder she had been leaning on and walked carefully back into the water. She stepped in a hole and lost her balance, but Burke's strong arm reached out and scooped her to his chest.

"We don't want you to fall in before you're ready, do we?"

She felt the firm muscles of his chest against her softness and the iron bands of his arms around her. The heat emanating from him wrapped her in a blanket of warmth and spread out from her center, causing her to wrap her arms around his shoulders and pull herself tighter against him. He walked a few steps deeper into the ocean, holding her to him with his arms around her waist and then, as he fell forward still holding her, he pressed his lips to hers.

Lucia felt the warm sea wash over her as Burke's lips met hers. She could not separate the warmth generated by his kiss from the warmth of the water. Just as she began to run out of air, wondering if he planned to pin her to the sea floor, he rolled over and pushed her up toward the surface. She kicked once and her head popped up with his right alongside.

Both of them were laughing and sputtering.

"Do you always try to drown a woman with your first kiss?" she asked, sliding her hands over her face to sluice off some of the water.

"I didn't try to drown you," he said. "Didn't you feel me sending you to the surface?"

"Yes, I did."

They both turned toward the sailboat anchored off the

house next door and began to swim.

Burke admired Lucia's strength as a swimmer. She didn't seem to strain to keep up with him. Her long, lean form glided through the water as if she were in her true element. Their strokes synchronized, their pace slowed, and they moved as one through the warm water. When they reached the sailboat, they treaded water while they caught their breath. Burke needed it more than Lucia did.

He showed her the blue-green phosphorescence that trailed from her hands when she moved them.

"What is it?" she asked, fascinated.

"It's microscopic sea creatures that use tiny lights for defense. When you agitate them by pulling your hands, or any part of you, through the water, they light up."

They transfixed her, and she moved her arms and legs in graceful arcs. "Just beautiful," she said.

"Yes," he agreed, but his eyes were on her rather than the fiery water.

The swim back to their dock was at a much slower pace, and they swam most of the way on their backs to watch the sky and talk to each other.

As they swam along looking at the stars, Burke told her stories about the constellations. "See the Eel? Its head is there over Klein Bonaire. You can see its glowing eyes and long body twisting across the sky all the way to Polaris and the Little Dipper."

Lucia nodded. "I see it."

"The Eel lays in wait for its prey to come by. He can slurp up unlucky sailors on stormy nights."

"How do you know it's a he?"

Burke chuckled and swallowed a little seawater, which made him cough. "Sorry. My grandfather's foreman, Andrew, told me the stories when I was just a boy. I'd follow him around the plantation when he was working or supervising the other workers, and he told me many things about stars, animals, and plants. Andrew grew up on the island like me, and he'd heard all sorts of stories and legends from his people. My favorite were the night times when he'd build a fire with dried cactus, smoke a cigar, and tell tales."

Lucia swam alongside him, looking for the patterns in the sky. "That sounds like a great way to grow up. Do you know more?"

"Oh yeah. There, to the northwest, is the Flamingo. The brightest star is its tail, and its wings are spread in flight. Andrew always said it was flying toward the south end of the island to the salt pans. See how the long neck stretches to the horizon? Some people call it the Northern Cross, but that's not right. It's the Flamingo."

Lucia was impressed that Burke seemed familiar with every star overhead and could tell her Bonairean stories about each one.

When they reached the shallows, they stood for a few minutes talking until Burke noticed Lucia was shivering.

"I'll bet you never thought that you would end up chilled when you came down here tonight, did you?"

She laughed, a shaky laugh from the shivers. "No, when I started walking down here tonight, I was sure I would never be cold again."

He helped her out of the water, flipped open a fluffy towel, and draped it over her shoulders. Once he had dried himself off, he said, "Would you like to come up for a glass of tea?"

Her teeth were still chattering, but warmth was stealing down her limbs. She nodded. "I would love some tea. Thanks."

Lucia looked around curiously as Burke ushered her up the stairs and into his apartment over the boathouse. It was neat as a pin and reminded her of a ship's cabin. She kicked off her sandals and kept the towel to catch any drips from her still wet swimsuit.

Burke went into the small kitchen, opened the refrigerator, and pulled out a plastic pitcher. "I hope you don't mind that the tea is unsweetened," he said as he poured two tumblers of the beverage.

She admired the view of him in his racer's swimsuit. "That's fine," she said. "I don't sweeten my tea."

He brought the glasses into the living room and handed her one. "Have a seat," he said.

She looked around for a chair that wouldn't get ruined by her wet bottom. She settled on a canvas director's chair and put her towel down first. "I don't want to ruin your furniture. I hope this is okay. I'm still wet."

He set his glass on a side table and reached for a pair of jeans shorts he pulled on over his swimsuit. "There, now we're both in wet shorts."

While she sipped her tea, she looked around at Burke's apartment. It was tidy and decorated like she thought a man's place would look. There were nautical touches, but the décor was pretty plain and masculine.

Listening to him talk, she thought about the swim. The kiss had been a surprise. Lucia didn't expect it, and she didn't want it. Did she? Her breakup with Rob was too recent and too contentious for her to want to get involved with another man so soon. She had to admit that it had been a nice kiss, and she liked the strong feel of Burke's arms holding her. Rob had always held her as if she were a precious china doll that was easily broken. She had been wary of going to Burke's apartment after their swim, wondering if he thought it gave him permission to pounce on her, but he had been a gentleman and only served her a glass of tea and a towel. She thought he might make a move when she got up to leave, but he just took her glass, lent her a flashlight, and said good night.

Walking back up to the plantation house in the dark seemed long, even with the flashlight to light her way now that the moon had set. Lucia touched her fingers to her lips, remembering the pressure of Burke's lips on hers. She thought he tasted sweet and spicy, but that could have been his supper.

She heard the scrape of a shoe as she came up to her house, and a male voice said, "Where have you been?"

She gasped. "Rob, what are you doing here?"

He motioned to his suitcase on the porch. "I came to see you, to surprise you, and you weren't here. Where were you?" He reached out and touched her hip as if to pull her into his embrace. "You're wet. Why are you wet?"

She wriggled out of his grasp. "It's hot in the house, so we went for a swim."

"Who's we?"

"My neighbor, who lives in the boathouse down at the shore. It's not safe to swim alone, especially at night, so Burke came swimming with me."

"Burke? Who is Burke? Some old guy creeping around after a pretty heiress?"

"No. Geez, Rob, get a grip. Burke is a local fisherman who stayed in the boathouse to make sure Aunt Anneke was safe way out here away from town, and he is doing the same for me. He picked me up at the airport..." She looked around for another car. "How did you get out here?"

Rob folded his arms across his chest. "I got out here in the oldest, rattiest taxi I've ever seen."

"Yes," she said, "the taxis on the island aren't the best. Where are you staying? Not here."

"Yes, I thought I'd stay here. You must have room."

She was getting angry. "You fly down here without a word and expect to stay here? That took a lot of nerve." She shook her head. "You can't stay here. There's no room."

"What? I thought this was a plantation house."

"It is, just not an American plantation house. It's a Bonairean plantation house, which means single-story and small. There's one bed, and it's mine." She stepped around him onto the porch. "Give me a minute to change into dry clothes and I'll take you to find a room at a resort."

"But I thought…"

"You thought wrong, Rob. I have one bedroom with one bed and no air conditioning. You're not staying here, and I don't have time to tourist you around. I have estate work to do." She paused at the door. "You really shouldn't have come, Rob. We broke up, remember?"

He came onto the porch and reached out for her. "Oh, come on, Lucia. I know you really didn't mean it when you broke up with me. You were just mad because I got a little jealous. I've changed. You'll see."

She pushed his hand away. "No, I won't see anything. Rob, I told you when I broke up with you, I didn't want to see you again, and I meant it. Now, wait here while I change, and I'll take you to find a place to stay."

A deep voice came out of the dark. "Everything okay, Lucia?"

Lucia let out her breath. "Oh, Burke, everything is fine. This is Rob, and he decided to surprise me, not knowing that I don't have room for guests."

Rob stood gaping at the other man. "This is the fisherman you went swimming with?"

"This is my neighbor Burke, who lent me the flashlight and towel so that I made it back in one piece." She handed the flashlight and towel off to Burke. "Thanks for the light. It made getting back up the driveway a lot easier than having to rely on the moon." She turned to go into the house.

"This is your fisherman neighbor?" Rob said again.

Lucia turned back. "Yes, this is my neighbor, and yes, he's a fisherman. What's the problem?"

Rob stepped right up close to Burke. "You keep your mitts off her, you hear? She's not here for you to fool around with."

Burke looked into Rob's eyes and didn't blink. "I'm not planning on fooling around with Lucia. She's my neighbor. We took a swim; that's all. We've become friends since she's been here, and I'm helping her find her way around the island. Back off."

Rob took half a step forward and pushed Burke back a step. "You just back off yourself. This is my girl you're fooling around with."

"Stop!" Lucia stepped up and used her arms to separate the men. "Rob, I'm not your girl. I broke up with you over two months ago. I meant it." She turned to Burke. "I'm so sorry that Rob is acting like an ass. Thank you for the swim and the flashlight. I can take it from here." She turned to Rob, one finger poking his chest. "You. Stay right here. Don't talk. Don't move. I'll get my keys and my purse, and I'll take you to a hotel near the airport so that you can fly away tomorrow. I've had it."

Lucia didn't bother to change into dry clothes. She was too worried that Rob would follow her into her room or follow Burke home and make more of a scene. She drove around the house, put Rob's suitcase in the back, motioned him into the passenger seat, and got into the driver's seat.

"Lucia, baby, I just…"

She raised her hand to stop him. "Don't 'baby' me. I'm not your baby, not anymore." Without another word, she coasted down the driveway and turned toward town.

It was a long drive from Karpata to town because of the one-way road along the leeward coast. Rob filled the time with protestations of his undying love. Lucia answered as little as possible, reiterating that she had broken up with him and meant it.

She made sure he could go by taking him straight to the airport from her house. His ticket was open-ended, and the mid-morning flight to San Juan had seats available. Lucia dropped Rob off at the Plaza Resort. They had a room and would get him to the airport in the morning for his flight.

Rob tried to kiss her in the lobby as she prepared to leave, but she dodged out of the way.

"No kissing," she said. "It's bad enough you showed up uninvited and unannounced after I broke up with you weeks and weeks ago, but there's no kissing." She didn't care that the desk staff were standing at their places, silent and interested.

"But I'm in love with you," he said.

She shook her head. "I'm not in love with you. I never was. Goodbye, Rob, have a safe flight home."

As she reached the door to the outside, he called, "I hope you get a disease from that fisherman you're hanging around with."

She stopped, turned to look at him for a long moment, and then walked out into the Caribbean night.

As she opened the car door, her phone rang. It was Rob. She let it go to voicemail.

"Lucia," he said, "baby, I didn't mean that. You hurt me when you said you had never loved me. You told me you loved me before. I know you did. Why don't you love me? I love you. I'll love you forever, for the rest of my life." There was a long silence. "You'll be sorry that you sent me away. That fisherman Burke is a bum, I can tell." Another long pause, and then, "You go to hell, Lucia." He hung up.

She looked sadly at the phone in her hand. Rob was a nice enough man, but he was too clingy and too needy for her. His jealousy was over the top. She knew if she hadn't broken it off, it would only have gotten worse until she was isolated from everyone and everything. His showing up here on his own was just a sign that she had done the right thing. She felt a sense of lightness as she drove north through downtown Playa. Traffic was heavier because there was a cruise ship in port, so she took her time getting on the road to Rincon and home.

****

A few days later, Lucia looked up in surprise when Manning walked into the study. "How did you get in here?" she said.

"The door was open, so I walked in." He shoved a stack of ledgers away from the corner of the desk and perched there.

Lucia watched her carefully sorted documents slide out of their tidy piles. "What are you…? Stop that." She pushed him off the desk and put the ledgers back where they were. "Now I have to sort these all again. Go away, Manning. Whatever you're selling, I'm not interested."

He reached over and held her chin between his thumb and forefinger. "I'm selling riches beyond your wildest dreams, darling."

She twisted her chin out of his grasp. "I'm not interested in your dreams or anything else. You're trespassing. Get out of my house."

"You can't be serious." Manning brandished the gold doubloon on the chain around his neck. "You aren't interested in treasure lost under the sea for hundreds of years?"

She shook her head. "I'm not as gullible as you think. I don't believe you've found treasure. I think you're running a scam. I'm not falling for it. You might have fooled Jack Spencer, but you're not fooling me."

Manning stood looking at her. "Well, all right. I guess I know where I stand with you. I won't be wasting any more time." He gave the pile of ledgers one last shove before turning and walking out.

CHAPTER 14

Manning sat with his back against a boulder; black binoculars held to his eyes. With elbows on bent knees, he was motionless, focused on the horizon. He looked like a part of the landscape with hair bleached pale blond by sun and salt water, khaki shirt and shorts, and tropical tan. He had arrived in the cool pre-dawn, picking a sentinel spot that would give him a little protection from the midday sun. As the sun rose, so did the wind, swirling the sea into a white blur on the shoreline rocks and sending a cooling spray that sparkled in the light over him. As the day aged toward noon, the surface of the ocean, flat at dawn, wrinkled and crumpled into small waves and then whitecaps. Five-foot waves exploded in geysers as they met the coast, finally convincing him that no rendezvous would happen today.

****

A few days later, Manning stood on the yellow sand at Boca Onima, feeling the warm saltwater swirl over his feet. He had a good feeling about this little bay, about the broken and jagged boulders that littered the stretch of beach. It seemed realistic that a sailing ship full of treasure would have filled with water and sunk rounding the point out there where the water foamed white, and the gulls soared on the updrafts. There, right there, where the turquoise of the shallows plunged into the navy blue of the abyss, that was the place where he and Santiago had planted the broken pottery and encrusted metal that had come up entangled in the Venezuelan's nets. Santiago's fishing spot was too deep to be visited by most divers and therefore too deep and too far offshore for setting up the "investment opportunity" they had used to snare Jack.

Part of Santiago's argument against the plan was the dishonesty, but Manning convinced him that making the artifacts more accessible would make it more fun for the rich investors. Manning banked on Santiago's English not being up to the wild yarn he planned to spin to reel in Jack and his money.

****

When Lucia left Pietr's office after a long, tiring session, she looked across the parking area and thought she saw Rob in an aqua car parked at the edge of the lot. It couldn't be. A few days ago she had taken Rob to the airport, made sure he had a seat on the next flight out, and put him up at the Plaza Resort right across from the airport. There had to be a lot of pasty-faced brunette men on the island. She put him out of her mind and headed up the island toward home. It wasn't until she turned into her driveway that she realized the aqua car had followed her from town. She breathed a sigh of relief when the car went on past her place. He was probably a junior executive up at the oil tank farm on the north end of the island.

When she went to the market that afternoon with a list from Susanna, there was an aqua car following her. It didn't follow her into the parking lot of the More For Less market, so she ignored it.

She kept seeing that aqua car behind her over the next few days and got suspicious. When she walked across to the beach in the afternoons, it was parked at the pullout at the entrance to the park less than a hundred yards from her house. A man was standing next to the car, holding binoculars and looking her way. Lucia looked closer and thought he looked like Rob, but it couldn't be. Rob was back home in the States, not on the island.

Lucia put on sunscreen and spent a happy hour snorkeling around the dock pilings, enjoying the life of the creatures colonizing the sponges that grew there. After her snorkel, she lay on her towel, basking in the sun and listening to the soft sound of the waves rattling the coral rubble on the beach. She heard footsteps and squinted up to see Burke smiling down at her.

"Enjoying the afternoon?"

"I am. I snorkeled for a while and now I'm soaking up a few rays before I go home to tackle the piles of papers again."

Burke stooped down and rested on his heels. "I can still ask my sister-in-law Louise if she'd be willing to help if you need it. It seems to me this is too big a job for just one person."

"I'll think about it." She heard a car passing slowly on the road up the slope from the beach and saw the roof of the aqua car creeping by. She sat up fast and jumped to her feet. Burke was so startled that he fell over on his back.

"What's the matter?" he said as he scrambled to his feet.

"That aqua car has been following me all week." She pointed at the receding vehicle. "The guy in it looks like Rob. I think the creep didn't go home when I told him to."

Burke put his hand on Lucia's arm. "Don't jump to con-clusions. Tourists drive all over, slow, fast, around and around. Maybe it's just some guy trying to find his way."

Lucia shook her head. "No, I'm sure it's Rob. This is the sort of thing he'd do. He's so jealous and controlling. I'm ashamed it took me so long to figure it out." She shook out her towel and stuffed her snorkeling gear in her bag. "Time to get back to work. See you later."

When she walked up her driveway, there was the aqua car parked in front of her house.

Rob was on the porch, arms folded across his chest. "Been spending time with your fisherman boyfriend?"

"I thought I told you to go away and stay away."

"It's a free country. I can stay here if I want, and I want to stay with you. I know I can convince you to come back to me."

"Not by following me around and spying on me. I broke up with you weeks ago, Rob. Get it through your thick head. You're not the man for me. And don't you have to be at work?"

"I quit my job so I could stay here with you. So I could be here when you come to your senses and realize I'm the man you want." He looked over Lucia's shoulder, and his eyes got big.

Burke's voice came from behind her. "Is everything okay, Lucia?"

She shook her head.

"Rob, I don't know you, but I know Lucia doesn't want you around," Burke said. "You need to get on a plane and leave the island, or things won't go well for you."

"Are you threatening me, big man?" Rob stepped off the porch and raised his fists.

Burke took one step around Lucia and loomed over Rob. "If that's what it takes."

Rob stepped back, tripped on the edge of the porch, and fell flat on his back, knocking himself out when his head hit the concrete.

Lucia and Burke looked at him in horror. "Oh my god, it'll be just my luck he's really hurt, and he'll sue me or the estate. That's the kind of guy he is," she said.

"He'll come around in a minute. He didn't fall that hard."

Lucia stooped down and looked back at Burke in horror. "He's bleeding."

"Oh, for God's sake, I'll call the rescue squad." He pulled out his cellphone and hit 9-1-1.

Rob didn't wake up while they waited for the ambulance, and the pool of blood kept getting bigger.

"I don't like it. He's still bleeding," Lucia said.

"If he's bleeding, that means he's still alive. Head wounds bleed a lot. I wouldn't be too worried."

It took a while for the rescue squad to come screaming up the road and pull into Lucia's driveway. The attendants jumped out and rushed to the porch. They carefully examined Rob's head and asked questions about what had happened. Lucia explained that he had tripped over the edge of the porch and fallen.

"He fell backwards?"

"Yes, he was backing away and tripped."

"Is he your husband?"

"No."

"Is this man your husband?" He looked at Burke.

"No, neither man is my husband. I'm sure you'll find Rob's insurance information in his wallet, which will be in his back pocket. Can't you just take care of him without all these questions?"

"Yes, ma'am. We can do that." They eased Rob onto a stretcher and rolled it into the back of the rescue vehicle. "We will meet you at San Francisco Hospital."

"Meet me? Why do I have to meet you? I'm not involved with him. I'm not a relative."

The paramedic smiled at her. "He was injured on your property. You meet us at the hospital." He eyed Burke. "Maybe we need to call the police." He climbed into the back with the stretcher and closed the door. The driver backed down the driveway and turned toward Playa, sirens wailing.

Giving in, Lucia got in her car and followed the ambulance into town and to the hospital. She sat in the waiting room, refusing to be coerced into sitting in Rob's cubicle, saying that she wasn't related to him and wasn't responsible for his injury.

After an hour of sitting, a nurse came out to say that Rob was asking for her. She grudgingly followed the woman through the swinging doors and down a corridor to a curtained cubicle where Rob lay, head swathed in gauze.

"You stayed," he said with a sigh. "That proves you love me."

"No, it doesn't. It proves that I'm a nice person, unwilling to leave you alone in a strange place when you're hurt. As soon as you're released, I'm taking you to wherever you're staying so you can pack, and I'll take you to the airport so you can fly away home."

He reached out to grab her hand, but Lucia backed away. "Wherever you are is my home."

"Don't be melodramatic, Rob. I broke up with you over two months ago, and you need to face the fact that I do not love you. No matter what you do or say, I'm not getting back with you. Never gonna happen."

She heard a small indrawn breath from the nurse in the corner of the room and shot her a look. "Rob is a jealous, clinging man who doesn't listen," she said to the woman. "He chooses not to hear me when I say I don't love him and never will. Maybe you can make him hear sense. Get someone to take him to the airport when you release him. I'm through with him." She turned on her heel and left the room. She walked down the hall, out through the swinging doors, and out into the parking lot. Lucia drove back to her house, muttering to herself that she never wanted to see Rob again as long as she lived.

Faced with the aqua car in her driveway, she searched the glove compartment for the rental papers and called the company to ask them to pick up their car. "Hi. The man who rented this car," she read off the description, "is leaving the island. Can you come pick it up?"

"Where is the car located?"

"It's in my driveway in Karpata," Lucia said.

There was a pause, then the agent said, "There will be a charge for picking the car up so far from our agency."

"That's fine. Just charge it to Rob's credit card. He won't mind."

****

Driving on the narrow road that traces the southern end of the island, there isn't much to see. The Solar Salt works is just about the biggest thing on the horizon, with its long conveyor to load the white salt onto cargo ships. Beyond the salt mountains there are no more houses, only what look like fishermen's shacks made of old boat planks and billboard parts, and the old slave huts. At the red huts and the white huts, each cluster separated from the other by about a half mile, there is also an obelisk. The red and white obelisks aren't the only ones on the island. There are half a dozen of them on the extreme southern shore. Mariners used them, lined them up in a certain order to sail into the correct patch of shoreline to pick up or drop cargo. Like a finger pointing the way, the red obelisk stands sentinel over a deserted stretch of shoreline. No longer do mariners use it as an aid to navigate in to pick up cargo. Now it stands as an oddity, a curiosity poked and examined by sun-burned tourists. They lean against it, embrace it with a lascivious look on their foolish faces, or pose looking stiff and uncomfortable having their picture taken. How many albums hold photos of the red obelisk? How many people remember the story of the hardships it represents?

Manning sat in the arrow of early morning shade cast by the obelisk at Red Slave, a small pile of cigarette butts at his side. His eyes were slits as he squinted offshore, straining to get a glimpse of the *Santa Marta*, one of the boats that came over every week from South America laden with fruits and vegetables for the island's tables. He had first met Santiago at what some called the Venezuelan Fruit Temple, a twenty- by thirty-foot area with a peaked cement roof supported by Doric columns at the pier in the center of town.

****

You must dive Red Slave at dawn if you don't have a boat. And even if you have a boat, dawn is still the best time because that's when currents run slowest. Red Slave is a collection of huts at the extreme southern end of the island, and the currents run strong. So strong that gray vase-shaped sponges grow in a flat fan-shape there. There's a lot of detritus around, mute evidence of just how challenging it is to dive there. Broken fins lay where desperate divers flung them onshore, eager to lighten their burden as they staggered and struggled through the building waves to the safety of shore. If I wanted to dispose of something, this is where I'd do it, Manning thought as he sat waiting for Santiago's boat to appear on the horizon.

Trying to walk in the sandy places in the shallows, he moved out of the cleft in the ironshore rocks and shone his flashlight at the white fiberglass boat purring on the horizon. Ready with a story in case the dawn light was playing tricks and instead of Santiago in the *Santa Marta,* the boat carried the Coast Guard or, worse yet, the fish police. Manning thought about how he had gotten into this mess. Throughout his whole life he had attracted, let's say, a more interesting class of people. His mother, his social-climbing, money-loving mother, hated his friends, forcing him to live his life in the shadows to avoid her disapproval.

A sly grin lifted the corners of his mouth when he saw the flash of Santiago's smile when the *Santa Marta* reached the edge of the drop-off. Manning waded out, swimming the last few yards. He slipped over the gunwale like an eel, pulled the zippered plastic pouch out from under his shirt and counted out the pile of guilders.

"I said dollars," Santiago said, his smile draining away from his eyes and lips.

"You want me to explain to the bank manager why guilders aren't good enough? 'Dollars are what smugglers want, sir.' Yeah, that'd be great." The hard light in Manning's blue eyes and the clenched fist under Santiago's chin stopped his complaint.

****

Glint of gold. It caught Manning's eye as he swam down the reef that night. He stopped and finned nearer, only to find it was a broken bottle glittering in his light. The pale glow of the moon lent its cold light to the warm beam in his hand as he swept it over the reef. Looking for the clues, the markers Santiago claimed were there made Manning's heart rate slow. He knew even without the treasure the Venezuelan swore was there for the taking that he had all he needed to keep Jack on the string long enough to part him from a good bit of his money. Many fools like Spencer, who imagined they were smarter than Manning, had regretted it.

He was back looking the next morning. He'd gotten out of the water long after midnight when he felt nitrogen narcosis building, what they used to call the rapture of the deep. Back at the site where Santiago swore there was a treasure ship, Manning prepared to dive again. He was diving alone. He always dived alone, even though the diving instructor in his class emphasized over and over that they should never dive alone. No way would he share his purpose for diving the same site over and over. If there was a treasure there, it had to be his because he'd worked for it and wanted it so badly. He swung his scuba unit onto his back, buckled it, picked up his mask, snorkel, and fins, then entered the water.

From the shore, it looked like a large cloud shadow shifting over the sandy seabed, but once he was underwater and swimming out toward the drop-off, he could see the fish. A school of silver fish called Boga, each about six inches long, was flashing like falling coins in the tropical sun. The colors shifted from white to green to blue with the angle of the school, and they moved with frantic energy, as if predators were nearby.

He hung there, nearly hypnotized by the flickering fish, startled when a Barracuda almost as long as he was came knifing through the blur of Boga, trailing scales like glitter in its wake. Manning folded his arms across his middle and made himself as streamlined as possible when he swam through the school. Periodically, he checked his compass to make sure he was swimming in the correct direction, and he glanced at his depth gauge so he wouldn't miss Santiago's landmark. Bubbles spiraled up as he laughed at himself. Landmark, ha. He wondered whether something could be called a landmark if it was underwater.

His icy blue eyes darted from the reef passing on his left, looking for the "you cannot miss it" stand of staghorn coral tangled with lush yellow tube sponges. Santiago swore it marked the edge of the shipwreck, and the deep dark blue of the open ocean yawned on his right. He had dived these waters many times without incident, but there was always the chance of something coming out of the abyss.

****

Lucia was lost. On a tiny island twenty-four by seven miles, she had gotten lost. She wanted to go to the fruit and vegetable market, La Portuguesa, and must have taken a wrong turn. Lucia saw nothing familiar and had seen no one to ask. She had gone past this purple house at least twice, once each way, and kept hoping that someone would come out onto the porch to ask for directions. Lucia thought she should have asked Susanna to ride along, to make sure she went the right way, but Lucia had been confident she knew how to get there. Surely someone was around to ask. The brown dog lying in the middle of the dusty road would be no help. And how had she gotten off the paved road and onto this gravel and dirt road? She needed to stop and get her bearings. What time was it? Two o'clock, which meant the sun would move westward. That meant south was straight ahead. She wanted to go south. South of her house was the town, and south of the town was La Portuguesa. All she had to do was find the paved road again.

Wait. Was that a restaurant out in the countryside? There was a Coca Cola sign, and cars nosed up to the building. She pulled in. As soon as she stopped the car, a head popped around the corner of the building. Thank goodness, a human who would be sure to know where she was and where she needed to go.

"Can you help me?" she asked.

The man nodded and motioned her closer.

She got out of the car and stepped to what she saw now was a service window. "Can I get a Coca Cola, please?" She dug in her purse for a few bills. The soda was icy cold and tasted great. "Oh, thank you. That's what I needed." She took another drink. "Now, can you tell me how to get to La Portuguesa?"

The man laughed. "You're really lost, aren't you?"

She felt the blush rise in her cheeks. "I am. I'm new on the island and thought I knew the way, but I got turned around and now I need help."

"You're Miss Anneke's niece, yes?"

She nodded. "Wow, this is a small island. Yes, I'm Lucia, Miss Anneke's niece."

He smiled a gap-toothed smile and reached his hand out to shake hers. "I am Hardy. I'm Susanna's husband. She tells me all about you coming to deal with the estate."

Lucia shook his hand. "I'm glad to meet you, Hardy. Yes, there's a lot to do with the estate. I find more every day." She finished her Coke.

"Now, about you being lost."

Hardy gave expert directions, and she wasn't that far lost, but far enough. It only took about ten minutes to find the paved road and, following Hardy's sketch on the back of a paper bag he gave her, soon she was at La Portuguesa. She bought some onions, carrots, bananas, oranges, chayote squash, and a loaf of brown bread. She also bought herself a bottle of water, which she had forgotten to bring along, and a small dish of ice cream as a treat. She was careful returning to town, swiveling around to see where the turns were. Once she was in the middle of town, she was more confident knowing where to go. She passed The Everything Store and doubled back to see if it had a fan. It did. Lucia got the last one and even asked the clerk to plug it in to make sure it worked before paying for it. It worked. She couldn't wait to put it in the corner of her bedroom that night.

She was even brave enough to drive home up the windward side of the island, through Antriol and Rincon, to get back to the plantation house. Lucia told Susanna about meeting Hardy, and Susanna laughed at her being lost enough to find his little snack restaurant out in the kunuku, which she told Lucia was the countryside.

Susanna offered to make her supper, but Lucia said, "It's too hot for cooking. I'll have some toast with cheese and fruit for supper, but thank you."

Later, she made her small supper as the sun dipped in the west and the shadows grew long down the hall. It had been a good day.

CHAPTER 15

They spent all afternoon in Pietr Smit's office, going over official forms to settle Aunt Anneke's estate. The longest one was called a quitclaim deed that officially ceded the land and house over to the island government.

"Does this include the docks and boathouse?" Lucia said.

Pietr frowned. "Yes, it includes all of Miss Boon's property, the boathouse and docks, too."

It was her turn to frown. "But what about Burke's business? Where will he live and dock his boat?"

"That's not your problem, Lucia. Burke knew the terms of the agreement when he moved into the boathouse. Miss Boon let him stay there for some handyman help and just having someone else around that far out of town."

Lucia had never thought of that. Her heart beat a little faster. "Do I need to be worried that someone will come out to the house looking to break in or vandalize the place?"

Pietr patted her shoulder. "No, no, there is very little vandalism on Bonaire, and as far as break-ins, well, the rich houses up in Santa Barbara are sometimes broken into, but not regular houses."

"But Aunt Anneke's house isn't a regular house. It's out in the middle of nowhere with a single woman living in it. People knew Aunt Anneke was a rich woman and might think she kept valuables in the house. Now I'm afraid."

Pietr laid his hand on her arm. "Don't be afraid. Miss Boon didn't keep money or valuables in her house; she kept them in the bank. I could come out and sleep on the couch or in the spare room if that would make you feel safer."

"Thank you for the offer, but with your broken ankle, you'd probably fall over your cane and break a wrist or your neck. No, I'll just lock up better and put up with roasting at night." She looked around the air-conditioned office. "I wonder where I could buy an air conditioner for my bedroom. Would The Everything Store have them?"

Pietr shook his head. "No, not The Everything Store, but James Hardware, just across the road from there, might. It has been so hot and still lately that I doubt there is an air conditioner for sale on the whole island. But you can try."

Lucia picked up her purse and pulled her car keys out of her pocket. "Thank you, Pietr. I'll stop there on my way home."

"But we're not finished." He motioned to the drift of papers that covered his desk.

"We're finished for today," she said. "I'll call another day, and we can start on the rest of the paperwork. I'm in no hurry to be homeless or to make Burke homeless, either."

The heat and bright sunlight slammed into Lucia as she left Pietr Smit's office on the major downtown street. There was a cruise ship tied up at the Town Pier, and the street was thick with roving groups of shopping tourists. She realized she'd been lucky to come into town early enough to get a parking place. Not that the cruise ship passengers had cars, but when a ship was in port, the town parking lots were full too. Lucia wondered why. She would ask Susanna when she got home. Home. She hadn't been on the island long, but already it felt like home. She pulled out of her parking place and turned toward Kaya Korona, where the hardware store was. When she got to James Hardware, the parking lot was nearly full. She had to park at the very back and walk across the hot, dusty gravel to the store. She was surprised when she entered that the store was dimly lit and not air-conditioned.

"Oh please," she said under her breath when she saw the empty spaces on the shelves.

"May I help you?" said a male voice to her left.

She saw a middle-aged man standing behind a counter, smiling at her. "Yes," she said, "I hope you have a window air conditioner that I can buy."

The smile melted off his face. "I am sorry to say we don't have an air conditioner for you. I have a few fans I can show you."

Lucia's shoulders slumped. "Thank you, but I have a fan. I was hoping for an air conditioner."

He shook his head. "I don't believe there is an air conditioner for sale on the whole of the island. Since the wind left a few weeks ago, everyone is hoping for an air conditioner."

She thanked him for his help and went back to her car, which had turned into an oven in the short time she had been in the store. She rolled down all the windows and reached in to start the car and turn on the fan before getting in. She grabbed a beach towel from the back seat to sit on, so she wouldn't burn the backs of her thighs when she sat down in the driver's seat.

The drive back to Karpata was slow because of the traffic. People were going home from work, stopping at the market, or going for a drink with friends. As she drove through the town of Rincon, she remembered there was an ice cream store off the main street, if she could only remember the name. Her foot came off the accelerator while she thought. Prisca's, that was it. She stopped next to the children playing in the schoolyard and asked where Prisca's was. Of course, children knew where the ice cream store was. The oldest girl gave her good directions, and she drove right to it. One scoop of mango and one of coconut cooled her off and made the rest of the drive bearable.

Later that afternoon, she thought of her conversation with Pietr Smit about being so far out of town and living alone, Lucia stood in her bedroom looking at the windows. They were tall, nearly floor to ceiling, and wide open to catch any breeze. The house was cooler than outside in the sun, but not by much. She stood looking toward the Caribbean Sea, down the hill and across the road. She could see the boathouse roof and thought about Burke. What good would he be if someone came into the house? He wouldn't be able to hear her scream, especially if he had an air conditioner. Did he have an air conditioner? She was too far away to see or hear. She supposed he had a phone, but she didn't know the number. Maybe Susanna knew, or maybe it was written somewhere, perhaps on that tiny telephone table in the hall. If she closed the windows, it would be even more stifling than it already was. Where had the wind gone?

She heard a noise in the kitchen and looked at her watch. It was too late for Susanna to still be there. She went to check, her heart in her throat.

"You need to cook this today," Burke said when she walked into the room. "Do you know how to cook fish?"

She put her hand on her heart. "Oh, you scared me. What?"

He gestured at her with a dead fish. "Do you know how to cook fish? This needs to be cooked today."

She shook her head. "No, I don't know how to cook fish. Susanna does, but she's gone for the day."

He flopped the fish onto the counter and looked in the lower cupboards. "Then I guess I'm making supper. See what there is in the refrigerator for a salad. That should be a good supper, snapper and salad."

Lucia gaped at him. She didn't want a babysitter, and she hadn't asked him to make her supper. Why was he here with fish at this hour?

"What are you doing here so late?" she said. "I thought you fished in the mornings."

He looked at her over his shoulder. "I usually do, but today I had an appointment to see an apartment with a dock, so I don't end up homeless when this place goes back to the government. I know you and Pietr spent the afternoon filling out estate papers, and I figure sooner rather than later, I'll need another place to live and park the boat."

"Yes, we did some paperwork," she said, crossing the room to stick her head in the refrigerator. "Do you like avocado?" She reached in and pulled out a head of lettuce, a carrot, and an avocado.

When Burke didn't answer her question, she shrugged and figured he could pick it off if he didn't like it.

"Hand me an onion," he said, his hand reaching back toward her. She took an onion out of the basket on top of the fridge and gave it to him. "You should pay attention to the way I do this, then you can make your own supper instead of relying on a cook or a fisherman to feed you."

That made her angry. "I didn't ask you to feed me. You came into my kitchen uninvited, waved around a dead fish, and you took over. I would have managed just fine."

"With a dead fish?"

That stopped her. "Well, maybe not with a dead fish, but no one asked you to bring the fish up here so late in the day."

He slammed his knife down onto the cutting board. "Oh, excuse me for worrying that you might be alone and hungry. I forgot that you have been here all of a month…"

"Two months."

"Really?" He looked down at his hands on the counter. "Sorry, two months, so you have the island and island life all figured out."

Tears spurted from her eyes. "No, I don't have it all figured out, but someone was kind enough to leave cheese and bread for me, so in a bind I can make a cheese sandwich and if I'm feeling especially brave, I can make a grilled cheese sandwich. I make a mean grilled cheese sandwich."

His shoulders relaxed, and he picked up the knife to continue slicing the onion. "Will you make me a grilled cheese sandwich someday?"

She turned away and sniffed. "Sure. Man, that onion is strong. My eyes are tearing up."

"Yeah."

Lucia made the salad, and Burke cooked the fish in a cast-iron skillet he found in the oven. They shared the meal seated at the scrubbed wood table in the kitchen as the last rays of sunlight poked through the window.

She put down her fork after eating the last bite of her fish. "That was excellent. Thank you."

He wiped his mouth with the napkin on his lap. "You're welcome."

"Burke," she said.

"Yes?"

"This afternoon Pietr talked about you staying at the boathouse to keep an eye on Anneke's house and her because it's so far out in the country and so alone up here."

"That's right."

"I don't know how to get in touch with you if I need to, like if something breaks…"

He looked her in the eye. "Or if someone breaks in."

"Well, yes. It never occurred to me until Pietr talked about you and the boathouse today. I thought maybe the boathouse and the docks weren't part of the agreement, but Pietr said they are. Where will you live? Where will you keep your boat? What will happen to me?" That last part came out involuntarily.

"I looked at a place down toward town that has room for my fishing equipment in the shed, a mooring for my boat, and a small apartment for me to live in. You? You'll go back to the States and get on with your real life."

"Oh, yes, back to real life. Soon I'll leave here and go back to work and cold weather and my real life." A little voice in the back of her mind said, but what if being on the island is your real life?

It was obvious Lucia couldn't stay on Bonaire. She had tried to work remotely, but the internet at the plantation house was not up to it. She would be in the middle of a meeting, and the service would drop. She tried to get more capacity and greater speed, but they were not available, and it would have been too expensive if they were. Oh, but she wanted to stay. She loved the slower pace of life on the island and the long but scenic drive into town. She had even grown to love the adventure of shopping, of not knowing what would be in the store when she went to the grocery. People knew each other. People knew who she was even though she had been on Bonaire for just two months. And there were those two older ladies who had seen her with Burke on a shopping trip and now nodded at her when they met in the grocery store aisle.

She needed to meet with Pietr Smit again and again until all the estate paperwork was done, and she was free to go home. Home, where it was cold and snowy, not hot and sunny like here. She didn't want to go home. She wanted to live the carefree island life forever. But that wasn't reasonable.

True, she had broken up with Rob, so she didn't have anyone to go home to, and avoiding Rob would be easier if she stayed on Bonaire than if she was back in her old neighborhood. He had called her daily since she first broke up with him, pleading for another chance to be the man she wanted. She had told him he was not the man she wanted and would never be, to please stop calling her. He had persisted until she told him she was going away to settle an old aunt's estate on an island in the Caribbean. He had nearly flipped out at that news. He raved. He said he was sure she would meet a beach bum and have her heart broken. She had met no beach bums, mostly because she had not been to the beach.

Rob had shown up unannounced at her front door twice, but she had hurried him, protesting and cursing, off the island. Even after he had nearly cracked his skull falling on her front porch. But he kept calling every day. She should really block his number on her phone.

She would have to ask Susanna about beaches on Bonaire. Every section of shore she had seen was rocky, not sandy. There had to be some sandy beaches on the island, didn't there?

"Good morning, Miss Lucia," Susanna said, coming in the back door. "I see you have made coffee and toast. Did you have enough breakfast, or can I fix you something?"

Lucia put down her coffee mug. "I've had enough breakfast, thank you, Susanna. I'll finish my coffee at the desk and get out of your way."

"You are not in my way, Miss Lucia. I will start in your bedroom so that you can enjoy your coffee undisturbed." She reached into the back closet for the broom, dustpan, and dust rag, then left the kitchen humming a tune.

It occurred to Lucia that Susanna would be out of a job when the house reverted to the government. She would have to ask the housekeeper and cook what she planned to do. Maybe she had another job lined up. Lucia followed the noise of the broom into her bedroom.

"Oh, Miss, I'm not finished. You should have said that

you would come here next, and I would have cleaned else-where."

"No need. I just wanted to ask if there are any sandy beaches on the island. All I've seen are rocky shores, and I thought it might be nice to go to the beach one day."

Susanna leaned on her broom and smiled. "Most of the coastline is ironshore and coral rubble, but there are a few natural sandy beaches on Bonaire," she said. "At the west end of the airport runway is Windsock Beach." She waved a hand to show the beach was to the south of Karpata. "A lot of the locals go there on the weekend, and the cruise boat passengers get dropped off there when there's a ship at the Town Pier or the Customs Dock." Susanna looked at her with a smile. "You should come to Windsock on Saturday. A bunch of us are having a cookout. It would be a good time for you to meet people."

She waved in the other direction. "At this end of the is-land, the dive site Ol' Blue is sandy and has a nice little beach. There is good snorkeling there, too." She shifted her broom to her other hand. "And way down south of the airport is Pink Beach. It's the biggest beach on the island and the most popu-lar."

Lucia laughed. "If I'm going to snorkel, I'll need a wetsuit or something to cover me, so I don't get sunburned again. I don't want a repeat of that pain."

Susanna started sweeping again. "You should probably go with Burke or Mr. Smit so that someone watches you. They could put sun lotion on your back and the backs of your legs to keep you from getting burned."

Lucia swept her hair off her neck and let it fall. "It's hot today. Mr. Smit has a broken ankle, remember, so he won't be able to go to the beach, and I don't think Burke would be inter-ested in spending an afternoon watching me snorkel. I prom-ise I'll stay in the shallows and not go too far from shore." She slid her feet into sandals and picked up her purse. "I'm going down to the dive shop at Habitat Resort to see if I can rent a wetsuit. I'll be back for lunch. There's still some of the salad you made the other day. I'll finish that." Lucia started to walk away, but then turned back. "Thanks for the cookout invitation. I'd love to come. Tell me what I can bring and when to be there."

Susanna smiled and nodded. "All right, Miss. And you don't need to bring anything on Saturday. Just come to meet some islanders."

Lucia was glad to be in motion. The air coming in the car window was hot, but at least it was moving. Her wheels kicked up a cloud of dust that hung in the air over the gravel drive. She wondered when the trade winds would be back. It was too hot.

At the Habitat dive shop, she found a rack of thin wetsuits that were more than she wanted to spend.

"Can I help you?" asked the clerk.

"Yes, I got sunburned snorkeling and wonder if you have a wetsuit or something that I can rent to keep it from happening again."

The clerk smiled and led her to a rack of thin, short-sleeved shirts and shorts. "These are for sun protection. You should find something here that would fit your needs."

Lucia looked at the price and said, "Do you rent these?"

The clerk shook her head. "No, I'm sorry, we only sell them."

"Do you rent wetsuits?"

"Yes, we do."

Lucia was not thrilled with the faded and tattered wetsuits that were on the rental rack and decided that she would be happier with her own suit. She found a full-length wetsuit on the first rack that fit for just over a hundred dollars and bought it. As she put the suit into her car, she said, "Happy birthday to me."

****

Pigeon-toed and armor-plated, the iguana stamped down the middle of the road, a line of cars and trucks trailing behind it like a retinue. The first car would have passed, could have passed the tiny dinosaur when it came up behind him (it could only be a "him" with the line of spikes down the spine). As the lady driver put on her turn signal and prepared to zip around him at the next wide spot in the one-lane road, he turned and fixed her with such a glare that her foot came off the accelerator and she remained in her proper place. The driver, a lady trying very hard to stay in touch with her island roots, took on the task of keeping anyone else from passing just as a proper courtier protects other, more human royalty. Three cars back, Bunny sat enjoying the slow pace of the ride. At the other end of the island, Manning checked his watch for the tenth time and cursed the day he had hired such a laid-back helper. Maybe if he didn't pay Bunny on time, made him wait for his money, the guy would be there when he needed him.

****

On Saturday, Lucia felt like she would be an intruder as she drove down to Windsock Beach for Susanna's cookout. The housekeeper had reminded her on Friday that the party was the next day, and she was expecting Lucia to be there. "I want you to meet my friends and family. They have all heard about Miss Anneke's niece, and they want to meet you."

"Are you sure I can't bring anything?" Lucia asked. "I'll feel like a freeloader."

"You will be my guest, and guests don't bring things to parties." Susanna was very firm on the subject. "Hardy will have his grill there, cooking chicken and burgers. My friends are bringing dishes to share. I'm bringing you."

So, Lucia packed her sunscreen and hat, put on her swimsuit under her shorts and tee shirt, slid on her flip-flops, and set off to be there at the appointed time. She had to park on the opposite side of the road from the beach because there were so many cars, pickup trucks, and vans there. It didn't take long for Susanna to spot her. As soon as she set foot on the sand, her housekeeper was at her side.

"I'm so glad you came, Miss Lucia. Come meet my mother and aunties."

Making her feel like a show pony or trophy wife, Susanna introduced her to everyone there. "This is Miss Lucia," she said. "She is Miss Anneke's niece. Miss Lucia hasn't been on the island long, but already she fits right in."

It was funny, but within an hour Lucia felt as if she'd always been a part of this family. They were all welcoming and interested in her life in the States and on the island. Susanna's mother and aunties were curious about her love life, just like her aunt was at home. They asked questions about what kind of man she liked and would she like them to set her up with a few likely candidates.

She thanked them but said she wouldn't be on the island long enough to form a permanent relationship, so she focused on the estate work.

"We hear that a man came around saying he was your boyfriend and telling anyone who would listen that you were his property," Susanna's mother said. "I would worry about a man so confident of a woman."

Lucia was shocked. "Where did you hear that?"

"My nephew works at the front desk at the Plaza Resort, and he said you dropped off a man who professed his love for you and got angry when you left him there."

Lucia put her hand over her mouth and then pulled it away. "That was an old boyfriend who was very controlling. He didn't want to believe me when I broke up with him before coming to Bonaire, but I think he got the message, eventually." She reminded herself to block Rob's number when she left the cookout.

Susanna came up and put her hand on her mother's arm. "Mama, stop taking up all Miss Lucia's attention. I want her to meet my friends and have something to eat."

"All right, all right. But you come again, Miss Lucia. We love having you here."

"Thank you. I'm sure I'll see you again."

For the rest of the afternoon, Lucia met and talked with a whirl of islanders, each one friendlier than the last. She ate some delicious food and even took a cooling swim with some of the kids in the crowd. It was a fun afternoon and made her want to be a part of the island community for longer than a few weeks.

****

Santiago steered the *Santa Marta* out of the little bay on the north coast of Venezuela he called home. The stink of the aging diesel was pulled out of the cabin when he reached the open ocean and pushed the throttles all the way forward. He took one last glance over his shoulder to bid farewell to the orange spot that was the fire his wife Marta always lit on the beach when he left, but he'd waited too long to turn. He couldn't see it. A bolt of panic shot through his gut. The superstition of bad luck at the change in routine churned his stomach and made his knees feel loose. "Stupid peasant," he said, running his fingers over the religious medal he wore around his neck, making a little bow to the statue of the Virgin duct taped to the console. He pictured the warm orange light of Marta's fire as he looked out at the waves painted pale blue and white by the cold light of the stars. Manning would be waiting, and he, Santiago, would soon be rich enough to buy a new engine for his boat, with a bit left over for a few sparkly things for his Marta.

The local fishermen went out just after sunset five nights a week. They putt-putted out of the anchorages to their favorite fishing grounds, navigating by the stars. No fancy GPS to keep dry or out of the bilge water in the bottom of the shallow boats. All they needed was a view of the stars to lead them out and home. Not that they needed to go all that far offshore. The waters around the island had been declared a marine preserve over thirty years before, so there were plenty of fish to catch. The rules said they could only fish with hand lines, not nets, but Santiago figured what the fish police didn't know wouldn't hurt him. He always trailed a net behind the *Santa Marta* on his way from his little bay on the coast of Venezuela to the Town Pier. He hauled the net in, put the fish in the well, and stowed the net before getting too far into Bonairean waters. If anyone asked, he had plenty of fishing line scars to brandish to prove how he caught the fish. The nets were good for covering the other cargo Santiago carried, the things the gringo Manning waited for on the beach every Tuesday night.

Santiago moved with speed and grace from his boat, moored as close to shore as was safe. He slid over the gunwale into the water, his feet in their gray canvas shoes barely making a splash. The Venezuelan eased away from the boat, sliding his feet along so he wouldn't churn up the water and leave a telltale line of white behind him. He carried an old burlap sack that had begun its life full of coffee beans, destined for the lucrative American market. Then it had been reduced to carrying ganja for a while along the Jamaican coast. Now it held a few ballast stones and a clump of what might be Spanish silver pieces of eight welded together by a couple of centuries of immersion in the sea. He tucked the bag into a corner of the fourth slave hut from the south end of the row. It would look so much like run-of-the-mill trash that the casual observer wouldn't notice. It should be safe there until Manning retrieved it to prove to Mr. Moneybags, Jack Spencer, that he, Santiago, really had found something valuable. The sun was just tinting the eastern horizon with the thinnest pale gold line as Santiago re-boarded the *Santa Marta* and resumed his journey to the Town Pier with his official cargo of pineapples and potted palm plants for the weekly market.

****

Lucia found another mention of someone named Burke in Aunt Anneke's papers. She went in search of Susanna and found her changing the sheets on Lucia's bed.

"Susanna, was there a planter named Burke years ago? The name keeps cropping up in Aunt Anneke's ledgers, and I found a reference to a party at Burke's when she was a young woman."

Holding two of the corners, Susanna flung the sheet out and let it fall softly on the bed. "Oh yes, Miss, old Mr. Burke had a place way up at the top of the island in what is now the national park. The Burke family were some of the earliest settlers from the Netherlands on Bonaire, just like the Boons."

Lucia sat at the desk in the study, surrounded by old letters and yellowed papers from the last century. She vaguely heard a male voice in the back of the house and thought it must be Susanna's husband, Hardy, dropping something off for her. Frowning over how to organize the drift of papers she'd found in an old dresser in the second bedroom, she didn't notice Burke come into the room.

"Susanna asked me to bring you this." He held out a plate of banana bread slices. "She says you skipped lunch, and she's worried you're not eating enough."

Lucia glanced up at him, hoping he didn't see the heat of the blush turning her cheeks pink. When would she stop feeling like a teenager around him? He was her neighbor, for God's sake, not someone interested in her. And she wasn't interested in him. She had a life in the States and didn't have time to waste on an idle flirtation on a Caribbean island she'd probably never see again once she'd settled the estate.

"Thank you. I usually eat only two meals a day, so I'm trying to get back into the habit. Just set it down here." She slid a pile of old bills aside. "I'll nibble on it later."

Burke leaned a hand on the back of her chair. "Have you found any letters from my grandfather? There are family rumors saying that when they were young, they had a torrid affair that ended badly."

She sat up straight to avoid touching his hand with her sweaty back. "I've found some, yes. They don't seem to be very torrid, but they certainly are friendly. Would you be interested in reading them? You could have them since they're personal, not estate related."

He caught her by surprise when he reached across her shoulder and slid a small pile of papers toward him on the desktop. "Here's his handwriting. I'd recognize it anywhere. Do you mind if I read them now?"

"Be my guest. You can sit at the kitchen table where there's more room to spread out and better light."

He crossed the room and sat in one of the side chairs across from her. "This is fine. The fan is making a nice breeze. I won't bother you."

But his presence did bother her. She watched the smile on his face and the expressions that made his eyebrows lift and fall. Who knew eyebrows could be so distracting?

Lucia couldn't keep herself from glancing up at Burke whenever he made a sound. It was obvious he was enjoying the letters. He was smiling, chuckling, and there were crinkles at the corners of his eyes.

Burke looked up and caught her looking at him. "Did you read these?"

"I read some of them. Why?"

"It sounds like they're having an affair."

"Really?" Lucia stood up and went to stand at his shoulder so she could read with him. "What gives you that idea?" She leaned forward to decipher the old handwriting and felt the heat radiating from him. He smelled of soap and sunshine. His tanned cheek was right next to hers. The nearness gave her butterflies.

"Here." Burke pointed to a line. "He says, 'You looked like

an angel in your pale pink dress at the party. I could barely keep my eyes off you.' That sounds like what a boyfriend would say to a girlfriend, don't you think?"

He turned to look at her, and his lips nearly grazed her cheek.

Lucia stood up abruptly and stepped away from him. "They certainly sound like close friends." She walked back to her seat behind the desk. "Why don't you take these with you? Then you can read them at home whenever you like."

"Oh, I'm sorry if I'm bothering you." He gathered up the small pile of old letters from his lap and stood up. "I didn't mean to interrupt your work. Have a good afternoon." He sketched a small wave and left the study, saying goodbye to Susanna on his way out.

Lucia thought that maybe her relationship with today's Burke might echo his grandfather's relationship with her great-aunt Anneke.

CHAPTER 16

Lucia didn't need to stay on the island. Soon, she and Pietr would have all the estate paperwork finished, the government would take possession of the house and property, and she wouldn't have a place to sleep. There was no publishing house on the island where she could get a job, and remote working was not, well, working. She wondered how long her boss would put up with her being away. She'd brought her work tablet along, so she had manuscripts to read and could communicate with authors and the office, but it wasn't the same.

Lucia may not have needed to stay on the island, but she wanted to. In the short time she had been there, she had fallen in love with Bonaire and its people. Even the stark simplicity of the landscape pleased her. She was supposed to have gone to Pietr Smit's office that afternoon, but he had called to cancel. Now she was free to do whatever she wanted to do, and that was to go to the beach. She packed a couple of bottles of water in a bag along with her towel, mask, fins, snorkel, and her sun protection suit, along with sunscreen and a bag of trail mix. Then she changed into her swimsuit, grabbed a hat, and set off to find a beach.

Lucia went back to Windsock Beach at the end of the airport runway, where Susanna's cookout was held. When she arrived, the beach was filled with people scuba diving, groups on guided snorkel tours, and more people having cookouts. She found a parking place at the south end of the beach, walked a few steps onto the sand, and laid her towel in the shade. At first, she sat and watched all the activity while she had a snack. Once she'd drunk a bottle of water and eaten some trail mix, she pulled on her wetsuit and waded into the shallows with her snorkel gear. There was a small reef right offshore from where she had left her towel so she could keep an eye on it.

She'd bought a plastic box on a lanyard for her keys and money, which she put around her neck and tucked into the top of her suit. She swam out to the edge of the drop-off and just floated there, watching the activity of the reef fish. Lucia enjoyed riding the surge, which pulled her in toward shore and then pushed her away. She tried to mirror the small school of Yellowtail Jacks that rode the surge looking for something to eat, but she kept moving too much and losing her place. She saw a tiny fish, no bigger than a pea, finning rapidly in the shelter of a coral head. A Bar Jack swooped in and ate it. "Oh no," she said. She watched a cleaning station at the edge of the drop-off. Fish of different species lined up like cars at a Saturday car wash, while tiny shrimp crawled all over them, eating away parasites and dead skin.

The sun was scorching, and she needed to get back to the shade, so she turned toward the shore and saw someone sitting by her towel and bag. Swimming closer, she saw it was a man. As she waded out of the water and started up the beach, she noticed the man was Burke.

"Hi," she said. "What are you doing here in the middle of the day?"

He stood, shook the sand off her towel, and handed it to her, taking her fins and mask. "I was down here looking at a place, saw your car, and thought I'd stop."

She stripped off her wetsuit before drying her face and hair. "How'd you know it's my car?"

"You're driving Miss Anneke's car. I'd know it anywhere since I helped her pick it out."

She laughed. "I forgot." She put the towel on the sand and sat on it. "Did you find a place?"

He sat on the sand next to her and shook his head. "No. Places down here are too rich for my blood, and there's no good mooring nearby. I'll have to keep looking."

"I hope you find something before the estate is settled. I'd hate to think you were homeless because of me."

He squinted out at the ocean. "I won't end up homeless. There are places available. I just have to find the right one." He turned to smile at her. "Are you planning the estate sale to get rid of the furniture and things?"

"Pietr and I talked about it, and that'll be the last thing before I file all the papers. I don't want to sell all the furniture and have nowhere to sit or sleep."

"Good thinking."

"How was fishing this morning?" she said.

"Good. Now that the wind has picked up a bit to ruffle the surface of the water, the fish aren't hiding from the sun, so I catch fish and can fill my restaurant orders." He nudged her with his elbow. "I already gave Susanna fish for your supper tonight."

She smiled at him. "Thanks, but you don't have to feed me. I can get my own supper at the market."

"Yeah, but wouldn't you rather have fresh fish than store-bought fish?"

"I think the fish in the store is fresh too, isn't it?"

"Not as fresh as mine."

"Ah. Okay, thanks then."

While they talked, Lucia gathered up her belongings and repacked her bag. Burke shook the sand out of her towel and folded it before handing it to her. They walked the few steps to the side of the road where their vehicles were parked. Burke opened the door of the car for Lucia, then went to his faded green pickup truck and climbed in. He waved at her as he pulled out and drove away.

Instead of turning around to go back through town, Lucia continued on south. She had never been down to that end of the island and wanted to see how it compared to her end. Soon the houses petered out, and the land flattened until it was barely above sea level. The road hugged the shore on her right, and there were dive sites marked by yellow-painted rocks with the site names on them in black. On the left were large pink ponds separated by dikes. Those must be the salt pans she'd heard about, she thought just as she caught sight of great big white piles of salt ready to ride a long conveyor over the road to be loaded on a freighter and shipped to the States. She had read that the salt was used for road salt and water softener salt, not salt for food. There was a big ship anchored at the end of the conveyor, so she pulled over to watch. Bull-dozers moved alongside the big piles of salt, lifting buckets of it and dumping it onto the belt for the trip across the road to the ship. She wondered if there was a tour of the saltworks that she could go on. She would ask Susanna, or maybe Burke.

As she drove further south, there were more dive sites with small pickup trucks parked nearby with pairs of divers gearing up to dive or coming out of the shallows to take off their gear after a dive. Lucia thought about learning to scuba dive or maybe just taking a tryout dive. They had to have things like that, right? She was a good enough swimmer, so that wouldn't be an issue, and she had a mask, snorkel, and fins. She could probably rent a tank and breathing apparatus. She would look into it before she had to go back home to the States. But Bonaire felt like home, too. She pulled into one site called Tori's Reef, where a couple was just coming out of the water. Once they had removed their scuba equipment and were drying off, she walked over to talk to them about what they had seen.

"Hi," she said, "would this be a good site for snorkeling?"

The woman smiled at her. "It would be a great site for snorkeling." She turned to point behind her. "This channel where they let seawater into the salt ponds is like a swimming pool, so if you are not very confident, you can stay in here where it's shallow." She motioned to where the waves crashed around some boulders at the entrance of the channel. "Then if you swim out there, it's shallow for a long time with patches of coral and little critters all around."

The man chimed in. "This would be the best place on the island to snorkel. It's a great place to dive, that's for sure."

She smiled at their enthusiasm. "I don't know how to dive. I only snorkel, but I'll come back here one day while I am here."

"Are you here on holiday?" the woman asked.

Lucia shook her head. "No, my great-aunt lived here and just passed away. I came down to settle her estate."

The woman reached out and touched her forearm. "Oh, I'm sorry for your loss."

"Thank you," Lucia said, "but I didn't know her well. The news that I am her sole relative and in charge of all of that was a big surprise."

"How long have you been here?" the man asked.

"Just over two months. Bureaucracy moves slowly here. I'm already in love with the island and the people. It's too bad–I can't stay here, but Aunt Anneke's property reverts to the island government upon her death, so I have a lot of legal wrangling and mounds of paperwork to do. In fact, I should be going. The house is at the entrance to the park, way on the northern end of the island." She walked back to her car and waved as she got in. "Enjoy your time on Bonaire," she said.

"And thanks for the snorkeling info."

The couple waved back.

On she went, passing windsurfers gathered at a place along the shore, then small white huts with an obelisk nearby, and a lone house beside a cluster of red huts. Next came a lighthouse that sat close to the shore with waves spouting up behind it. She figured she had turned from the leeward side of the island to the windward side. There were no houses and no divers along this shoreline, just dark jagged rocks and pounding surf. On the left were still salt ponds with a few wading flamingoes. She passed some windmills, then the road turned away from the shore and headed straight across the island through stands of large cacti with bright green birds with yellow heads flying between them.

Soon she came to a neighborhood of small, single-story houses, many with beautiful flowers spilling over the walls of the garden. At the stop sign, she turned right and was soon passing the backside of the airport runway and Windsock Beach. Lucia followed the road into town, stopping at the market for some cheese and a loaf of bread. She took the road out of town and up the eastern side of the island to avoid some of the tourist traffic. Besides, she liked the peace and open spaces on the road to Rincon and then home to Aunt Anneke's plantation house. When she got home, Susanna's scooter was gone, but Burke's faded green pickup truck with its tangle of fishing poles in the back was parked in front. She eased around him and parked her car outside the back door. Lucia took out her wet things and her shopping and went in. She walked through the house and out the front door.

"Hi Burke, what can I do for you?"

He looked at her. "I thought you got lost."

She shook her head. "Nope. I drove around the south end of the island since I'd never been down there before. I stopped at Tori's Reef to talk to some divers, then at Warehouse Market in town for a few things." Lucia smiled. "Were you thinking of sending out a search party? Someone told me the morning I arrived that it was hard to get lost on an island this small."

He shook his head. "No, I said it's hard to hide on an island this small. It's easy to get lost when you don't know the island."

She nodded. "Agreed. But today I stayed on the main roads and didn't get lost." She folded her arms across her middle. "Thanks for worrying."

He snorted. "I wasn't worried. I just, well, I was concerned when you didn't turn up in good time. All right, I was worried. I didn't want to have to tell Pietr that I'd lost you."

"Pietr's not in charge of me." She stepped toward the house. "Would you like some iced tea? Susanna made some this morning."

He stood up. "No, thanks. I need to shower and clean up. I'm meeting friends for a drink." He turned to get into his truck. "Hey, do you want to come along? Meet some new people on the island?"

She thought for a minute. "Yes, I'd like to come along. What time?"

"We need to leave here around five thirty."

"Great, I can shower and be ready. Thanks for the invitation."

By five fifteen, Lucia was ready. Hoping she was dressed right, she had fifteen minutes to stew about it. Burke had not said to dress up, so she wore cotton slacks and a sleeveless button-down shirt with a collar. That seemed like a neutral outfit for drinks with friends. She paced up and down the hall, wondering if Burke was usually on time or perennially late. She bet he was on time, maybe even early, and she was right. Just then she heard tires crunch on the driveway gravel and headlights shone on the front of the house. He parked and got out to open the truck's door for her.

"Hi," she said, "thanks."

"You're welcome," he said. "Do you have a sweater or a jacket you can leave in the truck? We'll be outside, and you might get chilled."

She got out and retrieved one. When she came back to the truck, she said, "I can't imagine getting chilled. It's been so hot at night since I arrived."

He started the truck, backed around, and drove down the driveway. "We'll be near the sea, and it could cool off enough that you might need a light jacket. You can leave it in here, and if you need it, I'll fetch it."

"Thank you."

They drove for a while in silence. Then Lucia asked, "Who are we having drinks with? You didn't say."

He glanced at her. "Oh, they're a couple of expats from England, Charles and Amelia. She buys fish from me, and he used to do something in the fisheries business in England. We have a fish connection." He smiled at her in the dark, his teeth flashing white in the headlights from oncoming cars.

"I've met them. Don't you remember? We saw each other at the appetizer table at their party."

"Right. I forgot."

They drove through town on the road along the shore. The street was crowded with tourists and locals dressed for an evening.

"There are a lot of people out and about," she said.

"Downtown is popular. There are a lot of restaurants and bars within walking distance around here. Have you come down for a meal since you've been here?"

She shook her head. "No, I've stayed home at night. I'm

not sure enough of my directions to drive around in the dark. I haven't even tested the car's headlights. I'd hate to have one or both out when I need them."

He bristled. "Do you think I would let Miss Anneke's car have bad lights? I would never risk her life like that."

"I'm sorry," she said. "I didn't mean to accuse you of not taking good care of Aunt Anneke's car. I'm just a nervous Nellie about getting lost, especially in the dark."

"That's okay. I get defensive when people accuse me of being careless."

"I never…"

He held up his right hand. "I know you didn't accuse me of anything, but I took my responsibilities to Miss Anneke seriously."

"And I appreciate it. I should have said so before. Thank you for taking such good care of the place and of her. I would have done my part, but until Pietr called me, I knew nothing about her or this place." They drove past the airport.

"My pleasure. We're almost there," Burke said.

"Tell me about Charles and Amelia," said Lucia. "I didn't really talk to them at the party. There was such a crush."

"Well, Charles is a retired businessman, and Amelia was a wife and mother to their children because Charles traveled a lot for his job. They retired down here to get away from the rain and dreary fog of England. Charles organized a snorkeling group. Amelia is in the art appreciation group with a lot of other expats and a few locals."

"Have you known them long?"

"Pretty much since they arrived. I used to sell fish at the morning market in town, and Amelia came to buy fish for supper. She and I got to talking, and I started saving a bit of the fish I knew she liked. When my restaurant orders picked up and I stopped selling at the market, I kept fish aside for her. I still do today."

They had cocktails with Charles and Amelia Eastman and then the four of them went out to supper at Fredo's Barbecue. The restaurant was in the carport and backyard of a house on a side street in downtown Playa.

"How did you ever find this place?" Lucia asked.

"Burke told us about it," Amelia said.

Burke said, "I've known Fredo for a long time. He and I worked together on a fishing boat before he opened this place, and I got my boat."

The waiter brought their meals and drinks. Lucia had a combination plate with ribs, chicken wings, satay, fries, and coleslaw. She looked at the platter in dismay. "This is too much food," she said.

Burke leaned toward her. "I'll help you eat it."

She put a protective hand over her plate. "Oh no, I see a couple of excellent lunches coming from the leftovers."

Everyone laughed and got down to business.

Lucia enjoyed the conversation with Amelia and Charles. They had been on the island for over a year and did their best to convince Lucia to stay.

"You need to come snorkeling with my group next Tuesday," Charles said.

Lucia smiled. "I would love to. Do you know where you'll go?"

Charles looked up as if the dive site's name might be written between the branches of the trees. "I think we are planning to go to Tori's Reef down past the Salt Pier."

She clapped her hands together. "Oh, I would love to come along. I stopped there earlier today, and a pair of divers told me it's an excellent snorkeling spot." She looked at him uncertainly. "Will it be okay for a nonmember to attend? I can pay something toward refreshments or whatever is provided."

He waved her offer away. "No, no, you'll be my guest. Many guests come on our snorkeling outings. People will be happy to meet you and show you the site. Your diver friends were quite right. Tori's is a perfect spot for snorkeling. Do you have your own gear?"

Lucia nodded. "I do. Do I need to bring anything else?"

Charles turned back to his meal. "Just a bottle of water and a towel. Someone will bring fruit and something else for a snack. We take turns."

She protested that she should bring something, so Charles relented and asked her to bring some bottled water. "Just a few bottles in case people forget."

"I can do that, and thanks for the invitation."

Amelia leaned across the table. "Why don't you come to our house, then ride with Charles? That way, there will be fewer cars at the dive site."

"Is that okay, Charles?" Lucia asked. "I don't want to interfere with any arrangements you might have already made."

Charles waved away her protests. "Not to worry. I will pick up only one other person, so there will be plenty of room for you in my vehicle."

Amelia snapped. "Are you picking up that David Flemming again?"

Charles patted Amelia's hand. "Calm down, my dear. David is harmless, and yes, I am picking him up, as I do every time. They have only one vehicle, so this way Verna is not stuck at home while he is away."

By then, everyone had eaten as much of their meal as

they could. The waiter came by with to-go boxes for Amelia and Lucia.

"Dessert?" he said.

Lucia leaned back and patted her stomach. "Not for me; I'm stuffed."

Burke spoke up. "I'll have chocolate mousse. What about you, Charles?"

Amelia spoke for him. "We'll split some. I would like just a taste." She leaned across the table to Lucia. "They make excellent chocolate mousse here. You might want to reconsider."

"Well, I'm pretty full, but I could probably make a small serving of mousse disappear."

"Three mousses it is," said the waiter, and he walked away to fetch them.

The chocolate mousse lived up to its reputation. It was creamy and cold and extra chocolaty.

"Oh, this was a good idea," Lucia said. "I'm glad I got my own serving." She looked at Burke. "Maybe I should jog home behind the truck. I ate so much tonight with appetizers at Charles and Amelia's, drinks, all that barbecue, and then mousse on top of it. I'll have to watch what I eat for a week."

Charles leaned toward her with a glint in his eye. "But worth it, right, my dear?"

Lucia smiled back at him. "Totally."

They had arrived in two vehicles, so the couples said their goodnights, gathered up their to-go boxes, and went their separate ways.

"We should do this again," Amelia said. Lucia agreed.

As they drove away, Burke said, "So, did you like my friends?"

Lucia smiled in the darkness. "I did. Thank you for introducing me to them."

"I wish I could go snorkeling with you, but I have to work."

"We could go snorkeling another time," she said. "There must be sites closer to home where we could go when you come back from fishing." She could see him nodding in the dashboard lights.

"Oh, there are. We could snorkel right off our dock if you want to. There are small patches of reef right there."

"I've been there and seen them. I liked it," she said. "Can we go tomorrow?"

Burke laughed. "Yes, we can go tomorrow. I'll call when I get in from fishing and we can set a time."

"That's great. I can't wait."

****

Manning pried the lock of the back door of Lucia's plantation house. He'd watched her leave with Burke and figured they'd be gone long enough for him to search the place. He started with the desk in the study, pulling out drawers, rummaging in each corner before dumping the papers out onto the floor. The doubloon had to be somewhere. He'd sent one to Anneke Boon, hoping to entice her to invest in his treasure scheme, and he wanted it back. Too bad the old lady had kicked off the day after his letter should have arrived. He got a reply from her tight-ass attorney saying no thanks for the deal and thanks for the doubloon. But Manning wanted the gold coin back, and he was determined to find it. It had to be there.

When he'd been through the things on the desktop and all the drawers had been emptied, he started on the shelves of books. Anneke Boon had been an old lady. Old ladies kept money stashed in their houses, didn't they? Manning ruffled the pages of each book, dropping them on the floor, and kicking them aside. Maybe there'd be a safe he could twiddle the lock on and find all sorts of cash and his doubloon.

He had been through every place in the study and was about to move on to the other rooms when he heard a truck pull into the gravel drive. Manning dashed to the kitchen and slipped out the back door just as he heard voices on the porch and a key in the front door.

****

They drove the rest of the way in silence, each of them lost in their own thoughts. Burke dropped Lucia at her door. She thanked him for the evening, and he waited for her to unlock the door before driving away. She hadn't gotten to the kitchen before there was a knock at her front door.

"What is it? Is something wrong?" she said.

A silent Burke held out her sweater and to-go box.

"Oh, thank you. I'd miss this at lunchtime tomorrow."

She began to close the door, but his hand stopped her. He stepped up to her, placed his hands on her shoulders, and bent down to kiss her cheek. When she didn't protest, he moved his lips down to the corner of her mouth and kissed her there. When she still didn't move or speak, he took the sweater and Styrofoam box from her, laid them on the hall table, and kissed her full on the lips. She put her hands flat on his chest and kissed him back. As the kiss went on, she slid her hands up and pulled his head closer to hers.

With his hands still on her shoulders, he stepped back, looked down into her eyes and said, "Good night, Lucia. Sleep well."

Lucia closed the door behind him and stood in the dark hall. He kissed me, she thought, and touched her lips with her fingers. I kissed him back. She shook her head. Neither of them had drunk much, so she didn't think that was the reason. She picked up her box of leftovers and walked down the hall to the kitchen, where she had left on a small light. She put the box into the refrigerator and glanced over to see the back door standing open. Had she forgotten to close it before she left? No, she was certain she had checked the doors before leaving. Had someone been in her house? She fumbled her cellphone out of her purse and called Burke.

"What?" he said. "Do you want me to apologize for kissing you?"

"No," she whispered, "I think someone's been in here."

"I'll be right there."

Lucia stood in the center of the kitchen, in the pool of light from the lamp on the table, and listened for Burke's truck. In a very few minutes, she heard footsteps on the gravel drive. Running footsteps. There was a knock on the door.

"Lucia? Lucia, it's Burke. Open the door."

She hesitated for a moment, then hurried down the hall and opened the heavy wooden door.

He gripped her upper arms. "What makes you think someone has been in here?"

She turned and gestured toward the kitchen. "The… the door is standing open. I know I closed it and locked it before I left. I know I did." Tears filled her eyes and spilled down her cheeks.

"Did you check the rest of the house?"

She shook her head.

He turned away and walked through the rest of the house, turning on lights wherever he went. Lucia followed him, not speaking. All the rooms looked the same until they came to the study. Someone had pulled open the desk drawers, and papers were scattered everywhere.

"Oh no," she said in a small voice. "What were they looking for?"

Burke stood in the doorway with his fists on his hips. "Money."

"Surely not. There's no money here."

"But people don't know that. Everyone knew that Anneke Boon was a rich old woman who lived alone, and people assume old people keep money in their homes."

Someone had knocked the books off the shelves, leaving them in a drift on the floor.

"Why knock all the books down?" she said.

He toed the edge of the nearest volume. "Looking for a safe would be my guess."

"A safe? There's no safe here. All of Aunt Anneke's stock certificates and deeds are in a safe deposit box in the bank or in Pietr's office safe."

He looked down at her huddled in the doorway. "People don't know that either. You should call the police, make a report, so there's a record of this home invasion."

She sniffed back tears. "Okay."

Burke stayed with her while she waited for the police to come. When they arrived, they didn't offer any confidence that they could find out who had been in the house.

"Probably young opportunists," said the police officer. "Are you certain you locked the door before you left?" He glanced around the kitchen. "Maybe you left it ajar, and the wind blew it open."

"What wind?" she asked. "There's been no wind since I arrived. People keep talking about how hot and windless it is at night. No, the wind didn't blow open the door. And it surely didn't yank out the desk drawers or knock all the books off the shelves in the study."

She had left everything just as she had found it and had double-checked that her room hadn't been ransacked. If her things had been strewn about, she didn't know what she would do.

"I will file an incident report, and you will need to stop at the station tomorrow to verify what it says." The policeman touched the brim of his cap and left, leaving Lucia standing in the middle of her house.

Burke touched her arm and made her jump.

"Oh, sorry. I had better get this cleared up and then get to bed." She looked at the mess around her feet. "Get to bed. I don't know if I'll be able to sleep tonight after this."

Burke put his hand on her shoulder softly. "How about I sleep in the other bedroom tonight? You can get new locks, and we'll install them tomorrow."

"That's unnecessary. I'll be all right."

"You look like a startled animal. You need someone around tonight, and that someone is me. I'll go home and close things up. I'll be right back."

She nodded and watched him go down the hall and out the front door. She went into the kitchen to close and lock the back door. It wouldn't close. She looked at it closely and saw that someone had pried the lock out of the doorjamb. "Oh, no." She sat down at the table, put her face in her hands, and cried.

Soon she heard tires on the driveway, and Burke came in the front door with a backpack over one shoulder. "Look at the back door," she said, drying her eyes.

"Aw man, that's terrible. We'll have to repair the wood frame and get a new lock." He sat down next to her at the table. "I'll get up early to go fishing, but I'll be back soon, before noon, and I'll get this fixed. We'll put in a new lock and a deadbolt and make you feel safe in here."

She sniffled, pulled a paper napkin out of the holder on the table, and blew her nose. "I don't know if I'll ever feel safe in here again."

CHAPTER 17

Lucia lay awake, staring at the ceiling. She couldn't shake the feeling of dread at having her home invaded. Burke and the police officer said they thought it was kids looking for money, but what if it wasn't? What if there was something else they were looking for? The only room torn up was the study, so there must be a reason they chose it. Was there someone in the house when she got home? She shuddered to think she might have walked in on them if Burke hadn't stopped her at the door with his kisses. And those kisses. What did she think about those?

Burke lay asleep in the next room. Lucia was glad he had volunteered to stay the night. She doubted she would have slept at all without his comforting presence. Lucia wondered if she could fall asleep with him there. She thought about his broad shoulders and the way they had felt under her hands when he held her and kissed her cheek, then her lips. He had tasted of salt and sunshine. Maybe she would go into his room and kiss him back. Or maybe he'd come here for a repeat performance. With that thought, she drifted off to sleep.

The next morning the sun was high, and Susanna was rattling around in the kitchen, humming a tune. Lucia slipped into her robe and, after combing her hair and brushing her teeth, she peeked into the next room, but Burke was gone, and the bed was made. She smiled to think that he was protecting her reputation by making the bed.

"Good morning, Susanna," she said as she walked in from the hall.

"Good morning, Miss Lucia," Susanna said. "Would you like some coffee?"

"I would love some, thank you," Lucia said.

While she sipped her coffee and ate some toast that Susanna had made for her, she told Susanna about someone breaking into the house the night before.

"Oh, no," Susanna said, her hand over her open mouth. "Were you here when they broke in?"

Lucia shook her head. "No, Burke and I met some friends of his for drinks and then went out to supper, so we didn't get back until after ten o'clock." She had a bite of toast and a sip of coffee. "I came into the kitchen to put my leftovers in the fridge and saw that the back door was standing open. I knew I hadn't left it open, so I called Burke, and then he called the police when we saw that the study had been ransacked."

"Ransacked?"

Lucia nodded. "Yes, all the drawers were pulled out and all the papers were on the floor. A lot of the books were pulled off the shelves, too. It's a mess. It'll take me days to get it all back in order."

Susanna shook her head at the thought. "I can help clean up the room."

Lucia smiled at her. "Thank you, but I think it would be just as easy if I did it myself and got Pietr to help me organize the papers. You and I can shelve the books today if you don't mind. That will be a big help. The papers need to be looked at and sorted."

Susanna turned to the sink and ran hot water to wash the breakfast dishes. Then she turned back around. "How did you sleep here with the back door unlocked?"

Lucia smiled a small smile. "Burke got the doorjamb back into place and locked the door."

"Even so, I would have been awake all night with worry that they would come back."

"I would have, but Burke offered to sleep here, so we made up the bed in the second bedroom and he slept there. I suppose he got up early to go fishing."

Susanna pointed to a piece of paper tucked between the salt and pepper shakers on the table. "There's a note." She shuffled her feet. "It was on the counter by the coffeepot when I got here. I put it on the table."

"Oh, thank you." Lucia reached for the small piece of paper.

Good morning. I hope you slept well. I'll come back after work and see if you are okay. Burke.

"What time is it?" Lucia asked.

"It's nearly ten thirty," Susanna said.

"Oh, it's late. I had better take a shower and get dressed." She finished her coffee and toast and went to clean up for the day.

After her shower, she and Susanna went into the study to clean up the mess. Lucia thought it looked worse in the daylight. She nearly cried, but Susanna stepped forward and started lifting books and shelving them, so Lucia did the same. She swept up piles of papers and laid them on the desk for sorting later. It didn't take them long to get all the books off the floor and onto the shelves. Lucia thanked Susanna and then sat down to sort the papers. She was relieved to see that the old ledgers and journals were not damaged.

A few minutes later, Susanna stuck her head in the door. "Miss, there's a folding table in the back room that might make it easier to sort the papers. Would you like me to bring it?"

"Oh, that would be great. Thank you. Do you need help to carry it?"

"No, Miss Lucia, I can get it."

Lucia cleared a place on the floor and helped Susanna set up the table.

Susanna dusted it off and patted Lucia's shoulder. "There, that should help you."

Lucia spent the next few hours sorting papers into piles by decade. Once she had them all off the floor, she took the most recent ones and got them into chronological order. She found some empty manila folders and started labeling them. After a couple of hours, Susanna popped her head around the corner and asked if she wanted lunch.

"Lunch, is it time? Yes, I want lunch. I brought home leftovers from Fredo's that I'll heat in the microwave. Thanks for reminding me to eat."

Lucia was just finishing her lunch when Burke knocked on the back door. He carried a wrapped fish steak in one hand and his toolbox in the other. "Hi Burke. How was fishing this morning?" She stood and opened the screen door to let him in.

"Good," he said, handing the wrapped fish to Susanna. "I hooked a dorado, so we'll all have mahi mahi for supper tonight."

"What's the toolbox for?"

He set the old metal box down next to the back door. "I want to putty the crack in your door frame and get it back in place so the putty will dry before we put in the new lock. It might be a good idea to add a deadbolt to the front and back doors too, so I brought my hole-cutter bits."

She carried her plate and glass to the sink and rinsed them. "That sounds great. What can I do?"

Burke handed her a small flathead screwdriver. "Take this and carefully pry the crack open so we can spread putty all over the break. Try not to chisel off any of the wood when you do it."

Lucia took her time to lever open the split in the old wood. "Are you sure this will work?"

"It has before. I've used this kind of putty to repair split wood for years. We'll get it pushed back together, and then we can go pick out some new locks at James Hardware."

Once she got the wood pried apart so they could see all the raw wood, he handed her a putty knife and said, "Use this to smear putty all over the break on both sides."

She looked at him in surprise. "Why are you having me do it? You do it." She tried to hand the putty knife back to him.

"You can do it." He came up behind her with the can of wood putty. "Dip the end of the putty knife in the goop and spread it over the raw wood. Use your finger to smear it in all the spaces. Your fingers are smaller than mine, so I thought it'd be easier for you to do it."

"All right." She leaned over and concentrated on getting putty all over the broken wood. "Both sides?" She felt his breath on the back of her neck.

"Both sides. Put on enough so that when we shove the wood back into place, the putty oozes out. We'll clean it off." He put his hand over hers on the handle of the putty knife and guided it. "That's right. Nice and smooth."

She turned her head to find they were nose to nose. Lucia quickly straightened up and handed off the putty knife. "You finish it. I'm sure I'm not doing it right." She stepped away from the doorjamb to put some distance between them.

Burke shrugged. "Okay. But you were doing just fine." He bent over to finish spreading the putty, then he eased the wood back together and pounded on it with a fist to make sure it was tight. Just as he'd predicted, the putty oozed out. He used an old rag to wipe the excess off. "Get me a wet paper towel so I can remove the rest. We don't want it to dry where it doesn't belong."

After they'd both washed their hands, they got into Burke's faded green pickup truck for the drive to James Hardware on the road into Playa. Lucia didn't mind the long drive when she was with a friend. In the store, they picked out a pair of new locks and a pair of deadbolts to add to the doors for extra security. When they got to the checkout, Burke put his hand on his hip pocket to pull out his wallet, but Lucia stopped him.

"It's my house, so I need to pay for them. Well, the estate will pay for them. I'll save the receipt to get reimbursed. Thanks for helping me."

They'd left the windows of Burke's truck open, so it wasn't unbearably hot when they got in to ride back to Karpata. Lucia still pulled a towel from behind the seat to protect the backs of her thighs from the hot seat.

Back at the plantation house, they tackled installing the deadbolt in the front door first to give the putty more time to dry. They also replaced the doorknob so that both front and back doors used the same key. "So much easier than having to remember which key goes where," Burke said.

"I'll miss using the skeleton key to get in, though," Lucia said with a smile.

"True. It isn't period correct, but it's a lot safer to have modern locks. They're less likely to be picked. Especially with the deadbolt added, too." He drove the last screw into the deadbolt strike plate. "There. Now don't forget to lock these when you leave the house or turn in for the night. There's an extra key, so you can give one to Susanna, so she has it when she comes to work."

The putty was dry enough, so Burke had Lucia sand all around the crack. Again, he put his hand over hers to show her the sanding motion that was best. She shrugged him away, elbowing him back. "I know how to sand. My uncle was a woodworker."

He put up his hands and backed away. "Whatever you say."

When she finished, he swung the door into the frame to make sure that it fit. "Fits like it belongs there. Let's get the deadbolt installed, and then we can install the new doorknob."

It didn't take long to finish the job.

Burke packed up his tools after cleaning off the putty knife.

"I don't know how to thank you for all you've done for me," Lucia said. She put her hands on his shoulders, raised up on tiptoe, and kissed his cheek.

He turned his head so that their lips met, and Lucia froze. Burke's hand slid from her shoulder to the back of her head to hold their lips together.

She relaxed into the embrace and pulled his shoulders closer.

"Miss Lucia, I'll just get that fish cooked for you before I go." Susanna came through the kitchen door talking and stopped when she saw them. "Oh, I'm so sorry." She turned on her heel and left the room.

At the sound of her voice, Lucia and Burke sprang apart, looked at each other, and turned away.

"Thanks for all you've done today," she said. She felt the heat of her blush rise from her neck to her cheeks. "I mean, thanks for fixing the locks."

"You're welcome. Always happy to help." He picked up his toolbox, waved, and left through the open kitchen door.

Neither of them remembered their plan to go snorkeling that afternoon.

CHAPTER 18

Once Jack got the hundred grand transferred into Manning's bank account, he started looking for results, hounding Manning for details, times, places. He wanted to have something—recovered metal encrusted with barnacles, a piece of cannon shot, a tankard, anything that he could touch and feel the hundreds of years on it.

Manning was shocked and unsettled by Jack's vehement insistence that he be kept informed of every single move that was made. Jack sounded like he wanted to take over the operation, wanted to be the big cheese instead of the silent money man. In less than a week, Manning thought Jack had been a very poor choice to make for his first shipwreck scam mark.

Jack wanted to be in the thick of things. He discounted Manning's warning that the site of the sunken wreckage was too deep and swept by currents too dangerous for a new diver. Jack had gone to Lora Divers, the dive shop at the Plaza Resort, and started taking Open Water scuba classes so he could dive on "his" wreck.

Manning needed to do something fast to get back in control of the situation.

****

Burke steered the *Miss Ana* along the northern coast of the island. He usually fished the southern end of the island but decided to try his luck at the northern end, just past the fuel depot. There had been a rumor floating around town that Manning and Santiago were salting a wreck site or even setting up a fake one. Burke heard whispers they were working off the northern, more treacherous end of the island, so he thought he'd check it out. But he also wanted to be able to get back home quickly in case Lucia needed him. He'd checked the shipping schedule and knew there weren't any tankers expected that day, so he wouldn't have to worry about being rammed by the interisland tanker that brought fuel to Bonaire.

The sun was a pale promise in the eastern sky when he rounded Malmok, the northern point of the island. He saw another boat up ahead, so he slowed down to find out if another fisherman had the same idea. Burke stopped and, by the small running light on the boat in front, he saw two figures moving about. One of them wore scuba gear, and the other was helping him over the stern. Once the diver was in the water, the man on the boat handed over what looked like a piece of an old ship's railing.

Burke doused his running lights and picked up his binoculars. It was challenging to hold them still on the shifting boat, but he settled his eyes on the scene ahead. He thought it was the *Santa Marta,* Santiago's boat. Burke had seen it frequently tied up at the Town Pier and easily recognized it.

All thoughts of fishing fled as he watched the man in the water sink beneath the surface with the piece of railing clutched in one arm. It wasn't long before the diver's head popped up and Santiago reached over the stern to hand him a heavy cloth bag. The diver descended again and was gone longer. When the diver surfaced a second time, he handed up his weights and fins, then climbed up the outboard and over the stern into the boat. When he pulled off his hood, Burke caught his breath. That was Manning. No one else had golden curls like that. He remembered there was a rumor going around that Manning and Santiago had found a sunken ship and were planning to bring up treasure. And Jack Spencer was paying for it.

Burke lowered the binoculars for a second and then put them back to his eyes. He saw the two men pull up the anchor, turn into the sunrise, and speed away at full throttle into the gathering dawn. "I wonder what those two are up to," he said to himself. "Nothing legal, I'll wager."

The brightening sky made him realize he was wasting prime fishing time. He figured the spot he was in was as good as any, so he rigged his lines and got down to the business of catching fish for the tourists' suppers. But he kept wondering what he'd find if he fished a little farther to the east.

CHAPTER 19

"Necklace, Mister? Only fifteen guilders."

Jack pushed away the hand that thrust the shell necklace at him. One look at his face and the middle-aged woman vendor withdrew her hand and took a step back.

His eyes, dark brown and darting from side to side, kept everyone at bay. All the vendors in Queen Wilhelmina Park across from the Town Pier were glad he wasn't looking for them. He smoked the harsh island cigarettes one after another. Just another reason to take revenge on Manning, Jack thought. Eight years of not smoking and within three months on this god-forsaken outpost of an island, he was back smoking over a pack a day. Damn Manning. And damn Nora for nagging him about it.

****

Silent flyers swooped out of the night to glide through the swarms of delectable bugs that congregated around the security light. Times had changed on the island. Where once you could have left the door unlocked and trusted that a light-sleeping dog would keep your house safe, now every door had a couple of locks. More and more windows sported bars screwed right into the frame, and lights turned on at dusk, drawing moths and other tasty treats for the island's bats. The security lights turned off at dawn just as the furry flyers were gliding back to their crowded, comfy roosts in the caves on the wild windward coast.

****

Nora sat on the patio watching the sunrise behind her in the east send pastel shades of rose and gold in streaks across the sky, painting the tops of the iron gray clouds crouched on the western horizon behind the little offshore island. She watched the curl of steam rise from her cup of mint tea and smiled at the drops of dew that trembled on the ends of the palm fronds. Tiny emerald and brown lizards splayed themselves on the stucco wall, did their morning push-ups, and displayed their orange throats at each other. The vivid red and yellow verbena that screened her patio from the neighbor's view reminded her of early morning at a busy airport. The squadron of black and iridescent green hummingbirds swarmed around, jockeying to be the first to sip the nectar from each tiny trumpet. Nora mourned the fleeting moments of perfect stillness she felt as she sat there every morning that were so quickly lost when the maid Yana arrived.

The large robin-sized bird perched on the garden gate, glaring at Nora. She couldn't get over how vivid orange the bird's breast was and how the contrast of its black head feathers made the orange even brighter. There was a yellow ring around the shiny black eye that gave the bird a horror-film look. Nora studied the elegant-looking creature as she sipped her tea and toyed with the toast that Yana set before her.

"You see the Trupial, Miss?" Yana asked.

"I wondered what it was—a Trupial."

As if responding to its name, the bird stretched its neck, threw its head up, and gave a loud clear call, flung at the blazing morning sun like a gauntlet. Almost before the note stopped ringing in the heated air, there came an answering call from a nearby tree.

Yana laughed. "Just like a man. He calls her to come to him." She cocked her head to the side. "You watch," said the younger woman, "pretty soon a female will come and flutter down beside him."

Sure enough, another Trupial flew over and landed on the gate. "How can you tell males from females?" Nora asked.

Yana crossed her arms and shook her head. "Easy. You see, he is all duded up. She is just a little drabber. I figure to soothe his ego."

The women looked at each other and burst out laughing at the universal truth of those words. The Trupials flew away unfed.

****

Manning told him that Spelonk Cave was where he could see them working to raise parts of the shipwreck. The low-ceilinged space reverberated with the irritated squeaks of fruit bats jostling for space. Jack glared up at them to make sure he was not in line for any falling guano to stain his pristine khaki shirt. He had arrived at the cave an hour before sun-rise, nestling in a small niche off to the side of the main cave chamber. The rising sun had revealed yellow and red ochre prehistoric paintings of sea creatures on the walls and ceiling and had also heralded the swirling arrival of more bats than he had expected. Their little dog snouts sniffed the air, and their translucent ears constantly swiveled like small radar dishes. Those ears, combined with their unexpectedly intelligent eyes, made him think that if he had not been there to disturb their roosting that they just might have talked to each other.

****

Nora lost patience sitting at the villa waiting for Jack to return. She had Yana drop her at one of the car rental kiosks at the airport, where she rented a compact car for a week. It only cost her ninety-nine dollars. Not even Jack could argue with that. She drove through town and up the coast to one of the pull-off parking spots along the little cliffs that line the north-ern shore of the leeward side of the island.

She got out and walked along the cliff path, watching the waves march in and collapse at the base of the cliff, and marveling at the frigate birds riding the thermals. How does the sea grape grow? she wondered. You find it in the most un-likely places. Here on top of the cliff overlooking the ocean, for example. There was precious little soil anywhere on the island for plants to grow in, and none she could see up here. The thick fleshy gray roots lay curled on top of the rock like long growths, not the white threads she saw when she planted be-gonias with her grandmother when she was a kid. Those hours spent with Grandma had been the only normal parts of her life so far.

****

Every one of them watched the same sunset. Every one alone.

Nora stood on her patio holding a drink and staring at the fiery ball sinking behind the small, low island smeared on the horizon. She listened intently for Jack's car to stop on the gravel out front. The phone rang, and, thinking it might be Jack, Nora hurried to answer it. It was Amelia. After the initial pleasantries, Nora confided her worries to her new friend. "I don't know where Jack is, and I'm afraid that Manning is lying about the shipwreck."

"Jack's a big boy. He can take care of himself," Amelia said. "Although I wouldn't put it past Manning to be working a scam."

Lucia sat on her front porch with a glass of ice water and watched the sunset, debating whether to put on her swimsuit and go down for a swim. She knew Burke was at home, but it was so hot she was past caring. She went to change.

Bunny sat with his back against a tree in front of his ramshackle house behind the big supermarket, slapping at the occasional mosquito brave or foolish enough to fly through the cloud of herb smoke. He listened to Bob Marley wail and nod-ded his head at Brother Bob's words.

Jack had spent the day sitting in the cave's mouth. He had been sure in the morning that he was in the perfect spot to catch Manning pulling a fast one, salting the submerged wreck just offshore, but he had been wrong. He stood, stretched, and watched the bottom of the sun's disc touch the horizon. As it did, there was a rustling behind him and suddenly a huge stream of bats flew out of the cave, swirling like smoke. Jack was too startled to do anything more than stand still and let the bats fly around him.

Burke was at his window watching the water and beach, thinking it would be good if Lucia came down for a swim. He'd go down and join her.

Santiago sat on the deck of the *Santa Marta*, a cigarette in one hand and a Polar beer in the other. The rest of the Venezuelans who came over with produce to sell were either on the dock or on the stinkpot diesel trawler *Abierto* he had tied his boat to. They were all laughing and calling out to the women walking down the waterfront to the restaurants further into town. Santiago was quiet and watchful.

Manning stood among the raucous tourists celebrating the sunset in the bar cantilevered out over the ocean at the Sand Dollar resort, his eyes darting like lasers. He made it a habit to cruise the resort bars once a week to keep a lookout for his next pigeon, and he thought he'd found a live one to replace Jack Spencer, who was getting all too suspicious and would have to be cut loose. This one was fat, pink, and balding, wearing a sickly yellow aloha shirt printed with mutant flowers and worn unbuttoned enough to display the outsized gold doubloon necklace that told Manning that the wearer imagined himself a pirate. He downed the rest of his beer and got ready to move in.

****

Jack Spencer was becoming too insistent about diving on the wreck. Manning and Santiago had put another piece of the old wooden wreck from Santiago's home harbor in the place where Manning said the treasure ship had gone down. They'd haul it up tomorrow morning so that Jack could witness it from shore.

The only trouble was Jack didn't want to sit on the shore watching from a distance with binoculars. He insisted on joining their next trip to be present when they raised pieces of "his" wreck.

So far, Manning had held Jack off, but Jack's patience was wearing thin. Manning was afraid that Jack would rent his own boat and scuba gear and head out there on his own. Part of the time, Manning thought that wouldn't be the worst idea. The place where they'd salted the site was rife with currents and was really too deep for a novice diver. It would serve Jack right if he got into trouble underwater and drowned.

"I saw you out on the water the other day. What you're doing is illegal." The voice came from over Manning's shoulder. He whirled around to find Burke looming over him, an amused look on his face.

"What are you talking about?"

"I saw you on Santiago's boat hauling ship pieces down to your supposed wreck site before dawn."

Manning took a step toward Burke. "You don't know what you're talking about."

"I do. I was out fishing off Malmok and saw you diving."

"You think you're such a big man because your family has been on the island for years, but you can't tell me what to do." Manning pushed his finger into Burke's chest. "Stay out of things that don't concern you."

Burke stood his ground and leaned into the finger poking him. "But they do concern me. I don't like your setting up a scam to cheat a man out of his money, and I don't like that you've been sniffing around Lucia Vandersteeg."

"Oh, now we come to the point." Manning threw back his head and laughed. "You don't like the fact that I might be competition for Lucia's attentions. Pietr Smit's already in the race, and now you think I'm coming up on the outside. Did you think you'd have the heiress and her money all to yourself? And as far as Jack Spencer and his money are concerned, that's none of your business. Besides, he can afford it."

Burke crowded the shorter man. "It doesn't matter what he can afford. Your lying and cheating isn't going to end well."

"You think so?" Manning set his drink down on the nearest table and shoved Burke away. "We'll just see about that." He wound up and took a swing at Burke, who ducked and jabbed Manning in the gut.

In a heartbeat, the two men were rolling on the floor, punching for all they were worth, and bar patrons were backing away to avoid being knocked down, holding their drinks in the air. Almost immediately, powerful hands pulled Burke off Manning, and others held Manning away from Burke.

"What's going on, friends?" Bobo, the bar's owner and bartender, held each of them by a shoulder and frowned. "I do not allow fighting in my bar. It's bad for business. If you have a beef with each other, take it outside."

Manning wrenched out of the man's grip and, wiping the blood from his split lip on his shirttail, said, "I don't know what his beef is. He started it."

Burke lunged toward the other man. "And I'll finish it too when I have the chance. Stay out of my way, Manning, and stay away from Lucia."

Manning left his half-empty beer on the bar and stalked off.

"Now, Burke, you don't want me to tell you to stay away. Put your anger aside and move on. You know I don't allow fighting. It scares the ladies." Bobo held Burke's arm and grinned down at him. "You're going to have a lovely black eye tomorrow, I wager. Better go home and spend some time with an ice bag." He shoved him toward the door. "Go on now."

Burke picked up his drink from the edge of the nearest table, downed it in one swallow, and put the empty glass in Bobo's hand. "I'm sorry, my friend. I won't let it happen again."

Manning walked to his Jeep parked on a side street, talking to himself. "You don't know what you've started, Burke, but you can bet I won't forget. You can't order me around or tell me who I can and can't see. Lucia isn't your private property. You just put your name on my list."

CHAPTER 20

Lucia was excited about going on a trip to Tori's Reef with Charles and the snorkeling club. She gathered her mask, snorkel, fins, booties, and wetsuit. She packed some water for herself and a few bottles to share with the others, as well as a bag of trail mix to help get the saltwater taste out of her mouth. She plunked her straw hat on her head, put on her sunglasses and drove down the island to Charles and Amelia's house in Belnem. Amelia came to the door.

"Right on time," she said. "Charles will be pleased. He sets great store by punctuality."

"I like to be on time," Lucia said. "I gave myself extra time to get all the way around the north end of the island and back down here, just in case there was traffic in town."

Amelia smiled. "If there isn't a ship in port, traffic will be reasonable. When there is a ship tied up at the Town Pier, all bets are off."

"I've noticed."

"Here she is." Charles came into the room, rubbing his hands together. "Are you ready for a world-class snorkel? Tori's Reef is one of the best I've ever seen."

"I'm ready. I spent most of the last few days sorting and filing papers, and I'm tired of it. I need to be out in the fresh air and sunshine."

Charles took her bag and touched her elbow. "Let's go then." He led her out the kitchen door and over to his Range

Rover. "We have to pick up David Flemming on the way."

Lucia stopped with her hand on the passenger door. "Oh, well, in that case, I'll sit in the back seat."

Charles came around and opened the front passenger door. "Oh no, you'll sit in the front. David can sit in the back. He won't mind."

She hesitated. "Are you sure? I can happily sit in the back."

He persuaded her to sit in the front, and they were off. In about two minutes, Charles slowed down at a small pink house in a pleasant neighborhood a few streets back from the sea. "Here we are." He tooted the horn, and a tall, thin man came out with a large bag that looked like he was going away for the weekend.

Charles got out and opened the back of the Rover, hoisted David's bag in, and closed the back. "I hope you don't mind, David, but Miss Lucia is coming today and is in the front seat."

David tipped his ball cap to Lucia. "I don't mind. I'd sit in the wayback if need be. I love to snorkel at Tori's Reef. Let's go." He hopped into the back seat and closed the door, folding his long legs like a flamingo.

It was a short drive to the site. There were a dozen cars parked on either side of the seawater inlet when they arrived. Charles pulled into the last remaining space and cut the engine. "Here we are," he said. "Let's go get wet."

They joined the group of older men and women gathered near the inlet. "Folks," Charles said, "this is Lucia Vandersteeg. She is from the States and is on the island taking care of some family business."

"Hi Lucia," said the white-haired man beside her. "I'm Edgar. Have you done much snorkeling since you arrived?"

She shook her head. "I've only gone twice, once around the dock across from my house and once at Windsock by the airport. I'm looking forward to today's outing. I hear this is a wonderful site."

The groups on either side of the inlet divided themselves into pairs, and one pair from each group volunteered to stay with the vehicles while the others went first.

"Why are they staying out of the water?" she asked Charles.

"Because there are young people who make their living breaking into cars and trucks left at dive sites. People bring only what they can carry into the water and little else. It's easier to have someone guard the vehicles than to lose things while you're in the water."

"Oh, that's too bad."

"But the fact remains…"

David volunteered to stay on shore with Edgar while Charles and Lucia went into the water.

She quickly put on her wetsuit, spread sunscreen on her face and the back of her neck, and then sat on a boulder to put her booties on.

Edgar told her, "Next time, bring cheap flip-flops instead of these nice sandals. They would be stolen in an instant."

"Thanks for the tip," she said.

Carrying her mask, snorkel, and fins, she found it easy to climb down the boulders and into the inlet. The water was chest deep on her and was the perfect place to get ready to go. Charles was right beside her.

Charles and Lucia moved away from the entry point to put on their fins and get their masks settled. A woman named Deb came along. She was new to snorkeling and worried about seeing a shark.

Edgar assured her she'd be lucky to see a shark in Bonairean waters. "My dear, a few people have seen a Nurse Shark here, but not at this end of the island and not lately. Despite what you see on cable television, the ocean is not paved with sharks. I'm a retired marine biologist, so you can trust what I say."

Charles offered to buddy with her, too. He and Edgar talked about the waves and the current to plan in which direction they would start out. The water felt cool and refreshing on Lucia's face as she put it in the water to look around. They had to swim over coral boulders at the inlet's mouth, which acted like a breakwater. The boulders knocked down the surf, so the waves didn't wash into the inlet and erode the sides. The breakwater made it a perfect area for getting ready to swim out or for beginners to get comfortable.

Charles asked Lucia and Deb to wait while the others swam out so that Deb wouldn't be jostled in the crush. She held Charles's hand as they swam through the whitecaps. Lucia enjoyed timing the surge, so she moved with the water and made it out into the ocean without scraping her belly on the rocks. The sea floor was covered with white sand that looked like powder. Lucia dived and lifted it up to see it trail away from her fingers. It felt like powder, too. She looked around to see Charles and Deb moving along the shoreline, so Lucia turned that way. She noticed they were swimming across the waves, and there was a small current pushing against them. Charles had said something about going out into the current and swimming back with it when they were tired.

There were small patches of coral and sponges where little fish and baby eels cavorted. Lucia wanted to stop at each one to see the daily life of each reef, but Charles and Deb were getting ahead of her, so she kicked after them. Suddenly, she saw a black diamond shape in the distance. It was close to the bottom and coming her way. She caught her breath when she realized it was a stingray. It was beautiful and so graceful with its wide wings and long, string-like tail. The ray swam under her, and she twisted around to watch it go. She turned back to see Charles giving her the okay signal. She signaled okay back and kept swimming.

Lucia caught up with Charles and Deb and motioned that she wanted to head toward the drop-off. Charles nodded and steered them all away from the shore toward deeper water. The reef was much larger and lusher at the top of the drop-off. There were purple tube sponges and orange barrel sponges. Schools of Yellowtail Snapper hung motionless over the coral, and navy blue and purple Calico Wrasse swam in long streams across the reef. Lucia took her time swimming slowly, peering into each sponge to see if anything lived there. The waving sea fans had small snails and little fish hiding in them. Multicolored Parrotfish swam by, munching on the coral and pooping out sand. She laughed when she realized where the soft white sand came from.

Deb pulled Charles back toward the shore. She wasn't comfortable in the deep water. Lucia trailed behind, reluctant to leave the action-packed area of the reef at the top of the drop-off. She thought she would stop at a dive shop and inquire about the possibility of a practice dive. Lucia wanted to be down with the fish, able to stop close enough to watch them go about their business.

She swam over a small coral head, and a little Damselfish swam up to warn her away. Lucia stopped to watch and saw that the little fish was tending an algae garden in the hollow of the coral head. As she watched, a Blue Tang swam by, and while the little Damselfish eyed Lucia, the Blue Tang dipped down to munch some algae.

Lucia looked up to see that groups and pairs of snorkelers were headed back toward the inlet. She thought maybe it was time to dry off and put on more sunscreen. The inlet was busy with people going in and coming out when she got there, so she swam off to the side to let people pass. When she swam around a coral head, she saw long red antennae waving from under the coral. She took a breath and dived to see a row of lobsters backed under the rock. She thought it was too bad that they were in a marine preserve. Otherwise, she would have lobster for supper that night. If she could catch one, that is.

When the stream of people lessened, she swam around the breakwater boulders and again timed the surge to carry her over and into the inlet. She stopped in the shallows to take off her fins and climbed up the exit in her booties. She was glad she had bought fins that needed booties. They protected her feet when she had to cross hot sand and rough coral rubble at dive sites. She felt sorry for people who had elected to get the full foot fins because they had to walk barefoot into the water.

"Well, how did you like it?" Charles asked as she walked up to where he was standing.

"It was terrific. Did you see that stingray? It was huge."

"That was a Spotted Eagle Ray," Charles told her. "You were lucky to see it."

"I saw a line of lobsters under a coral head when I was waiting for the inlet to clear out. Oh, I would love lobster for supper one night."

Charles laughed. "You'll have to go to a restaurant for that. All the waters around Bonaire are a marine preserve, so it's against the law to catch any of the sea creatures."

"Yes, I know," she said. "But I was tempted to try for one just the same."

Someone had set up a snack table on the tailgate of a pickup truck. Lucia got her extra water bottles to add to the spread. She opened a bottle and drank, pouring part of it over her face to wash away the salt. She helped herself to fruit and cheese and happily talked to the others about things she had seen and things they had seen. She was tempted to put her snorkeling gear on and go back into the water, but David said his wife expected him home soon, so they packed up and left.

Lucia decided to join the club even if she'd only be there for a few more weeks, and next time she would bring her own car so she could have a second snorkel if she wanted to.

****

It looked innocent, the mound of broken coral pieces shoved up by the waves at Margate Bay, but try to walk across it and you find out differently. The stuff rolled and slid, never firm, never stable. Jack clambered up toward the blue Caribbean sky, arcing cloudless overhead. He felt undignified and awkward, which made him angry that Manning was forcing him into this island-wide scavenger hunt. He got to the top, disturbing a pelican as he did. "Out of my way, bird." He stood up, staggering a bit on the shifting coral rubble, and looked around. Nothing. No Manning, no treasure, no further instructions. Oh wait, something was fluttering stuck to a piece of driftwood. Jack slipped and stumbled over to grab the paper before the ever-present trade winds blew it to kingdom come. *Not just yet,* it said.

"Damn him." Jack crumpled the paper and threw it—into the wind—so it blew back in his face. He caught it and shoved it into his pocket, looking around, sure that Manning was somewhere nearby laughing.

****

For the next few days, Lucia settled into the study to work on sorting all the papers that the vandals had pulled out of the drawers and off the shelves. She was glad she had been smart enough to start with the most recent papers because there were fewer of them. Her tidy piles for the last couple of decades made her feel like she had accomplished something.

One afternoon, a woman from the Bonaire Historical Society came calling, just as Pietr predicted someone would. She wanted to know what Lucia planned to do with all the papers that Aunt Anneke had kept.

"Miss Boon always told me she would donate it all to the society, the furnishings too. I, uh, we plan to use the house as a historical museum of the days of plantation life on the island," she said.

Lucia smiled at her and said, "I'll keep that in mind. For now, I must get everything in order so the attorney and I can meet with the government representatives and work out the exchange of deeds and funds."

The woman's hands clenched on her purse. "Funds? There are no funds for a museum. Miss Boon was kind enough to donate the property to us."

Lucia shook her head. "I'm sorry, but the terms of the will and the agreement with the Bonaire government say that Aunt Anneke promised to deed the land and the buildings to the island for fair market value. There will be an estate sale to disperse the contents of the house. I'm very sorry to disappoint you, but the death duties and the upkeep of the property make it impossible for me to donate it to your organization."

The woman's face fell, and tears glittered in her eyes.

Lucia said, "I'm certain the government won't be interested in all the ledgers and journals of the running of the plantation for all those years. Would those interest you?"

She sniffed and dabbed her eyes with a floral handkerchief. "Perhaps. Yes, I am sure they are interesting, but we had hoped to add the plantation house to our exhibits in the park."

"Maybe you should contact the island governor or whoever will be the one to decide the disposition of the house. That may be their plan, too. I'm sorry I can't be of more help to you."

She ushered the woman down the hall and out to her car. Lucia tried to resume sorting, but the visit of the woman from the Historical Society distracted her. She looked at her watch. Four thirty. She wondered where Burke was, if he was done fishing for the day. It seemed like on other days, he had been here to drop off a fish or two and was gone by now. She got back to work.

Lucia was deep in sorting the papers in the study when the phone rang.

"Lucia, it's Pietr Smit. I was wondering how you are doing getting the papers organized."

She gave a short laugh. "I was doing all right until someone broke in the other night and threw everything on the floor. I'm back at square one."

There was a long silence. "Someone broke into your house? Were you there? Did you call the police?"

"Yes, someone broke in. No, I wasn't here. And yes, I called the police. They don't think they'll figure out who broke in, but Burke fixed the doorjamb and put in new locks. Of course, with the windows open, someone could just cut the screen on a window and step over the sill."

"What did they want?" He sounded shocked.

"I don't know. The police officer thought they were looking for money, but all they ransacked was the study. Maybe they didn't have time to go through the rest of the house. None of the other rooms were touched, and I had my purse with me."

"Do you still have your passport? That's a popular item to steal and sell."

She had a moment of panic and tried to remember the last time she had seen it. "Yes, it's in the zipper pocket of my purse," she said with relief.

"Your purse isn't a safe place to keep a passport. What if your purse gets stolen?"

She looked at the ceiling. "You're not helping, Pietr. If you want to help, come out and sort papers with me. It's a monumental job, and I don't know what I am doing. I can't tell what's worth saving and what's trash. Oh, and a woman from the Historical Society was here trying to tell me that Aunt Anneke had promised the house, contents, and the land to them. I think she expected me to just hand everything over."

Pietr clicked his tongue. "They are shameless. They'll say and do anything to get donations. Miss Anneke wouldn't have promised them everything. She may have said she would donate ledgers and journals and other historical documents and maybe a few artifacts, but never the entire estate."

Lucia let out a breath. "Well, that's a relief. I didn't want to think Aunt Anneke would have promised them everything when it said in the will that the land goes to the island government. They'll have to pay something for the buildings, right?"

"That's right. Miss Anneke wanted you to have the house and the boathouse to sell to the government and to sell the contents. Uh, Lucia, would you like to have supper with me tomorrow night? I have gotten permission to start driving and thought we could have a meal."

The invitation surprised Lucia. "I think I would like that, Pietr." She heard the smile in his voice.

"Wonderful. I'll pick you up at six o'clock. Is that too early?"

"No, that's fine. I'll see you at six o'clock. How dressed up should I get?"

Pietr laughed out loud. "This is Bonaire, Lucia. Dressing for supper means ironing your khaki slacks and linen shirt."

She laughed along with him. "I can do that."

****

The trade winds had come back. Lucia was glad that she had closed the windows in the study, or the wind would have blown the papers all over again. She spent the morning sorting and organizing another year's ledger pages and letters. In the afternoon, she took a shower in the old claw-foot bathtub and got her clothes ready for her date with Pietr. She decided to wear her sundress and take a light sweater for when the night cooled off.

Burke stopped by after she had showered and dressed, and Lucia noticed he had a black eye.

"What happened to you?"

He looked embarrassed. "I got into a fight, and the other guy punched me."

She grinned. "Aren't you going to say, 'but you should see the other guy'?" Lucia stepped closer and lifted her hand to touch the bruise. "Does it hurt?"

Burke shied away. "Yeah, it hurts when someone touches it."

"Sorry. Why did you stop by?"

He lifted his hand. "I brought fish. I'll grill it for you."

"Thanks, but I'm going to supper with Pietr."

His shoulders slumped, and he said, "Where are you going?"

"I don't know. Pietr didn't say," she said.

"Oh. Well, enjoy yourself," he said, and he left, taking the fish with him.

The sun was setting when Pietr arrived to pick her up. "You look very nice," he said when she opened the door. "You might need a sweater or a jacket when the sun sets."

She turned to the hall table and picked up her purse and sweater. "I have one right here," she said.

Pietr escorted her to his car and opened the door for her.

"Thanks," she said. She noticed he was still limping. When he got into the car, she said, "How's your ankle?"

"It's healing. The doctor said I'm a fast healer, so he allowed me to drive since I have an automatic transmission in my car."

"That's lucky. You'd still be stuck at home if you had a standard transmission car."

"Yes." He concentrated on navigating the narrow road in the gathering dusk.

They drove in silence for a while, over through Rincon and down into Playa. Lucia brought up the pile of ledgers she still needed to go through.

"Don't worry about them tonight," Pietr said. "I thought we could go to *Fishes From Heaven*. It's right on the seaside, and they have good food."

She smiled at him. "That sounds good to me. I'm hungry."

He parked on a side street not too far from Fredo's, where she and Burke had eaten with Charles and Amelia the week before, then they walked a couple of blocks to the restaurant. It was an open-air dining room with lots of metal fish hanging from the ceiling and seashells on the tables. They were lucky enough to get a table on the side overlooking the ocean.

"Oh, this is lovely," she said as she sat down to watch the sunset.

"Did you see the green flash?" Pietr asked.

"I forgot to look," she said.

"Next time," he said.

She nodded. "Next time."

They ordered drinks and discussed the menu. Lucia confessed she loved escargot, and Pietr encouraged her to order them. He ordered escargot as well, and they each chose the snapper with roasted vegetables as their entrée.

"We're not very adventurous diners," she said.

"Oh, but we are," he said. "We're having snails. Few people are having them, I wager."

Their drinks were delivered, and they chatted.

"How are you getting along with the sorting?" he asked.

She sighed. "Okay, I guess. I've found nothing of any importance. No deeds or stock certificates. I wish I knew what you think I'm going to find. It all looks like straightforward business to me."

He reached across the table and touched her hand. "That may be all you'll find. The deeds and important investment papers are in the safe in my office."

She frowned. "So, I wonder what the vandals were looking for when they broke in last weekend. Did people think that Aunt Anneke kept a lot of money in her house?"

"I imagine some thought Miss Boon was an eccentric, old rich woman who kept money in her drawers or between the pages of her books. That could explain why all the drawers were out and all the books were on the floor."

"Susanna helped me shelve all the books, and we didn't find even one guilder or dollar in the mess on the floor."

****

On a couple of days the following week, Pietr Smit came out to help her figure out what was important, what was historical, and what could be thrown away.

Lucia had the impression Pietr assumed his working relationship with her was translating into a romantic relationship. For her, nothing could be further from the truth. She relied on Pietr to help her with the legal work of settling the estate, and she agreed to go to supper with him a few times. The last time he took her home at the end of the evening, he leaned down to kiss her. She turned her head so that his lips connected with her cheek rather than her lips. He was disconcerted.

"What?" he said.

"I think we should keep our relationship professional, that's all," Lucia said. "We have a lot of work to do, and I don't want anything to interfere with that."

Pietr turned away, shoulders slumped, got back in his car, and drove away.

CHAPTER 21

Like frozen fireworks, the red and yellow bromeliad thrust its fleshy leaves outward from the center of the plant. The merest glisten of the pre-dawn rain shone in the center cup like life-giving blood. All around, as far as Nora could see in every direction, was dry ochre ground, crumbly rock, and cactus. Only this one plant held out the hope that there might be life surviving in this place.

Nora cursed the impulse that had pulled her out of bed at dawn and convinced her to drive into the park to watch the sunrise away from civilization. She had felt brave, even intrepid, as she dressed in cotton khaki slacks, a navy tank, and her never-worn hiking shoes. Taking pride in not being a complete fool, she stopped in the shadowy kitchen to fill a couple of two-liter bottles with water and tucked them in her backpack with a tangerine or two, just in case. Be prepared, her Boy Scout dad would intone as he slid his official Boy Scouts of America jackknife into his pocket. She had tried, Dad, she really had.

Knowing she wasn't in too much danger of being lost on the only road through the park across the old plantation, she drove boldly into the silver light of dawn. The muffled pop of the right front tire brought her to a stop. The discovery that some opportunist had made off with the jack and lug wrench from behind the seat left her in tears. But tears of frustration, only frustration, she told herself as she jammed her boonie hat down on her head. She pulled out a tangerine and a bottle of water and sat in the vehicle's shade to wait for the first Good Samaritan to come along.

****

Jack had driven away from the villa early, too. He'd gotten up to the turnoff at Boca Onima, where Manning had shown him he could see the boat at the wreck site from the shore, and then his vehicle had stalled. He felt an insect bite on the side of his neck and reached up to swat it away. That's the last thing he remembered.

****

Manning thought his plan to keep Jack from seeing the wreck site too soon was a good one. He slid the hypodermic needle that held a few remaining drops of sedative into a pocket on his Jeep's door, then he and Bunny pulled the unconscious man out of his truck. They slid Jack into the back of Manning's rusty blue Jeep. Driving Jack's truck, Bunny followed Manning down the island. They took the unpaved kunuku roads down the windward side of the island to the southern tip, where the lighthouse stood alone among the rocks. The two men not-so-carefully lifted Jack out of the Jeep and dropped him in the shadow of the tall structure. Then they drove to Jack and Nora's villa and parked Jack's truck in front of the house, putting his wallet, keys, and phone on the front seat. Manning was glad he'd gotten the muffler on his Jeep fixed. They made very little noise, except for the crunch of gravel under their wheels.

****

Jack lay at the foot of the Willemstoren lighthouse steps, pieces of broken coral flung onshore by the last storm digging into his back. He wasn't sure how he got there. A groan escaped his sun-dried lips as he levered himself up into a sitting position with his elbows, the rubble tearing and scraping his skin. This is the reason they call this stuff iron shore, he thought, there's not a hint of comfort in it. He looked around and saw a pair of eyes. Eyes set in a face out of prehistory, a scaly, cold face with amber eyes set under bony brow ridges and ragged spikes trailing haphazardly down its back.

He blinked, and the iguana gulped at him, as if contemplating a juicy smear of roadkill. The steady gaze of the lizard and the pigeon-toed confidence of its pale blue stance got Jack moving out of his stupor and swaying onto his feet. The weakness he felt must have been clear even to an animal as primitive as the iguana because it didn't shy away, didn't move a muscle as he grunted and shoved himself upright.

Jack stood trying to keep his balance on the suddenly tilting planet, and the lizard looked up at him as if to say, I could have eaten you if I wanted to. The world swayed dizzily as he looked around, hoping to see his rental truck parked nearby. Unless it was behind the lighthouse or beyond the rubble berm a hundred yards down toward the slave huts, he was screwed.

From the position of the sun straight overhead, he guessed it was siesta time on the island. The only people out and about in this blazing sun were crazy scuba diving tourists, and they were at least sane enough to be underwater where it was cooler, not frying their brains in the sun. While he stood there considering his transportation problem, he was checking himself for injuries. His head was pounding, but a quick feel of his skull didn't produce any bruised or squishy spots, thank God. He attributed his headache to having been lying broiling under the tropical sun for who knows how many hours. He scratched at a bite on the side of his neck.

His arms and legs seemed to work. He looked around again, hoping that from his lofty height of six feet he would spot his truck and, if not, then someone who might drive him to town. No glass or chrome winked at him from any direction, except for the shards of broken auto glass mixed with coral gravel. That was a common thing on this island of relatively well-to-do diving tourists and young native men who sought to balance things.

He shuffled into the narrow sliver of shade on the back side of the lighthouse and immediately felt better. His hands roamed over his pockets, hoping for a clue how he had ended up unconscious at the southern end of this desert island. His head lifted at the sound of an approaching vehicle. He stepped out of the shade and raised an arm to flag it down, but they returned his wave and drove on by. He went back into the shade and stood leaning against the old lighthouse, recently tarted up for tourists. His trembling hands made a more thorough inventory of his pockets, patting and groping, realizing with a curse that whoever had left him there had taken everything, even his smokes. No keys, no wallet, only a clean folded handkerchief came out of his hip pocket.

Deliberate footsteps from behind the lighthouse to his right brought his chin up and sent his eyes darting for a rock or a brick, something to use as a weapon, something for protection against further assaults. He edged left, away from the sound, sliding his feet, trying to move silently. The footsteps came closer, and now he thought it was more than one person. His stomach clenched as he looked at the feeble stone in his hand. Maybe enough to stop one attacker, but not much help with a gang of them. Now he heard their heavy breathing and muttering. He cocked his ear, trying to hear their words. Were they splitting up to circle the lighthouse? To squeeze him between them, cutting off his escape? Nearer and nearer came the stealthy footsteps. His sweaty palm slid on the rough surface of the rock nestled in it. He shifted it, trying to grip it tighter, pressing himself back into the brick base of the lighthouse as if he could melt into it and disappear. Close now. So close he saw a small stone dislodged by a foot roll into sight. The breathing of his stalkers was harsh and loud over the pounding of his heart.

He slowly raised his hand and narrowed his eyes to steel himself for the fight when a fuzzy muzzle came into view—three of them. The trio of wild donkeys paced by, their hooves crunching in the rubble and their dark questing eyes gazing at him as if to ask if he had food. His breath released in a short bark of laughter that caused the donkeys' ears to flicker, and he ran a shaky hand over his face. He dropped the rock, consciously loosening his grip finger by finger, feeling the blood rush back.

The lead donkey chuffed and shook himself, then turned and led his little herd down the coast in search of who knows what, food or companionship or perhaps merely habit.

****

It was late afternoon before either of them got back to the villa. When the couple from Wisconsin, Sam and Maxi, who had picked him up on the southern tip of the island near Willemstoren Lighthouse, dropped Jack at the villa, it surprised him to see his rental pickup truck parked out front.

He made an excuse not to invite them in but nodded politely when they told him they were staying "just down the street at Holiday Homes," Maxi, the wife, said. "We're in the orange bungalow."

Sam said. "We're staying for a month. Stop by anytime. Bring your wife."

Jack thanked them again for the ride, unlatched the gate, and went inside. "Nora," he shouted, but got no answer.

He went through the house, checking the patio to see if she was dozing on a lounge. Seeing no one, he went into the bedroom, stripped off his dirty and sweaty clothes, and took a shower. Before he stepped under the spray, he checked himself in the mirror to see if he had any scrapes or bruises from however he got from the northern end of the island near the shore to the foot of the lighthouse on the southern end.

While he was in the shower, Nora returned.

She too was hot and sweaty, looking forward to a shower and some clean clothes. She called for Jack but then heard the shower running, so she went into the bedroom. Just as she entered, the shower turned off. She undressed and tried to open the bathroom door to take her own shower, but the locked door surprised her. She was standing there, hands on hips, when Jack opened the door.

He looked her up and down as she stood there in the nude. "I like your outfit," he said.

"Since when do you lock the bathroom door? You never did before. Are you up to something shady?"

He looked at her. "In the shower? What could I be doing shady in the shower?"

The logic of that took a bit of the edge off her irritation. "Well… well, I don't know, but you've been acting oddly ever since you hooked up with that Manning character." She folded her arms across her chest. "What happened to you today?"

"What do you mean?" Jack asked.

She pointed at his right thigh and shoulder. "You are all bruised and scraped. Did you fall?"

He twisted to see his haunches in the mirror. "No, I didn't fall. I think someone knocked me out when I went up to watch them at the site. I ended up down at the lighthouse with no truck, no phone, and no wallet."

"Oh my God, Jack, what happened?" She dropped her arms and walked over to him.

"Hell if I know, Nora. I woke up hours after I left here, and it took me a while to flag someone down. I got here just before you did to find my truck parked out front with my wallet and cell phone on the front seat. I needed a shower, so here I am. Where did you get to this morning? Where were you all day?"

She snorted. "Not in much better shape than you, but without the conk on the head. I drove up to watch the sunrise in the park and got a flat almost as soon as I got there. I had to wait for someone to come along, and that took a while. Then I waited for someone to fix the tire, which also took forever. People don't work at any speed down here, you know?" She shook her head. "I'm going to take a shower. Will you make drinks, or do you want to wait for me to make them?" By the time she finished talking, she was already in the shower.

Jack made drinks.

After her shower, she met Jack on the patio. He'd made a pitcher of planter's punch, his favorite tropical drink. After her first sip, she said, "So who do you think knocked you out and dragged you down the island this morning?"

"It had to be Manning."

"Do you think he's strong enough to do it alone? How could he have moved you and your truck and not been stuck?"

"I figure he's got a helper, but I don't know who it'd be. Two guys could haul me around unconscious and move my truck here. The maid's useless. I asked her if she saw who parked my truck, and she said, 'No, Mr. Spencer, I don't see nothing.' Useless."

Nora finished her drink and got up to pour herself another. "Manning's a crook. You need to get rid of him."

"He's got a hundred grand of my money. I'll get rid of him when I get my money back."

For the next hour, they drank and argued. Nora thought Jack should write off the money and leave the island before something terrible happened to him. Jack wouldn't hear of it. He'd get his money back and, by god, stay on the island if he wanted to. By midnight they'd stopped speaking to each other and retired to their king-size bed in angry, semi-drunken silence.

CHAPTER 22

The ancient limestone thrusts its jagged and tortured bones above the sea that swirls angrily at its base. The grinding waves shove broken pieces back and forth, polishing them into a semblance of smoothness. You can tell how long the pieces have been exposed. The dark, just-revealed parts grasp the skin like Velcro, leaving hundreds of tiny cuts behind; the older pieces are smooth and bleached nearly white. Underwater, when a Parrotfish takes a bite of coral for the juicy polyps it contains, the scar left behind is white. But the cliffs that bare themselves to the pounding waves are nearly black. The dark color lends an air of menace to the already forbidding rocks that jut like rotten jagged teeth from the foaming salty saliva of the earth.

****

Nora sat gingerly on the softest place she could find, a little patch of sand caught in a depression after the last storm. Today the sea was nearly calm, well, as calm as it gets on the windward side of this scrap of an island. After last night's argument, she had slid out of bed, dressed in the bathroom, and driven away before the sun had sent more than the thinnest pink fingers of light to paint the clouds. Her headlong flight had carried her up the leeward coast to the petroleum depot and then down the hill into Rincon, nestled in the angles where ancient waves carved a hollow. Only a few dogs were stirring as she silently cruised down the main street of the town. Once she passed the grammar school and the soccer field, she squinted into the sunrise and turned off at the barely visible sign for Boca Oliva, her favorite wild little bay. The waves that pounded this piece of shore were born off the west coast of Africa and met no other land on their journey to these unforgiving cliffs. She loved the days when they pounded into shore with a booming crash and flung their edges skyward to patter down in suicidal blasts.

She made her way carefully down to the edge of the inlet to find a flock of flamingos just offshore in the shallows created by low tide. The scene had the air of an animated short film. The flock of pink flamingos all faced the same direction and, necks stretched, waded away from the splashing of a school of baitfish on the surface behind them.

Nora stared at the birds, an imaginary soundtrack running through her head. "Why are we running? Do you know why we're running? What are we running from?" The nasal honks, in no way synchronized, and the rigidity of their slender dark pink necks gave an air of panic to their movements. The realization struck her that the birds' knees bent backwards, that they worked more like elbows, and she frowned, trying to figure out why. It was easier to put all her energy into discovering the evolutionary reason behind the flamingos than to think about Jack and the dangerous game he and Manning were playing.

****

It flattered Lucia when Amelia Eastman called, inviting her to lunch. "I'd love to go. Where should we meet?"

"Well, on the windward side of the island is a little snack bar at the windsurfing center that has the best crab salad sandwiches I've ever had. Why don't you come here, and we can drive together? It'd be easier than giving you directions."

"Okay, it's a date."

They planned to meet the following Thursday and rang off.

****

On the drive from Amelia's house, Lucia was glad she

was riding along instead of having to follow directions. They went across the island on a road bordered by fields of tall candelabra cactus and lined with power poles. A trio of wind turbines among the cacti turned slowly in the trade winds.

Amelia pointed at the turbines and said, "Those things were standing still for the last few weeks. I've never known the wind to stop like that."

"I'm just glad the wind started up again. I was having a terrible time sleeping, even with a fan blowing the hot air around."

"Don't you have an air conditioner?"

"No, and there isn't one to buy on the entire island," Lucia said. "Trust me, I've looked everywhere."

"Oh, you poor thing." Amelia shook her head at the thought.

"Most evenings I walk down to the beach across the road for a swim. That cools me off enough so I can get to sleep. Sometimes Burke comes out and swims with me."

Amelia smiled and patted her hand. "I'm sure you enjoy his company." She turned off the pavement onto a gravel road that skirted a small bay. They passed a row of cottages behind a tall fence and then Amelia parked in a line of cars across from a cluster of thatched huts. "Here we are."

Lucia smiled to see colorful sails flapping in the strong breeze. She reached up and gathered her windblown blond hair into a ponytail, then secured it with a band from her pocket. "I can see why they put a windsurfing place over here. It's really windy."

"Let's find a place to sit where we can watch the windsurfers while we eat," Amelia said. "I'd never be brave enough to try, but I love watching them."

They ducked under a thatched awning and entered the

snack bar. It was built of bamboo and was open to the air. The islander behind the bar called out, "You're back, Amelia. It's good to see you again so soon."

Amelia laughed. "You know I can't resist your crab sandwiches, Joseph. This is my new friend, Lucia, from the States."

"Welcome, Lucia," Joseph said. He set two cans of soda on the bar. "I know Amelia likes her ginger ale. Is that good for you too, or would you like something else?"

"Ginger ale is fine." Lucia nodded. She gazed out at the windsurfers gliding across the shallow water of the bay. It was mesmerizing to watch them as they caught the wind in their brightly colored sails and leaped off the tops of waves.

Amelia guided her to a table under the thatched roof of the snack bar, which gave them a view of all the action. She set the sweating soda cans down on pasteboard coasters from a holder on the table. "There's a menu blackboard over the bar if you want to see what else they have." She pointed over her shoulder. "I'm having the crab salad sandwich and some chips."

"Sounds good to me. I'll have the same."

Amelia turned in her seat and flashed two fingers at Joseph.

The tall man laughed. "I'm already making your sandwich, Miss Amelia. I'll make the same for your new friend. Coming right up."

In less than five minutes, he rang a bell and called out, "Order up!"

"I'll get them," Amelia said, and she stepped up to the bar and came back with two plates, each loaded with a hoagie bun filled to overflowing with homemade crab salad. She also had two bags of Sun Chips. "Be careful when you open the chips. The wind is so strong it'll blow the bag right into your lap. Don't ask me how I know."

Lucia's eyes got big at the sight of so much sandwich. "I don't know if I can eat all this."

"Joseph has to-go boxes. I usually take half of mine home to have tomorrow. If Charles doesn't steal it for a midnight snack, that is."

Lucia reached for her plate. "I'm going in. Wish me luck." She took a big bite and, if anything, her eyes got even wider. After swallowing, she said, "Oh my god, this is so delicious. Thank you for bringing me here."

Amelia just nodded. Her mouth was full of bread and crab.

Once they had eaten their fill, they sat looking at a half-sandwich on each plate. They got to-go boxes right away to keep the pesky little black and yellow birds from stealing nibbles of their leftovers.

"These birds are crazy," Lucia said. "What did you say they're called?"

"They're Bananaquits, known around the Caribbean as sugar thieves, opportunists that hang around restaurants and patio tables trying to peck up what they can. They're supposed to drink nectar from flowers, but the birds have learned people leave crumbs on tables, and they're not above stealing food right off your plate." Amelia put her hands down on top of her to-go box. "Now, tell me about you and Burke."

Lucia felt a blush rising on her cheeks. "There isn't much to tell. We're neighbors, and he helped me replace the locks and install deadbolts after the house got broken into." She thought about the kisses they'd shared the night of the break-in and blushed even harder. "We had to use wood putty to repair the part of the frame that got splintered."

"You said you go down for a cooling swim in the evenings and sometimes he joins you. What do the two of you talk about?"

"Oh, you know, he tells me Bonairean folktales about the stars and stories of growing up on the island. Just regular stuff. I tell him about my job in publishing and about living in a big city. It's very different from being on Bonaire."

Amelia laughed. "Kind of culture shock, isn't it? We lived just outside of London, and moving down here required a serious attitude adjustment. It took me a few months to get used to the slower pace of life here."

Lucia shook her head. "I've tried to work here so I can stay longer, but the internet is too spotty. I'll be in a meeting, and the service will drop. My boss won't put up with it much longer. I can work on manuscripts, send my notes, and email authors. That works. It's the online meetings that are the problem." She looked around at the idyllic setting and sighed. "Home just doesn't compare to life here."

"I remember you came to our cocktail party with Pietr Smit. What about him?"

"Pietr's been a tremendous help in getting the estate organized and all the legal papers signed and filed, but that's it. He's a friend, although I think he'd like more than a friendship. Sometimes I feel we look too much like brother and sister to be in a romantic relationship."

"You do look quite alike." Amelia took a sip of her drink, and the condensation from the can dripped down her cleavage. "Ooh, that's cold." She dabbed at her chest with a napkin. "I saw you talking to Manning the other day downtown. Have you been spending time with him, too?"

"Heavens no. Manning scares me. There's a pirate air about him, and the way he looks at me gives me the shivers. He tried to lure me into investing in his shipwreck search, but I declined. I suspect he's only hanging around because he thinks I have bags of Aunt Anneke's money coming."

The older woman nodded. "That sounds like Manning.

He's amusing at times, but I know what you mean. There's something shady and menacing about him."

As they sat there visiting, a cloud passed overhead and loosed a sudden rain shower. People sunning on the sand hurried to gather up their towels and bags, but by the time they'd picked up everything, the rain was over. Amelia and Lucia stayed dry under the thatched roof.

"Now that the afternoon rain has passed, we might as well head home." Amelia picked up the empty aluminum cans and dropped them into the recycling bin next to the bar, then came back for her leftovers.

"I'll carry the boxes," Lucia said. "And even press my initial into mine so we can tell them apart." And she made a capital L in the cardboard container in her right hand.

"Thanks for coming, ladies," Joseph said as they walked past the bar. "See you soon."

Lucia lifted the stack of boxes she carried in salute. "Thanks for a wonderful lunch. You can be sure I'll be back."

CHAPTER 23

Nora couldn't bear to be in the villa with Jack pacing and muttering threats. He and Manning had had a huge argument the night before, when Jack had asked to be bought out of his share. Jack told Manning he thought five weeks was more than enough time for him and Santiago to find something more than the piece of railing and a couple of piles of metal that had solidified into a clump. Manning tried to convince him the clumps might be coins, but Jack wouldn't listen.

Jack spent hours on the internet and had even sent to the States for a new, high-speed laptop so he could do online research. When he had trouble even finding a reference to any treasure shipping or shipwrecks this far south in the Caribbean, he suspected he'd been had. He invited Manning over for supper and asked Yana to make a special meal, and that was when Nora knew Jack was setting a trap.

She tried to get Jack to share his ideas with her, but he just pushed her aside, telling her she was better off going to Art Appreciation with Amelia.

He even gave her two thousand dollars and told her to go shopping and not come back until she had spent it all. She looked at the money in her hand and thought unless she bought pricey jewelry, it would take her a long time to spend two grand in one day on Bonaire. But she would try. Or maybe she'd spend the afternoon away from the villa and stash the money.

****

Like a green arrow, the tall Caribbean pine pierced the bright blue sky at the south end of the Belnem neighborhood.

No clouds marred the blue as Jack drove toward it. To the tree, to the tree, he thought, feeling like a foolish child on a scavenger hunt. The clues that Manning left for him were just like that, clues fit for a child's game of pirates. Each time he followed one, his pulse pounding, his palms sweaty, only to find another taunt at the end, he resolved to stop. He hadn't told Nora where he was going when he went on one of Manning's wild-goose chases, and she had stopped asking.

Jack hated not being in charge of things. In all his other dealings, whether business or personal, it was he, Jack, who called the tune. He was the one who sent people running from pillar to post, beads of sweat dusting their upper lips, to do things and get things for him. No one sent him all over the place, only to be laughed at. No one laughed at Jack. Nora had once, right after he had acquired her. Jack immediately made her understand how wrong that was. Nora was a fast learner.

****

Lucia closed the curtains so that the sun wouldn't fade the old writing on the papers and went in search of something cool to drink. She found a pitcher of lemonade in the refrigerator. Susanna must have made it for her. Filling a glass with ice and lemonade, she went out onto the porch to look at the ocean. There was one spot on the porch that was in the shade. Lucia dragged a chair over and sat down. She could see across the road and down to the sea. A breeze swirled around the side of the house and blew her hair, cooling her off. There was a car coming up the driveway, but Lucia couldn't see it until it got to the top of the little hill. It was Burke's faded green pickup truck. She waved and waited for him to stop and get out, wondering what he wanted.

Lucia was very familiar with the look and sound of that truck. It was the first vehicle she had ridden in when she arrived in Bonaire. It was the sound she listened for when deciding whether to go down to the beach or to wait until he had left for town.

She stood up to greet him. "Hi Burke, what brings you here this afternoon?"

He stepped out of his truck and walked toward her. He rubbed his hands down the sides of his shorts and looked strangely shy. "I, um, I was wondering if you'd like to come fishing with me tomorrow. You'd have to get up before first light, but I think you might enjoy seeing the sunrise from the water. What do you say? Want to come fishing?"

A big smile stretched her lips, and she said, "I'd love to. What time do I need to be down at the dock? Do I need to wear something special? What do I need to bring?"

He chuckled at her eagerness. "Be at the dock at 5:30 A.M.; bring a ball cap and sunscreen and maybe a shirt to wear to keep the sun off. Wear clothes you don't mind getting wet and stinky. Fishing can be dirty, smelly work." He turned to go back to his truck but faced her again. "Oh, and don't forget shoes that can get wet. No sandals and no flip-flops. Old canvas tennis shoes if you have them."

"I don't have any shoes like that, but I'll get some. Where should I go?"

"Try The Everything Store. They have some of every-thing; that's why they named it that."

As soon as Burke's truck was out of sight, Lucia went inside and got ready to go to the store. She was glad she could get there without having to go into Playa.

In The Everything Store, there was a pile of shoeboxes in a corner. It looked like someone had tried organizing it once upon a time, but that system had gone by the wayside. Boxes were jumbled together, some without lids, some with shoes spilling out, and in no order at all.

"Can I help you find something?"

Lucia turned to see a young man behind her. "Oh, yes. I need a pair of canvas tennis shoes to wear on a boat tomorrow."

"What size do you wear?"

She told him, and they started hunting. He brought a stepstool so that he could search at the top of the pile first and work his way down. Lucia started at the lower left side of the pile and looked at every box.

"Be sure to look at the shoes in the boxes. Sometimes people put them back in the wrong place."

When she heard that, she went back to the beginning and started over. She took the lid off every box, looked inside, and either put it back on the pile or set it aside. All the shoes she put aside were canvas tennis shoes. Some high-tops, some low, but all canvas.

"Here's one pair in your size," the clerk said from his perch on the stool. He handed her the box with a smile.

Lucia took off the lid and recoiled. Inside was a pair of yellow and purple canvas shoes that looked like clown shoes. "Oh my, these are bright. Keep looking. Maybe we can find some in plainer colors."

For the next hour, they worked their way through every box in the pile but found only another pair just like the first one. They were both perspiring from the exertion, and the clerk was smiling.

"You're in luck. It's rare we find two pairs of the same size, and they are excellent looking shoes. Try them on."

Lucia sat down on the chair the clerk pulled from a corner and slipped off her sandals. The bright colors of the shoes hurt her eyes and offended her staid Dutch sensibilities, but she shrugged and tried on the shoes. Naturally, they fit as if they were made for her. Looking down at her crazy colored feet, she said, "I guess I'll take them."

"Do you want both pairs?" the clerk asked. "They're the same size."

"Ah, no. I think I'll leave them for another lucky customer."

Soon Lucia was back in her car on the way home with the yellow and purple shoes glowing in their box beside her. She wondered what Burke would say about them.

****

The rental truck rounded the curve where the road swung nearest the shore, and the setting sun almost blinded him. Barely able to see, Jack eased the pickup into one of the wider places carved through the scrubby brush and parked. Once the engine was off, the only sound was the shush of the waves as they ran up on shore, rearranging the broken coral pieces in the shallows with a sound like wind chimes. The rays of the sun quickly heated the interior once the air conditioner was off, so he cranked down the window to catch a breeze. Wishing he had a camera, Jack admired the way the clouds turned from white to pink to gold to iron gray as he watched. The silhouettes of the cacti on the horizon reminded him of hands reaching, clawing up from a fiery pit into the cool night air. A sudden step beside the truck made him jump, but it was only a nanny goat and her twin kids crossing the road to feed on the leaves of the thorn bushes that had unfurled after the morning's rain. He'd get back at Manning for running him around the island on this scavenger hunt game. His patience had run out.

****

Lucia set her alarm for 4:15 a.m. to give herself time to make coffee and wake up before walking down to the dock. Part of her wanted to drive down there, but she realized it was silly since she could see it from her front porch.

When her alarm rang in the morning, Lucia wondered why she'd agreed to go fishing because it was so early, still dark, and she'd probably be in the way. She dressed in her least favorite shorts and tee shirt, pulled on the crazy canvas shoes, and put a hat and long-sleeved shirt in a bag with her sunscreen and a bottle of water.

When she arrived at the dock, Burke was already on board the boat getting his equipment ready. "Good morning," she said. "It's awfully early."

"It is," he said, nodding to her. "But the fish are early risers, and if we get out early, we can be back early, and my customers will be happy." He walked to the side and held out a hand to her. "Welcome aboard." He looked at her feet as she climbed into the boat. "Nice shoes."

She blushed and said, "That's all there was in my size. Aren't they dreadful?"

Reminding her to apply sunscreen liberally, he untied the boat and pushed it away from the dock. "Have you been on a boat much?" he asked as he moved over to the wheel and engaged the throttle.

"Not much. Really only in rowboats on lakes or ponds. There aren't a lot of oceans in Ohio."

He grinned. "Then hang on." And he pushed the throttle all the way. The boat leaped forward. Lucia staggered and nearly lost her footing, but she grabbed the windshield and held on while they bounced over the small waves. "Is it safe to go this fast in the dark?" she yelled over the motor's roar.

"Not very. But I like to go fast."

Just like he drives his truck, she thought.

In a short time, they were offshore of Playa. Lucia could see the town's lights and a few early risers moving along the streets. Burke throttled back to a more reasonable speed and kept going down the coast. He slowed and let the boat drift once they reached the southernmost tip of the island. "Time to rig the lines," he said.

"Is there anything I can do?"

"Not really. Do you want to steer us toward the lighthouse? Keep us on track."

She went over to the wheel and kept the bow aimed at the lighthouse. Watching over her shoulder, she saw him hook small fish onto the lines and cast them out behind the boat. Before she could ask what they did next, one line made a sizzling sound, and Burke leaped to pick up the rod and crank the reel like a madman. He would crank, stop, pull up the rod, then lower it, and start all over. He did that until Lucia could see a white flash at the surface behind the boat.

"Hand me the landing net."

She left the wheel, looked around, and picked up what looked like a tennis racquet with very loose strings and held it out to him.

Instead of taking it from her, he said, "Hold it over the stern and scoop up the fish when I bring it close."

She wasn't too sure about leaning over the stern so far, but she did as he directed and soon a silver-white fish was there for her to scoop into the net. The fish was heavier than she thought it would be, and it kept flopping around, but she held onto the net and the fish. Burke set the rod in the holder and helped her get the fish into the boat.

"Good job! We caught a Snook. Thanks for your help."

Lucia looked at the fish that had to be at least two feet long. "It's huge. Is it good to eat?"

"You bet. It's pretty uncommon around here, but it's very tasty."

Just then, one of the other reels started to make that sizzling sound she had learned meant another fish on the line. "Here we go again."

The next few hours sped by as fish after fish was caught and landed. Lucia didn't notice that the sun had risen until

Burke reminded her to put on her hat and reapply sunscreen.

By the time he turned the boat around and sped back up the coast to his dock, she was exhausted and soaking wet. Her new shoes squelched every time she took a step, and her arms ached from hoisting the net with its wriggling cargo over the stern.

"What are you going to do with all those fish?"

"I'm going to clean them, fillet most of them, cut some into steaks, and deliver them to my customers as fast as I can."

"I'd offer to help, but I've never done anything like that before."

He grinned at her. "That's okay. I'm fast and careful. Maybe someday I'll teach you how to clean fish. It's a dirty job. You can watch if you want, though."

She looked down at the state of her clothes. "Maybe I'll just go up and have a shower. I'll watch you clean fish another time."

When he had the boat tied up to the dock, he reached a hand down to help Lucia out. She staggered a little as she stood there. "Whoa, be careful," Burke said. "Looks like you're a real sailor."

"What's wrong with me? I feel like the dock is moving."

"You've got your sea legs. Your equilibrium got used to the tossing deck, and now that you're on dry land, it thinks you're still at sea. It'll pass." He reached into the boat and handed her the bag with her sun shirt and sunscreen. "Thanks for coming today, Lucia. I hope you enjoyed it."

"It was fun and hard work. I'll never think of fishing as a relaxing sport again."

"Well, fishing for recreation and fishing for work are two different things. I fish for work, for my living. I'll drop off some of today's catch with Susanna for your supper." He reached out and touched her arm. "See you later." And he turned back to unload the fish from the live well.

Lucia walked slowly back up the hill to her house. She felt like she'd had a few too many drinks and hoped her sea legs would desert her before long. She didn't want anyone to think she'd turned into a day drinker.

After her morning on Burke's fishing boat, Lucia rinsed the scales and seawater out of her clothes and shoes. It was heaven to stand under the tepid spray of the shower and wash off all the sunscreen and salt. She hung her clothes on the line outside the kitchen and set her canvas shoes on top of the wooden table on the back porch to dry. Susanna teased her about starting a new career as a fisherwoman, but Lucia told her it would be a long time before she was a competent angler.

She had a quick meal of the leftover crab salad sandwich from lunch with Amelia, then settled in the study to resume sorting through the seemingly endless estate paperwork. An hour later, Lucia became aware of a deep voice coming from the kitchen. Burke must be here delivering today's catch, she thought. She tucked her hair behind her ears and smoothed her hands down her shirt so she would look nice when he came to see her.

A few minutes later, she saw him walk past the study window on his way back to the boathouse. He hadn't come to see her. He dropped off some fish for her supper, visited with Susanna, and left. She was disappointed. Had she been so much of a liability that morning on the boat that he avoided her? She had tried to be helpful and, once she understood what he needed, to anticipate when it was time to wield the landing net to bring the catch onboard. When her arms ached from the weight of the catch, she hadn't complained. When the struggling fish splashed seawater all over her, she hadn't complained. She'd worked hard and ended up soaked to the skin and smelling of fish. The least he could do was come to the study to thank her for her efforts. Catch her getting up before dawn to go with him again. Lucia huffed out her frustration and slid the next ledger toward her.

Susanna came into the study. "Here, Miss." She set a vase of fuchsia flowers on the corner of the desk and smiled at Lucia. "Burke brought these for you. He said you were a pretty good deckhand and deserved a reward. He must have gotten them when he finished delivering his catch."

"Thank you, Susanna," she said, wondering why he didn't deliver them himself, since he was just a few steps away.

"Don't touch the blooms and then put your fingers to your lips, miss," Susanna said. "Every part of the plant, flowers and leaves, is poisonous. But aren't they pretty?"

"Poisonous? Really? Why would he give me something that could kill me?"

"Oleanders are common on Bonaire. People plant them because donkeys and iguanas won't eat them, and because the flowers are beautiful." Susanna left the room, humming a tune and smiling to herself.

Lucia spent the rest of the afternoon squinting at the flowers whenever she looked up from her work. Was there a hidden meaning in Burke's giving her poisonous flowers? Maybe he was just stringing her along with his kisses, hoping she'd delay settling the estate so he wouldn't have to move.

CHAPTER 24

Scuba diving was not like snorkeling. Lucia had talked to Charles Eastman about an experience dive. He recommended the Dive Inn, so she stopped there and scheduled a Discover Scuba. There was a short classroom session, and then she and the instructor took their equipment across the street, climbed down the concrete steps to the beach, got dressed in the gear, and waded into the shallows.

At first, Lucia was afraid. It was hard to take the first breath with her face in the water, but soon the colorful fish distracted her, and she forgot to be nervous. She and the dive instructor, Michael, held hands as they swam up and down the reef, seeing all kinds of fish, shrimp, and even eels. Soon Lucia became comfortable with the gear and being underwater, so they didn't need to hold hands any longer. She had such an amazing experience that she immediately signed up to become a certified scuba diver.

The best part of the class was the fact that Dive Inn didn't have a swimming pool, so the confined water part of her classes was in the shallows where she'd had her Discover Scuba. She grew familiar with the denizens of the sandy bottom and the small pieces of coral that protruded there. The hardest part of learning to dive was how to hold her position underwater, not slam into the bottom or pop to the surface. She practiced her buoyancy by hovering in front of the rip rap wall that covered the side by the customs dock. Many small fish and critters lived in the nooks and crannies made by the big chunks of concrete tumbled together, so she was very motivated to hold her position in the water.

Once they had practiced their skills, they did a fun dive to the reef near the drop-off. Michael wouldn't let her go any deeper than twenty feet, but there was lots to see at that depth. The Pedersen's cleaner shrimp that lived in anemones and advertised their services by waving white antennae to attract fish that needed cleaning especially fascinated her. Lucia tried and tried to hold still long enough to have the shrimp give her a manicure, but every time she got near them, she would hold her breath and float to the surface.

Michael laughed at her frustration and showed her how to control her position by letting a little air out of her buoyancy device so that she could hold her breath for a very short time and not hurt her lungs.

She ditched appointments with Pietr Smit to take scuba class.

Her boss contacted her, wondering if she was ever coming back to work. It was an uncomfortable conversation.

"Lucia, I hate to say this, but you either come back for this major book launch in two weeks or you're out. I can't have you sending paltry excuses saying, 'things aren't settled' for much longer," she said in a rush when Lucia answered her phone. "You've been there for months. What's left to do? When were you planning to return?"

Lucia felt her cheeks burn. "I thought it wouldn't take this long, but the attorney had a broken ankle, so he wasn't able to work for the first few weeks. Now the government is dragging its feet about coming up with the money to purchase the house and property. I can't hurry them up; I've tried. When I push too hard, they stop understanding English. It's very frustrating."

"You know what this business is like, Vandersteeg.

You're either on top of things or you're not, and you're not anymore. This is unacceptable. Decide. You either work for me or you don't."

Lucia's hand was slick on her phone. "Yes, ma'am, I'll decide. Soon."

"It better be very soon." And the phone went dead.

****

Now that she had learned to dive, which had opened up a whole new world, Lucia thought maybe she would stay in Bonaire and just dive all the time. Lucia wondered how long she could stay on the proceeds of the sale of Aunt Anneke's house and its contents. She knew the government would pay her for the house and property and wondered how long that money would keep her on the island.

She enjoyed another outing with the snorkeling group at Tori's Reef, but spent most of her time diving to see the coral and the tiny critters close up.

Finally, Charles took her hand and kept her at the surface. "My dear, stay here. Your diving is disrupting the natural actions of the creatures of the reef."

"But I want to be down there watching it all close up. I want to look into the sponges, see what's hiding in there, and have the schools of fish swirling around me."

Charles nodded. "I know what you mean. But it's less expensive to snorkel. All you needed is a mask, snorkel, fins, and boots, and maybe a shirt to keep from sunburning your back, and you're good to go."

Lucia was smitten with the underwater world, and he understood.

When they got back on shore, he told her about dive trips that he had taken over the years. "I remember when I discovered Bonaire with my old dive buddy, Randy. We came down here for a week and were rarely dry. I'll be happy to dive with you once you're certified." Charles chuckled. "I'll even let you use my tanks if you'll let me come along."

"It's a deal," Lucia said.

The snorkeling outing made her pay more attention to her buoyancy in the next class. She asked Michael to help her get control of herself underwater. He showed her how controlling her breathing let her control where she was in the water column. And how he could blow bubble rings and then rise under them like they were a halo. It made her laugh and lose control of herself for a minute. That was when she learned she could fall underwater. Lucia bent over backwards, laughing, and within seconds was falling toward the bottom. She had the presence of mind to turn over and catch her balance, correct her buoyancy, and for once not fly to the surface or crash into the sand. Lucia looked down and realized that she was not over the sand; she was over the deep. As she realized where she was, a hand slid under her arm and tugged her upwards. Her depth gauge showed she was passing sixty feet. Too deep. Michael swam her back up the slope to the edge of the drop-off and had her kneel in the sand to get herself back in control. He gave her the okay signal, which she returned, and ended the lesson.

Once they had rinsed and hung their dive gear, they sat at the table outside the dive shop, filled out their logbooks, and talked about what had happened.

"I never imagined I could fall underwater," Lucia said. "Shouldn't the water hold you in place?"

Michael chuckled. "In laughing, you exhaled air from your lungs, so suddenly you weren't as buoyant as before and you fell. You did the right thing by turning over face-down, but you were way too deep for a beginner."

"Thanks for saving me from going any deeper. I'll try to be more aware next time."

They made a date to meet the next day for another lesson.

Driving home, Lucia thought Pietr wouldn't be happy that she'd blown off another meeting with him to go diving, but she couldn't help herself. She was hooked.

****

It was quiet at the museum in the afternoon. That was why Bunny went there at that time. His never-used anthropology degree made him appreciate the history on display there. In the heat of the day, the un-air-conditioned display rooms were often empty. No tourists roamed from case to case, skimming the little labels, and feeling superior. He hated to see the sour little smiles on people's faces that showed how the person thought where they came from was better than Bunny's adopted island.

Just because there were a lot of rich, educated people in America or Europe to pay money for scientists to search for artifacts and to build fancy museums didn't make them better. In fact, Bunny liked Bonaire's dusty and sparse displays better. The people who found shells and pottery, who saved the old photos, and who wrote the old stories did it out of love for their own history, not because they would get fame or be paid well. The things in these dim and dusty rooms were real, Bunny thought, not like the glittery trash that Manning and Jack Spencer kept arguing about.

****

Jack sat in the shade of the ruined house up on the hill overlooking the dive site called Weber's Joy, watching for Manning. From early morning, he sat there watching the trickle of diving tourists gear up and enter the water in pairs. He had thought when driving up from the villa in the pale dawn light that he would conceal his pickup somehow, but nearly every dive site he passed had at least one pickup parked there, windows open and no one in sight.

On an island full of tourists, he realized it was hard to

tell why someone was parked where they were. And with the number of divers on the island and their habit of independence, it meant no dive site was empty for long. Eventually, someone was bound to drive up and park, ready to dive. Jack figured that very randomness was his ace in the hole for staying undetected.

****

It was rare to find seashells on the beaches of Bonaire. There was plenty of coral rubble, especially after the latest hurricane wave had swept over the leeward shore and rearranged so much, both above and below the water. The Gaudy Natica shell that winked up at Nora in the early sunshine was a special find. Whole and unfaded, it looked fake, but when she held it up in the strong sunlight, she could see where a shorebird had pecked a hole right into it to devour the original inhabitant. Thinking that it had to have happened recently, she raised the shell and gingerly sniffed, but the clean smell of the sea told her that any traces of the unlucky mollusk had long ago disappeared. She tucked the shell into her pocket.

****

The donkeys stood looking at Jack as he drove off the paved road onto the barely visible track that wound through the cactus barren to end at the caves at Onima. Jack hated the wild donkeys that roamed the island. Their wise, dark eyes that stared down the brown furry muzzles seemed to judge him. The rigid posture as they stood motionless radiated disapproval. Foolish women tourists cooed as if the beasts were cartoons come to life, but Jack had rounded a curve in the coast road late one night and his headlights illuminated a pair of stallions fighting in the center of the road. The little mare had stood coyly on the roadside, fluttering her long lashes as the males reared and whinnied, gnashing their yellow teeth at each other's necks. Jack had sat in his pickup watching the primeval battle unfold in his headlights, shaken by the raw power of the fighting males caught in his lights. These were not petting zoo residents, content to nibble donkey chow from an outstretched palm. They were wild and dangerous animals.

****

It was hot in the study, and all the fan did was stir the heat around. It blew a stack of papers across the desk before Lucia caught them. She took her overheated and frustrated self into the kitchen for a glass of cold water.

When Burke walked into her kitchen holding a fillet of something fishy wrapped in brown paper, Lucia said, "What if I don't want fish for supper every night?"

"Uh." Burke was stunned.

"What if I want chicken or pork or even goat? Huh? What then? Do you show up at other women's houses carrying a smelly fish fillet instead of a bouquet or box of candy?" She stood with her fists clenched and her feet spread apart as if she were ready to fight. "Pietr doesn't bring me fish. He brings flowers, and not poisonous ones either. He brings candy. He takes me out for supper where I can order whatever I want. What do you bring? Fish."

Burke stood in the kitchen, baffled by the inexplicable change in Lucia's attitude. "I thought you liked fish."

"I do, but not every day. Every day it's the same thing— fish, fish, fish. I'm getting sick of fish."

"All right. I'll stop bringing fish. I'll even stop coming over to make sure you're fed and safe." He turned on his heel and stormed out the door, carrying his package of fish with him.

Susanna stood at the kitchen sink, her mouth hanging open. "Miss…"

Lucia said, "Don't start with me, Susanna." And she burst into tears and left the room.

"All right," the housekeeper said to the empty room. "But I think bringing fish is Burke's way of saying he loves you."

CHAPTER 25

Sunlight sparkled through the clear water in the pool behind the villa. When they'd arrived, Nora wondered why anyone would go to the trouble and expense of blasting out a pool when the ocean was right there, just down the stairs at the end of the deck. Now she loved the pool. Henkel, the pool man, cleaned it every day, and there was a beautiful big angelfish made of tiles in the bottom. She idly trailed a finger in the blood-warm water. Lying on the baking tiles of the pool deck made her empathize with how a sub sandwich must feel toasting on a grill.

Jack had left her early this morning; he'd kissed her shoulder in the dim cool morning, whispering he had a meeting. She vaguely remembered hearing the door close and the distant sound of his truck driving away. That was hours ago. When she arrived, the maid wondered where Jack was since his truck was parked out front. Nora couldn't imagine who Jack would have gone off with. Surely not Manning. Yana had come, cleaned and cooked, and gone. Yana had made a bowl of ceviche using fresh-caught fish from the local fishermen. She used limes and tomatoes from La Portuguesa, and big, sweet onions from the Town Pier vendors. Yana had even made johnny cakes to eat with it. Jack would have loved it. He should have been back for a late lunch. He said he would be back, but he hadn't returned. Nora had made a pitcher of planter's punch after Yana left and had drunk nearly half of it when she realized she was lying on the pool deck, telling her troubles to the pretty blue and yellow tile fish at the bottom of the pool.

****

After her outburst, Lucia couldn't look Burke in the eye. Not that he was around. Since her crazy, unfair fit of selfish anger, Burke had stayed away. Lucia stopped going down to swim from the beach.

Amelia Eastman stopped at the plantation house on her way to a gallery in Rincon. "What did you do to Burke?"

"What do you mean?" Lucia said.

"Well, when I've seen him lately, he's stopped smiling and chatting with me. Last Friday, he just dropped off the fish, took my money, and left."

Lucia looked at her. "Maybe he was late for an appointment."

Amelia shook her head. "I don't think so. Yesterday, he didn't even stay long enough to get paid. He's very unhappy about something."

"And you're blaming me? It's not my responsibility to keep Burke happy."

Amelia shrugged, lifted a hand as if to say, "Who else could make him unhappy?" and left.

Susanna moped around the house now that she didn't have Burke's daily fish delivery to look forward to. Even though the housekeeper was happily married to Hardy, she enjoyed the teasing and mild flirtation with the handsome fisherman.

Lucia let Pietr take her to supper more often, even though she knew it got his hopes up she might change her mind about him. One evening as she and Pietr stood at the host station waiting to be seated at *Chez Rendezvous*, Burke came in with a date.

He stopped short and frowned down at his date. "I don't want to wait," he said. "Let's go someplace else." And he took her arm, spun her around, and pulled her behind him out the door.

Pietr looked down at Lucia. "What do you think that was about?"

She sighed and looked after Burke's receding back. "I'm not sure. Maybe because he isn't patient." She turned to see the host coming to escort them to their table. "Or maybe because I told him I was tired of eating fish every day. He got angry, and I haven't seen him since."

Lucia noticed a sudden smile light up Pietr's eyes. Did he think that meant she was rekindling an interest in him?

****

Manning stood facing the cliff, sweat already trickling down his spine even though he had only walked from his Jeep, which was parked in the shade about fifty feet away. He was glad he had worn thick socks and hiking boots. Holes pocked the ground, and it was littered with ankle-twisting rocks that had fallen from the cliff face. Tucked in unexpected places were the globe-shaped Turk's Cap cacti, their vicious yellow thorns poised below the ridiculous-looking red and white pad on top that had earned them the name.

Manning thought the possibility of impaling himself on those thorns would be worse than losing skin on the rough limestone itself. He also knew he would have to be exceptionally careful when he was climbing. The Turk's Cap had a nasty habit of growing babies in every cranny. The young thorns emerged thick and sharp and would pierce leather gloves.

****

Nora walked slowly between the craft market booths set up on the square across the street from the Town Pier. Whenever a cruise ship docked, the little band of artists and entrepreneurs set up their tables and laid out their wares. Nora wasn't a cruise ship passenger, never had faced the prospect of being trapped in what amounted to a floating hotel with a couple thousand strangers for a week, steaming from island to island, striking each a glancing blow. The ships spent just enough time on each one for a hot cab ride to see the highlights and take a quick tour through the upscale shops that line the ports. The whole cruise idea seemed so artificial to her.

She had endured dinner conversations with avid cruisers who insisted they were familiar with nearly every Caribbean island. Judging by most of the people around her and the things she overheard, the packaged view they got of an island was just that—packaged. The real life of the island went on behind the Disney-esque sanitized experience that was trotted out before the ship docked and carefully folded away until the next ship was due. Even worse, Nora bet that ninety percent of what was for sale around her was made somewhere else. Pathetic. And where was Jack? He was supposed to meet her at City Cafe for supper.

****

Manning cursed as he looked at his hurting foot. A thorn from a cactus nestled in the rock had pierced the side of his shoe and worked its way into the soft flesh of his arch. He carefully scrutinized the next boulder he came to before sitting down. It took a moment for him to work up the nerve to begin gingerly working the devilishly sharp clump of thorns out. His breath hissed between his teeth, and his blood flowed fresh and red to splash on the rocks, where it was immediately absorbed. Manning tore a strip from his khaki shirt to stop the blood and act as a temporary bandage. Blistering the hot, still air with curses, he retied his shoe and, limping only a little, resumed his climb.

CHAPTER 26

A few more steps across the blackened rock, careful not to get tangled in the grasping branches of the sea grape colonizing the edge, and Jack could look down into the sea. Water the color of liquid turquoise lapped at the base of the rock where it plunged underwater, hissing and foaming in the spaces. The cliff face, all the rock on this tiny island, was an ancient reef pushed into the air by forces deep within the planet.

Jack used his hand to shade his eyes as he scanned the shallows for his quarry. The water was so clear and the sand so white beneath it that even the smallest movement was visible. He saw schools of fish going about their business. Jack watched groups of Bar Jacks hunting, darting to scatter smaller fish when they struck. He saw the silver blade of a solitary Barracuda patrolling the reef's edge, waiting for an opportunity to pounce on the unwary. All seemed normal.

He turned to the cab driver, standing nervously behind the open door of the white van. "Are you sure this is where you heard Manning ask to go?"

As the driver nodded, licking his lips to moisten them, his mouth dry from the threat of menace in Jack's voice, neither man noticed a hand reach up over the lip of the drop-off and slowly close around Jack's ankle.

Pulled off balance and flailing in the heartless air, Jack fell silently onto the tumbled boulders at the base of the cliff, then his unconscious form rolled into the cool water.

Manning clung to the ironshore rocks and sea grape roots for a moment to watch Jack's body being sliced and shredded by the waves until he noticed the first predators vector in from the navy blue of deeper water. He pulled himself up onto the top of the cliff, rolled over the seagrape and stood up, dusting his hands on his shorts. "Not a bad acting job, Bunny," he said, clapping the driver on the back.

Bunny gave him a mute look, went around the back of the van, and lost his breakfast in the thorny scrub, drawing an interested audience of lizards.

Manning climbed into the driver's seat and turned the key. "Mount up. I'll drive. I think we could both use a Polar beer, maybe a whole six-pack."

Bunny emerged from the bush, dragging a shaky hand over his mouth, got into the van and slammed the door.

Manning jammed through the gears and drove south in a flurry of gravel, leaving only a small dust cloud to mark Jack's passing. "You're next, Burke."

****

Sam and Maxi parked in the lot across the road from the dive site Thousand Steps. They had been on the island for nearly two weeks and were systematically diving their way up the coast from south to north. Some of their friends from the dive shop at home had given them advice on how to dive the island. They had pored over a diving guide and pulled a dive site map off the Internet, then decided they were just going to take them in order, and they had.

After all the dives they had done in the last ten days, it didn't take them much time to assemble their gear, put on their wetsuits, help each other into their scuba units, and get ready to go diving. They left the windows of their rental truck open and left nothing in it they didn't want to lose. They were certain their vehicle had been rifled at least once while they were on a dive so all they brought was a big bottle of water, a bag of trail mix, and some stained and torn tee shirts to put on for the drive back to their bungalow. Getting hot standing in the blazing sun in black wetsuits, they quickly crossed the single-lane asphalt road and descended the stone steps toward the cool turquoise water they could see below.

About halfway down, the steps took a right turn to cling to the cliff face, and there was a small landing with enough room for people to pass each other or stand and catch their breath on the long, hot climb. Sam had been making Maxi laugh on the drive up from the bungalow by telling her he was certain there could not possibly be one thousand steps down to the dive site, so he was counting the steps. Maxi had her head down and was slightly hunched forward to balance the heavy and awkward tank on her back. When she reached the landing, she turned to look back at Sam, and that was when she saw what she thought was a snorkeler in the water below them.

"Look, Sam, there is a guy down there snorkeling in a shirt, shorts, and sandals."

Sam came down the last couple of steps to stand beside his wife and looked down, eager to get into the water and cool off.

"Look at all the fish around him, honey," Maxi said. "Do you think he's feeding them?"

Sam lifted his mask with its corrective lenses to his eyes and peered down at the floating man. "Uh, Max, I don't think that guy is snorkeling." He put out his hand and turned his wife away from the ocean. "I think we need to call the police or the rescue squad."

She started to turn back to look again, but Sam gripped her arm. "Do you mean...?" Her eyes widened in horror.

He nodded.

Before he could answer, she had pushed past him and climbed up so fast she was almost at the top by the time he moved his feet. "Come on, Sam, haul ass up here and let's go get help."

By the time Sam's head cleared the top step and he could see across the road, Maxi had already shed her scuba unit and taken off her wetsuit.

"Come on," she said. "What's taking you so long?"

A thought struck him as he crossed the road. "Do you think one of us should stay with the body?"

She shook her head. "Uh-uh. No way am I going in there with a dead body. I mean, I enjoy seeing sharks and barracuda, but not when they're eating the guy next to me. No way. We are both going. Saddle up." As she was talking, she stripped Sam of his scuba gear and wetsuit.

Her strength and the speed with which she moved amazed him. It seemed to him that she had planned every move during the minute it had taken her to climb back up. Before he could protest, she had pulled his weights out of the pockets of his vest and tossed them into the truck bed. Then she twirled him around and slid his buoyancy control vest off his shoulders, tank and all, and then turned and laid it gently onto the tank rack next to hers. He was fumbling with the Velcro at the top of his wetsuit zipper when she pushed his hand aside and unzipped it for him.

She made shooing motions to get him to strip off the suit quickly. "Come on, slowpoke," she prodded, pulling the truck keys out of the dry box she wore on a cord around her neck. "You want me to drive?"

He nodded, surprised, because she had been reluctant to drive on the narrow island roads since their rental truck had a standard transmission. Today, however, getting help overcame her lack of confidence.

She slid into the driver's seat and turned to him. "Didn't you say that there is some sort of oil depot or tank farm up ahead?"

He pulled the map out of the glove compartment and unfolded it while she backed out and jammed the truck into gear. "Yeah, here it is." He held the map toward her, then he realized she was concentrating on the road ahead. "Just go straight and keep to the shore road when you come to an intersection."

"Got it."

Later, Sam thought it was a good thing that no big trucks or any vehicles at all were coming toward them that day. Maxi cut every corner and slid through every intersection in her headlong dash to report finding the body. He was certain that she had taken the turn onto the BOPEC Petroleum property on two wheels.

CHAPTER 27

Burke was driving home from delivering his catch of the day when he was nearly run off the road by a rusty white van. He recognized Manning and his Rasta pal, Bunny, as they passed and wondered where they were headed in such a hurry.

"God, Manning, you're a menace," Burke said under his breath as he pulled off the shoulder. He drove on up the one-lane road until he turned into the boathouse driveway. Glancing up at the plantation house on the rise across the road, he wondered what Lucia was doing. Then he shook his head. Nope. Not thinking of Lucia any more than he had to.

Burke still hadn't found the right house or apartment to move into when Lucia sold the property back to the island government. There was one place close to the Sand Dollar Resort that had possibilities. The dock was in pretty good shape, but the house was just about falling down. He supposed he could get the landlord to fix it up before he moved in, but did he want to live in a place so close to a beach bar? He wasn't a night owl, not with the hours he kept. Up before the crack of dawn to have the best chance of catching enough fish to fill his orders and have some left for the Eastmans and Lucia, he was sure that loud music and revelry would keep him awake.

He smacked his forehead with the heel of his hand. Why did he think of her again? Lucia didn't want his fish. She had told him explicitly she was tired of fish. She wanted no more fish, not from him anyway. Besides, as soon as the property was sold to the government and she'd had an estate sale to get rid of the contents, she'd be flying back to the States to resume her life. It wouldn't bother her one bit that a successful sale would make him homeless. She probably had a nice, cozy little apartment in the city where she could move back in and just take up where she'd left off. He, on the other hand, would be out of the home he'd lived in for close to fifteen years.

When his dad lived in the boathouse apartment, fished, and did handyman work for Miss Anneke, Burke had sometimes stayed there, bunking in the boathouse, especially in the summer when school was out. He had taken over the fishing and handyman work when Dad died ten years ago and moved into the bedroom of the apartment. Seamless. Painless. And now he had to find a new place to live.

Miss Anneke had been more like his auntie than an employer and landlady. She had told him stories of the old days when the north end of the island was all plantations and of the parties and business deals that she and his grandfather had brokered between them. Burke wondered if Lucia had found any more letters from his grandfather or if Miss Anneke had written about his family in her ledgers. If she did, would Lucia tell him about them or just toss them aside now that he'd offended her with his fish?

He noticed that Lucia had stopped coming down to the beach alongside the boathouse for a swim or snorkel. Not even on the hot, windless nights they've been having for too long. She probably snuck down when he was fishing or delivering his catch to his customers. Or maybe she was just up there in that big house sweating. The thought made him picture a bead of sweat running down her chest and into her intriguing cleavage.

Now he was sweating. Time to go for a swim before the storm looming on the horizon moved over the island.

****

Back in his apartment, Manning took a shower and

bandaged the puncture wound on his foot. "Damned cactus. If it wasn't for that, no one would ever know I was there." He stared off in the distance for a moment. "Except for Bunny, but he'll never tell. And who'd believe him anyway? His brain's too foggy from all the ganja he's smoked for years."

He dressed in clean clothes and left for Karpata plantation to see Lucia. She'd kicked him out the last time he'd shown up, but he was confident he could charm his way into her good graces. American heiresses were easy pickings. Burke and Smit weren't the only eligible bachelors on Bonaire. It was time he threw his hat into the ring.

Manning enjoyed Lucia's look of surprise as he stood at her front door brandishing a bottle of wine.

"What do you want?" she said.

He held up the bottle and grinned at her. "To welcome you to Bonaire."

"I've been here for over two months. You're a little late."

"Better late than never," he said as he stepped across the threshold into the dim entry hall, bumping her aside. "I found this bottle of wine at the store and thought you might enjoy sharing a glass or two." He dug in his pocket. "I even brought a corkscrew."

"I don't drink."

Manning's smile slipped a little. "You don't drink? What do you do?" He leaned toward her and leered.

"I don't do that either."

He took her arm and steered her into the parlor. Setting the bottle on the side table near the window, he opened the glass-fronted cupboard and pulled out a pair of cut-crystal glasses. "These'll do nicely." And he set to work opening the foil over the neck of the bottle.

Lucia stood her ground. "Manning, I don't want a glass

of wine. I told you; I don't drink. What part of that sentence is confusing you?"

There was a clear pop as he eased the cork from the bottle. "Well then, as my grandmother used to say, 'I'll just give you a little bit.'" He poured a healthy measure of the golden clear liquid into each glass, picked them up, and handed her one. "To getting things settled."

Humoring him, Lucia raised her glass to his and took a small swallow. "There. I'm welcomed. Now take your wine and leave. I have estate work to do."

He tipped his glass to clink with hers. "Oh, come on. You can do better than that. This is a celebration."

Susanna walked into the room. "Do you need me, Miss Lucia? I'm about finished for the day."

Manning nearly choked on the swallow he was taking. "Where'd you come from?"

"I work here." Susanna drew herself up to her full height. "Where did you come from?"

He held up his glass and pointed at the wine bottle on the table. "I came from town. I brought a little celebration drink for your boss here."

Lucia set her glass on the table. "What exactly are we celebrating?"

"We're celebrating having another beautiful woman on the island." He drained his glass and started to pour himself another, but Lucia stopped him.

"That's enough," Lucia said. "Susanna, Mr. Manning was just leaving. Please show him and his bottle of wine to the door." She turned to look at the dumbfounded man in front of her. "I appreciate the effort, Manning, but I'm not a drinker and I'm not interested in what you're selling. Good afternoon."

Lucia turned and left the parlor, leaving Manning stuttering in her wake.

Susanna motioned toward the front door. "This way, sir, and don't forget your bottle of wine." She reached past him. "Here's your corkscrew. You wouldn't want to forget that."

Almost before he knew what was happening, Manning was on the porch and the heavy wooden door was closed in his face. "You haven't heard the last of me."

CHAPTER 28

Being good citizens took up the rest of the day for Sam and Maxi. They told their story over and over to every police officer who arrived. Unfamiliar with the ranks of police in Bonaire, Sam never knew if the latest questioner was of a higher rank than the last or not. He tried to give the third one, or maybe it was the fourth one, their address at the bungalow so they could leave.

"I do not think that would be a good idea," Hale said, squinting at him as if measuring him for handcuffs.

Sam had reached the end of his patience and began yelling. "Where do you think we're going to go on an island this small.? We've paid our rent for the entire month and are probably going to stay for another one. We're not leaving."

The police officer pressed a hand on Sam's shoulder, trying to make him sit down again and behave, but Sam was having none of it. He dug in his heels and stayed on his feet. "You think we killed that poor guy, don't you?"

This police officer had been the first one not satisfied with Sam and Maxi's story. The officer questioned their statements over and over, had run at them from every verbal direction. Hale had even separated Maxi and Sam to grill each of them, hoping he would get the weak link of the pair to crack. The police officer had insisted that they accompany him back to Thousand Steps, driving them in his official car, the wrong way on the one-way road, with one of his underlings following in their rental pickup truck.

Officer Hale made them stand and watch the paramedics hoist the body up all those steps. When they reached the top, he stopped the paramedics, unzipped the end of the body bag, and asked Sam and Maxi if they knew the man. It was horrible. Predators had not hesitated to take advantage of the food source, and while Sam and Maxi stood staring shocked at the skeletal face, a crab scuttled out of what remained. That was nearly it for Maxi. Sam felt her totter, and he tightened his arm around her.

"This is enough," he said. "We were trying to be good Samaritans by reporting this, and you're treating us like criminals. I'm taking my wife back to the bungalow. If you or any of your superiors wish to speak to us further, we will be happy to speak to you there."

The police officer looked at his notebook. "Holiday Homes, the orange bungalow?"

Sam nodded. "That's right." He bent down and whispered, "We're going" into his wife's ear. Then they crossed the road to their truck, where he carefully helped her into the passenger seat. Sam got into the driver's seat, maneuvered around the various vehicles in the way, and drove off.

Sam and Maxi drove in silence until they had passed through Playa. Then Maxi said in a small voice, "Do you think that… that guy was a diver?"

Sam shook his head. "No, honey, I don't."

She turned as far toward him as her seat belt allowed. "Why not?"

"Because of his clothes. Those were expensive clothes and, I don't know, but to me, he looked like one of those rich guys you see in places like Nassau. You know, the ones with the trophy wife and the loud voice and always being rude to the natives and the waiters. A real jerk."

Maxi frowned. "What gave you that idea? You only saw the guy for about a minute."

Sam shook his head again. "I don't know, but I bet I'm right. He can't be a diver. Divers don't kill other divers. Divers are too nice."

She reached over and laid a small hand on his arm.

"You're too nice, sweetie. Thanks for getting us out of there. I know there'll be a lot more police officers coming to interview us, but I don't think I could have stood out there another five minutes before fainting or screaming. Most probably both."

When they got back to Holiday Homes, Sam backed the truck up to the gate of the orange bungalow. He and Maxi carried their scuba units onto the porch, made sure that the air was turned off, purged the lines, and went inside to make drinks. It wasn't even two in the afternoon, but they agreed the circumstances called for a drink.

Maxi made the drinks while Sam sliced Gouda cheese, tomatoes, and cucumbers for sandwiches. They each made a pair of open-faced sandwiches and carried their rum drinks and lunches out to the shaded porch to refresh themselves. They enjoyed watching the antics of the black and yellow Bananaquits as they swooped and squabbled over the saucer of sugar Maxi and Sam put on the half-wall every morning. When the sandwiches were only a memory, and they were just about ready to go in for a nap, a rusted-out blue Jeep driving by drew their attention.

"That Jeep is a disgrace," said Sam.

"I've noticed it going by a few times a day," Maxi said. "In fact, the other day when I was walking back with the clean laundry, he drove by, and I had to wait for him. The guy driving is pretty good-looking."

"Oh, really?" Sam looked at her with one eyebrow cocked.

She reached over and lightly swatted his arm. "Yes, really, if a girl likes that cheap, muscular, young kind of guy. Which I do not."

They laughed and squeezed each other's hand.

"What say we take a nap in the air conditioning?" Sam said.

Maxi stretched out her foot into the sunshine and felt the powerful heat. "Good idea. I still feel a bit overheated from having to stand out there all that time."

They carried their dishes into the kitchen, where Sam washed them while Maxi closed the bedroom windows and turned on the air conditioner. She drew the curtains and got undressed. She walked nude across the living room to the bathroom, and Sam whistled.

"Oh, thanks," she said.

"Hey," he said, curving an arm around her waist, "I like how you look." He dropped a kiss on her shoulder, and she purred.

The nap could wait.

****

Lucia stood in the study, staring out the window that overlooked the sea. She stood far enough back so she didn't think Burke could see her if he glanced this way. Burke. Lucia looked over her shoulder at the stack of letters from his grandfather to Aunt Anneke. How could she ever muster up the guts to tell Burke that she had them and would give them to him? Ever since the words spewed out of her mouth, she'd regretted her outburst that had driven him away.

It was bad enough he lived right across the road from her, and she could hear his boat and truck, so it was easy to track his comings and goings, but now he had invaded her dreams. She had awakened last night, all twisted in sweaty sheets, dreaming that Burke was standing in the doorway calling her and she couldn't get to him. After fighting her way out of the sheets, she'd lifted her wet hair off her neck and sat on the edge of the mattress. "I need a drink of water."

The tiles felt cool on her feet as she walked into the kitchen. She reached for a glass and was about to turn on the water when the back doorknob rattled. Lucia nearly dropped the glass. She set it down on the counter and tiptoed back into her bedroom. As she turned on her phone to call Burke, she heard laughter and young men's drunken voices. "I guess they fixed the door. Let's try the next one." Hearing the crunch of gravel under tires, she peered through the curtains to see a dark pickup truck with its lights off rolling backwards down the driveway.

She let out a breath and walked back to the kitchen for her drink of water. "It's too bad I don't have any liquor in the house. Now's the time I could use a belt." Lucia double-checked the door locks and deadbolts, front and back, and made sure the baseball bat Burke had given her was lying next to her bed. She crawled in between the clammy sheets, not sure she'd be able to fall back to sleep.

Staring at the gecko stalking moths across the ceiling, she thought about her first instinct to call Burke. Would he have come to her rescue? Or would he have told her to call 9-1-1 and hung up? Then she remembered what Amelia East-man had said about Burke not chatting or smiling or even waiting to be paid when he delivered fish to her lately. Did that mean he cared for her or just that he was depressed because he was losing his home?

Lucia turned over and pushed back the hair that stuck to her face. No more dreams about Burke. She worked hard to fall asleep.

She didn't feel rested when she woke up the next morning. Susanna was humming in the kitchen when Lucia walked in, hair all lank with perspiration and in her wrinkled sleep shirt.

"Can I make you some coffee, Miss?"

Lucia gave her a tired smile. "That would be wonderful. Thank you, Susanna."

While the housekeeper was busy making coffee, she said over her shoulder, "You don't look like you had a restful night, Miss. Wasn't your fan working?"

"Oh, the fan was working fine, but someone tried the back door again. I was in here getting a drink when I heard the knob rattle and drunks whispering by the door. I was just about to call for help when they left. Sleep was scarce after that."

"You should maybe let Burke know that someone tried to break in again." Susanna set down a mug of black coffee in front of Lucia.

"Thanks." She picked up the mug and took a sip. "Oh, I needed this." She set the mug down. "I don't think Burke would be interested in anything that goes on here anymore. He's just biding his time, looking for a new place, and waiting for the sale to go through."

Susanna shook her head and said nothing, but gave Lucia a look that said, don't be so sure.

Lucia sat going through papers in the study until late afternoon when the sun streamed through the sheer curtains and the room became stifling. She stood at the window, looking to the west and thinking how good it would feel to go down for a swim. Burke was home. She hadn't heard his faded green pickup truck leave since he got back from his deliveries, and he wasn't out on his boat. So swimming was out. Piles of dark clouds were gathering on the horizon. She wondered whether a storm was brewing. Was it hurricane season? Wasn't Bonaire outside the hurricane zone? Maybe she'd ask Burke. No, not Burke. Ask Susanna instead; she'd know. And Lucia thought maybe she'd take a shower. That would cool her off.

CHAPTER 29

Detective Inspector Joachim Rensburg was tired already, and it wasn't much past noon. He had gotten to the site where the Americans had found the body floating in the sea, only to find out his assistant, Sergeant Hale, had allowed them to return to their bungalow.

"I need them here, Hale," he said through gritted teeth.

"Yes, sir," Hale said, looking at the toes of his shoes. "I spoke with the American couple. I asked a few questions. Then I had them look upon the corpse to see if they knew the man, if the sight of him fresh from the ocean jogged them into confessing."

Rensburg sighed. Hale meant well. He was eager, almost too eager, and he worked hard. He watched too much American television, imagined himself a hard-boiled type who growled at suspects and swaggered at crime scenes. Hale was young and had not worked too many deaths. Rensburg could see that despite the bravado, Hale was nearly sick. Under the firm jaw, the muscles quivered.

"You interrogated them, didn't you, Hale? You bull-dogged those nice people until the husband got angry and took his wife home." The last was not a question.

Miserable, Hale nodded.

Detective Inspector Rensburg saw a smirk on the face of the patrolman loitering on the opposite side of the road. Rensburg gave Hale a break. "Didn't Sergeant Hale direct you to look for where the body may have fallen from, Officer Royal?"

The smile left the face of young Officer Royal, who squared his shoulders and turned to examine the state of the gravel along the road and check for scratches in the limestone wall leading to the dive site. Rensburg motioned for Hale to follow him into the shade.

"I'm not angry, Connor, but I am disappointed. We have discussed the proper way to extract information from witnesses, haven't we?"

Hale nodded, his eyes downcast.

"Look at me, Connor." The younger, taller officer raised his eyes. "I am calling you by your given name, not your official title. This should tell you I am teaching you, only chastising you a little."

Sergeant Hale opened his mouth, but Rensburg forestalled him, saying, "You are about to excuse yourself by telling me that the other Detective Inspector whom you work with uses intimidation to good effect and you wanted to try it out. Correct?"

"Yes, sir."

"Tell me, what sort of people was Detective Inspector Gerharts questioning?"

Hale dug the toe of his shoe into the sandy soil as if it helped him think. "They were young men, sir, whom he suspected of breaking into tourist vehicles."

"Ah, I see. So, do you think perhaps he would speak differently to young toughs than to middle-aged tourists?"

Sergeant Hale frowned and nodded unhappily. "Yes, sir."

Rensburg was not at all sure that his subordinate understood the point he was trying to make but the longer he stood here trying to mold Connor Hale into a serviceable police officer the longer the person responsible for the death of the man just pulled from the sea had to escape. If there were such a person.

Rensburg had to consider it was possible that a man in his middle years and, from all appearances, of the upper class, was taking a walk when he slipped and fell to his death. Of course, it would be logical if there were a vehicle abandoned at one of the parking areas along the cliff top, but there was not.

So how did the man get into the water? He thought he should set his officers to examining the cliff tops between here and the Oil Slick Leap dive site. And he should send out the police boat and have them examine the cliff face in the same area. As Rensburg made his way back to his official police car, he dialed his phone and set things in motion.

****

After the almost daily afternoon rain passed and the sky cleared, Lucia decided it was time to take an inventory of all the furnishings on the estate. She and Susanna went through the plantation house, counting every stick of furniture, every lamp and vase, all the pots and pans, and every plate, knife, fork, and spoon. It took them a full week—seven long days with a weekend off in the middle—to complete the job. Now, only the boathouse and apartment remained. Lucia stood at the end of the driveway. She knew Burke was home because his boat was tied to the dock, and she could see his faded green pickup truck. She didn't want to go down there. They hadn't spoken since her childish outburst over fish. How would he react when he opened the door to see her there? Would he slam it in her face? She clutched her binder tighter, took a deep breath, and crossed the road. Her steps were slow as she climbed the stairs to Burke's apartment door. She took another deep breath and raised a trembling hand to knock.

Burke opened the door, and his brows lowered when he saw her. "What?"

"I'm taking an inventory of the estate's furnishings. I need your help in the apartment because I don't know what's yours and what's mine."

"Yours? Nothing here is yours."

She glared at him. "Okay, the estate's."

He snorted a breath down his nose. "There are a few things." He stepped back and motioned her in.

They were both stiff and businesslike as Burke conducted Lucia around the apartment. He pointed out the few pieces that belonged to the estate. It was obvious to Lucia that he valued his possessions because the apartment was tidy and clean. The bed was made, and there weren't any dirty dishes in the sink.

When they reached the bedroom, he put his hand on the dark wood bedstead. "Miss Anneke gave my grandfather this bed. Even though it's old, it doesn't belong to the estate. It's mine. I inherited it from Grandfather Burke."

She made notes as they went along. "All right. I'll make a note that the mahogany bed is yours, so no one gets the wrong idea."

"And that's everything," he said as he turned to lead her back to the door.

"Is there anything down in the boathouse that belongs to the estate?"

He folded his arms across his chest. "No. Everything that was left in there rotted away from the salt air over the years. Do you want to check the title of my boat to make sure that's not part of the estate, too?"

She scowled. "Oh, for heaven's sake, no. I know the boat's not part of the estate."

"Well, I don't want you to feel like I'm trying to cheat you." He walked toward the door and leaned on the doorknob. "When's the sale? When do I have to be out of my home for good?"

"Pietr is in contact with the island government, and they don't seem to be in a hurry to cough up the money for the land and house and all." She held the binder tight to her chest. "Pietr said we won't have the estate sale of furnishings until just before the deal is finalized. I'll get back to you as soon as I know."

Burke glanced at her left hand holding the binder. "Pietr, Pietr, Pietr. Hasn't he put a ring on you yet? You spend enough time with him, always in his office, going out for meals. Isn't it about time he popped the question?"

Lucia's cheeks flamed red. "It isn't a romance. Not that Pietr wouldn't like it to be, but I'm not interested in him that way. Besides, it's none of your business what Pietr and I do. Or don't do."

He pulled the door open wide. "Is that all?"

"Yes, that's all I need. Thank you." She walked across the road and up the driveway, feeling surprisingly sad and lonely.

****

Nora's hand trembled as she lifted the crystal to her lips. The glass chattered against her perfect teeth. The villa behind her felt reproachful in its silence. She stood bathed in the sun's rays, wondering where Jack had gone and when he would return. The sound of tires on the crushed coral drive erased the minute wrinkle that had grown between her brows. Nora set her glass down on a palm leaf coaster and smoothed her hair before levering a smile up from the depths of her emergency bag of tricks. Then she turned to walk to the front door to welcome Jack home.

She ran her thumb over the surface of the shell in her pocket. The tiny ridges and whorls like fingerprints, each little bump and dip, were the only things that felt real to her. Events had spiraled so out of control that if it weren't for the little scrap of shell nestled in a teaspoon of sand in the pocket of her shorts, she would run away. It wasn't supposed to be like this. Her life was calm, serene even. She had played by all the rules, upheld her end of the cosmic bargain—kept herself trim, informed, well-groomed. She cultivated an interest in art and finance and even went to the tech school to learn about accounting. Jack said she was stupid, but she persevered, had spent time with her nose in books, magazines like Barron's, and even subscribed to the Wall Street Journal for a while, which she considered a kind of grad course in companionship.

"His companion" that's what Jack called her. At first, there had been a warm, intimate caress in his voice when he said it that made her happy, but lately there was a sharp, almost disgusted note to his voice that made her want to take a shower.

It had been hours since he had left on an unspecified mission. He didn't tell her where he was going or why.

If it weren't for the little scrap of seashell in her pocket, she would be screaming.

CHAPTER 30

Detective Inspector Rensburg got in his police car and maneuvered it around so he could drive directly to Playa. He was in no mood to drive north all the way into Rincon on the one-way leeward shore road and slingshot back to town by the windward shore road. He radioed the officer stationed at the place where the two-way road turned to one way to make sure he would not have to pull over. As soon as he got word that a body had been found, he sent an officer up to turn any divers back from the very popular dive sites arrayed along the northwest coast of the island. He was sure that doing that did not earn the police any points with the scuba diving tourists, who were the lifeblood of the island's economy. But it was of primary importance that the police had time to examine every place where the deceased could have gone over into the water.

Rensburg considered the possibility that the man had been pushed from or fallen off of a passing boat. He had heard whispers of underhanded doings on the island lately and wondered if this death was related. As he drove along with the hot midday air blowing through his open window, he thought about the negative publicity that a death like this could generate. He thought about the ripples of ill feelings that the necessity of questioning anyone suspected of having anything to do with the deceased could generate. And he thought about the effect all of it would have on an island of this size and population so small that everyone knew everyone else and news traveled faster than lightning.

Things had changed enough these days, he thought, what with the taint of the internet there to convince young people that the island ways were old ways, wrong ways. Convince them they were missing out on something important by living in such a backwater of a culture far from the advantages of Europe or America. Detective Inspector Rensburg had always thought that a small island with like-minded people made an excellent place to live. He got the news on the television when he needed it. Rensburg had contact with the wider world through the internet when he wanted it. And he could turn both off when his mind needed clearing, and his soul needed soothing. Today he couldn't turn off the news because he was right smack dab in the middle of it.

The hot, dry wind that blew in his window smelled of cactus from the little hills off to his left and the iodine and fish from the ocean to his right. If you drove him around the island blindfolded, Rensburg could tell you where you were by the smell. No one could miss the rank smell of decay that came from the marshy land across from Harbor Village, but it took a native to sniff out the aroma of curried goat from *El Fogon Latino* restaurant on the Nikiboko Road.

The curried goat there had a hint of Colombian spice, very different from the Caribbean version of the popular stew. The last time he had been at *El Fogon Latino,* it surprised him to see a middle-aged American couple digging into big plates of goat stew with enthusiasm. He even overheard the woman say, "Oh, the kids will be so jealous when we tell them we had goat." He thought they must be a rare couple because, in his experience, Americans liked only American things.

He swung over a block to the shore road, which took him through downtown, and then changed street names once the center of town was behind him. Driving that way forced him to slow down, to look at the roving tourists, and to watch the surge and play of the locals. It gave his mind a chance to go over the things he wanted to speak about with Mr. Spencer's companion and the American couple who had discovered the body. He stopped at San Francisco Hospital, down the street from Cultimara Grocery, to see if the coroner had any interesting information or if anyone had discovered the name of the unfortunate man.

Rensburg passed through the teeming lobby of the hospital with its crying babies and pacing mothers, down a long dim hallway to the lab and coroner's office at the rear. He pushed open the door of the morgue with his shoulder and reached to take a mask from the box alongside the door.

"Mask," a gruff voice called.

Rensburg saw the stooped back of Doctor Borremans spotlighted by the harsh lights over the autopsy table. "Yes, yes," he said.

The doctor turned to frown at him. "Don't be smart with me, boy. I remember you from when you weren't so important."

The dark brown eyes that peered at him over the mask could not hide a twinkle despite the sharp words. Holding the mask over his nose and mouth, the Detective Inspector crossed the room to stand at the older man's elbow. "And I remember you when you had more bedside manner," he said.

Doctor Borremans snorted. "Bedside manner, ha. I always had trouble with that. That's why I enjoy working with the dead. They don't complain about a man's lack of bedside manner."

"All I need to know is how this man died and who he was," Rensburg said to the older man.

"Oh, is that all?"

Rensburg could hear the sarcasm in the old voice and knew that his friend would not let him down. "I would appreciate anything else you could tell me, too, like the name of the killer, if this was not an accident."

The coroner's shoulders shook with silent laughter. "Of course, I'll discover all of that and more with one swipe of my scalpel." He brandished the surgical instrument like a sword, and then his eyes turned serious. "I have learned a few things for you, Joachim." He looked back at the body laid out on the cold marble slab. "This was a well-cared for man wearing expensive clothing. He was well nourished and groomed." His gloved hand moved to indicate the organs of the body's mid-section. "Our Mr. Jack Spencer had an ulcer that must have bothered him quite a bit."

"Jack Spencer? You know his name? Why didn't you tell me?"

"I just did. Give an old man a bit of credit." Doctor Borremans motioned toward the tray on the counter across the room. "His wallet was buttoned into his hip pocket. I teased the papers apart, a lot of money in there by the way, and found his American driving license, various membership cards, and all his credit cards."

"So, it was not a robbery," Rensburg said.

"It would appear not," the doctor agreed.

"Anything else you can tell me?"

Doctor Borremans was pleased to hear the note of humility in Rensburg's voice. "Well," Borremans said, drawing out his triumph, "Mr. Spencer drowned."

"Water in his lungs?"

Doctor Borremans nodded.

"Seawater?"

He nodded again.

"Anything else?" With each question, Detective Inspector Rensburg leaned further over Jack's open corpse.

"Down here." Doctor Borremans motioned to Rensburg to follow him down to Jack's feet. "Here." The coroner pointed at the right ankle. "See the faint bruising around the ankle?"

Rensburg nodded.

"Perimortem bruising. If you look carefully, you can see the shapes of fingers wrapped around."

Rensburg leaned over until his nose nearly touched the icy cold skin. "I see." He straightened up. "Can you take pictures of this? Is it possible to obtain fingerprints?"

"No fingerprints, but I have already taken pictures of the bruising."

Rensburg was silent for a few moments, staring off into

space. Then he asked, "Anything else?"

The coroner shook his head. "The amount of scraping and animal depredation has erased or covered any other injuries. He wasn't shot or stabbed; this I know. It looks to me as if he fell or was tripped onto sharp rocks, of which our lovely island has a large supply. Then, when he was unconscious, he was put into the water to allow the sea and the fish to finish the job. That's what I think."

"That will be your official finding?" Rensburg asked. "I don't want to go off searching for a killer, only to find it was an accident."

"I don't think you will find this was an accident, Joachim. The finger marks around his ankle tell me that. Now go find a killer." The coroner waved off the detective and went back to his work.

Rensburg replaced the gauze mask back on the shelf near the door and left the air-conditioned morgue.

CHAPTER 31

Lucia was glad they were meeting at Pietr's office. It was hot and still again, and the lack of trade winds let the humidity rise. She felt like she was walking through damp curtains in the un-air-conditioned plantation house. By that time, Lucia should have been used to the fact that the old Toyota's air conditioning didn't work, but she tried pushing the button one more time. Nothing happened.

Pietr's office was air-conditioned, so she'd brought a tote of files and ledger books for them to go through. Lucia had been through all of them once. These were the ones she had questions about. Were they worth saving? Would they be of any interest to the Historical Society? She already had a bulging file of letters from old Mr. Burke to Aunt Anneke to give to Burke if he ever forgave her for telling him she was tired of eating fish.

They were working at a table in a small conference room off Pietr's office proper. Lucia spread all the files out while Pietr went to get bottles of water. Sorting files was thirsty work. She finished laying out everything and sighed as she sat down.

"That was a big sigh," Pietr said, coming into the room behind her.

Lucia used her hands to lift the hair off her neck. "Even with the air conditioning, working on this stuff still makes me too warm. I guess I'm not acclimatized to Bonaire yet." She let her hair fall back onto her shoulders.

It surprised her to feel Pietr's hands gather up her hair and hold it off her neck. "I can get you a rubber band." Then she felt his breath on the side of her neck, under her ear. "I think you look very hot, even on the coolest days." He touched his lips to her skin.

Lucia jumped and stood up, shoving her chair into Pietr's midsection, making him grunt. "Oh, you startled me." She put her fingers on the spot his lips had touched. "What do you think you're doing? I'm here to work."

He grinned at her. "Your neck looked so tempting I had to take a little nibble. I'm sorry if I startled you."

"Well, you did. I surely wasn't expecting that." She picked up a bottle of water and touched the cold bottle to her temple. "Let's get to work. I only made an hour's appointment, and I don't want to waste the time."

"We can go longer. I cleared my afternoon when I saw you were coming in." He dusted his hands together. "Where would you like to start?"

"That was nice of you." Lucia picked up the first file. "I need to know if these contracts from the thirties and forties are worth saving."

They worked their way through all the files and ledgers she'd brought. Lucia was careful to keep her distance from Pietr. He kept trying to touch her hand or her shoulder. It was an awkward dance, but Lucia didn't want to give the young man any more ideas than he already had. She just wasn't attracted to him in that way.

****

After leaving the morgue, Rensburg visited the villa rented for the last few months by Jack Spencer and Nora Davidson.

"How can I help you, Officer?" Nora said when the Detective Inspector introduced himself.

"May I come in?"

She opened the door and ushered him in. "Jack isn't here if you need to talk to him, too. I don't know where he is."

"I am sorry to bring the news, but Mr. Spencer's body was found in the sea on the north end of the island. He drowned."

Nora's hand flew to cover her mouth, her knees buckled, and Rensburg escorted her to the patio table. "What do you mean? Jack's dead? But he left this morning... He was supposed to be back for... Are you sure?"

Rensburg looked at her eyes. They were dry. "Unfortunately, yes. A couple of divers discovered his body at Thousand Steps dive site. The coroner found evidence that he had fallen from the cliff, lost consciousness, and drowned. His wallet was in his pocket. That is how we made the identification."

Rensburg declined Yana's offer of lemonade in favor of plain water. He pulled a chair away from the table and positioned it in a spot where it would be impossible for Nora to look away. After thanking Yana for his glass of water, he started questioning. "How long had you and Mister Spencer been together?"

"Five years," she said, waving the time away with a languid hand.

"You're not married?"

She shook her head. "No. Jack had been married before and didn't like it. At least, that's the joke he made at parties. We never discussed it."

Rensburg questioned Nora Davidson for more than an hour, asking her what she had done earlier that day, who she had been with, and her relationship with Jack. He asked pointed questions about Jack's money. If she was in his will, what sort of investments did he have, and the value of his insurance?

"I don't know anything about those things." She gave Rensburg the names of Jack's attorney and his accountant so he could find out the information he sought. She told him Jack had been in a better mood, excited and energized since meeting Manning at Charles and Amelia Eastman's party about a month ago.

Nora said, "Jack would tell me to make myself scarce when he was meeting with Manning. And he wouldn't tell me what they talked about or what business they had together. I assumed it had something to do with shipwrecks, since Manning had talked about nothing else at the cocktail party where he and Jack had met. Jack made me stand next to him all evening while he listened, enthralled by Manning's tales of adventure and riches."

Nora told Rensburg she had struck up a friendship with Amelia Eastman and had joined the Art Appreciation group and made a few other friends on the island, but she didn't know of anyone who was angry enough with Jack to kill him. Maybe it was an accident?

They talked and talked. Rensburg was doing his best to get Nora to tell him something that would have gotten Jack killed. Nora admitted that she and Jack had been growing apart, that he hadn't shared what he and Manning were up to.

****

A short time later, Nora glared at the buildings on either side of the street as she followed the honey-voiced police officer into the island's government center. It was like nothing she had ever seen at home, even on TV. Not that she had all that much experience in police stations. Even in her extreme distraction, trying not to believe Detective Inspector Rensburg that Jack had drowned, some part of her recognized the comic opera aspect of her surroundings. There were wide yellow lines painted or taped three feet back from every reception window. There were signs admonishing people to have their forms notarized in triplicate. And there were posters with lists of safety suggestions and silly scenarios about how to avoid being a victim of crime. She thought the elaborate colonial architecture and bright tropical colors of paint used both inside and out were the perfect setting for the surreal situation she found herself in.

Once they reached the detective's office, he sat her down in a hard chair with one leg shorter than the rest and fired question after question at her until her ears were ringing and her brain was mush.

She repeated over and over her contention that she didn't know where Jack was going when he left. "No, I didn't see what he left in. Until I saw it parked out front, I thought he drove his truck. I can't tell you what the driver looked like because I was still in bed and, besides, Jack wouldn't have let me walk him to the door."

"Do you know anyone on the island who might carry a grudge?"

"No, I don't know who on the island might have a grudge against Jack." Nora clenched her fingers together to keep from flinging her hands into the air. "Lately, he's spent a lot of time chasing around after Dax Manning. They were in business together."

Rensburg's head rose, and for the first time, he looked her in the eye. "What kind of business?"

"Manning said that he and one of the Venezuelan fishermen had found a shipwreck with treasure off the northern coast of Bonaire, and Jack had invested in the search. Jack wasn't happy with how the search was going and was trying to get his money back." Nora pressed her hand to her forehead. "I don't know what else I can tell you. Jack was very secretive about the whole thing."

"There is no record of a treasure ship sinking around the island." Rensburg closed his notebook. "Thank you for your cooperation, Ms. Davidson. I will take you home. Please stay on Bonaire in case I have more questions." He ushered her through the door.

When Rensburg returned to the police station, he sent a pair of officers out in the police launch to scrutinize the shore from the water to see if they could find where Jack had fallen from. He assigned another officer to pace the boat from the shore so that they could coordinate their work. He fielded a few complaints about his using too many officers in one case.

The Detective Inspector turned to face the complainers. "And exactly how long do you wager this island will enjoy its excellent reputation if word gets out that tourists are killed here?" He looked each of them in the eye and stared them down. He knew he was right, they knew he was right, so they turned back to their cases and left Rensburg alone to coordinate his investigation.

Rensburg hated the idea that a tourist, a visitor to his island and a source of much-needed revenue for that beloved island, had been killed, and worse yet, murdered. As horrible as it is to say, he would rather it had been a local. The local life of the island was mostly lived underground, so that the lifeblood of the island, the tourists and their dollars or euros or yen were unaware of petty things. Not that losing a life was a petty thing, but people would not continue to come and spend money in resorts and dive operations, restaurants, food stores, and a host of other entertainments if they thought they might, just might, be in danger. A murder on an island this small would be as bad for publicity as a murder in a hotel.

He thought tourists were like a flock of flamingos; one would be startled and run, and all the others would run too, not really knowing why they were running. The Detective Inspector smiled at the mental picture of a flock of honking pink birds running this way and that, looking for all the world like a bunch of grannies getting upset after church. He shook his head at his own fanciful thoughts and got back to work. Checking the clock, he realized it was after one o'clock in the afternoon. Rensburg had missed lunch and supposed that Mr. and Mrs. Clark were napping after lunch or out at a dive site. He needed a vacation, he decided, as soon as this was done. Where were they staying? Ah, Holiday Homes.

He could call Lucille, the owner, and ask if they were in and have her give them a message to expect him around three o'clock in the afternoon. He called and left his message, then he took a short walk over to Julio's Snack on the corner downtown for a quick lunch and to stretch his legs. Rensburg had a feeling he would do a lot of sitting, interviewing people, and chasing reports for the next few days. He hoped it would not stretch into weeks, but he was afraid that it would if he didn't get a break today.

Just before three o'clock he drove south of the airport into Belnem, the neighborhood where Holiday Homes was situated and where Sam and Maxi Clark were staying.

He stopped first at the office to spend a moment visiting with Lucille and her husband, Marc. They had slowly built their little enclave of bungalows over the last twenty years, and they were very popular with visitors who didn't require a pool or a bar or restaurant. People who just wanted to pretend for a week or a month that they lived in this diver's paradise. After his brief visit in the office, Detective Inspector Rensburg pulled his unmarked official car across the access road to the back bungalows and parked on the gravel area next to Marc's workshop. He could see the front of the orange bungalow from there and noticed that the bedroom drapes were drawn. He smiled to think that the Clarks had so quickly adopted the old-fashioned habit of taking a siesta in the hottest part of the day. Backing his car into the wedge of shade cast by the workshop and getting ready to wait until there were signs of life in the bungalow across the way, he looked up to see a middle-aged woman opening the drapes. She was talking to someone he could not see, and as she opened the windows, he could hear the smile in her voice. Within minutes, a man a few years older than the woman came out the front door of the bungalow and stood looking at the birds clustered around the saucer of sugar on the short wall separating the patio from the crushed coral lawn. Rensburg thought he detected the self-satisfied look of a man who had just enjoyed more than a nap with his wife in the cool dimness of their bedroom. Rensburg hated to break the mood, but he had a murderer to find, and quickly.

He rolled down the passenger window of his car so it wouldn't be an oven when he returned from interviewing Mr.

and Mrs. Clark. In order to present a more friendly appearance, he removed his sport coat and tie and laid them carefully on the back seat. He unbuttoned the collar button of his shirt and rolled up the sleeves. He smiled at himself. When he was not on duty, casual meant cotton slacks and a tee shirt or polo shirt. He didn't know where he had gotten the feeling that he couldn't do a good job fighting crime and catching criminals when he wasn't in a tie and jacket. Casual dress was much cooler.

From the porch, Sam Clark watched the man cross the parking area toward him. He knew that the code of conduct in the Caribbean decreed a visitor stop at the gate of the property and give the people inside the chance to make themselves presentable, do a little tidying up, or, in extreme cases, pretend not to be home. Sam stood his ground, knowing that the man, who could only be yet another policeman, had seen him and, therefore, knew they were home. He didn't even pretend not to see the man advancing toward him. I have nothing to hide, Sam thought. Why would I run inside? Although he did step back and softly let Maxi know she needed to be decently dressed, as they had a visitor. Maxi felt that a loose tank top and a pair of panties were plenty of clothes when the two of them were alone. Personally, Sam thought the panties were superfluous, but when they were entertaining a guest, he supposed panties were necessary. Sam heard the shower, so he stepped into the house to make sure the bathroom door was closed enough and that Maxi had something to wear when she emerged.

"What the heck does he want?" she asked when Sam told her there was another policeman approaching. '

Sam shrugged. "I don't know for sure, but I'm guessing that this guy is as far up the ladder of cops as there is on the island. He looks like the boss."

Maxi giggled. "I guess that means I have to wear underpants with my sarong, huh?"

Sam leered at her. "Only while he's here." He ran a hand over his hair and picked up a tee shirt on his way back to the front porch. When he got to the door, the man he assumed was another cop was leaning on the gate, looking at the bougainvillea with interest.

Sam went out and said, "Can I help you?"

The man looked up with a smile that Sam thought looked a bit like a shark looked when it swam over you. "Am I speaking with Mr. Clark?"

Sam nodded. "Yes."

"I am Detective Inspector Joachim Rensburg. I'm in charge of investigating how the body that you and your wife discovered this morning came to be in the sea."

"How can we help you?" Sam asked.

Rensburg was still standing in the bright sunlight outside the gate of the orange bungalow. He thought either Sam Clark was very canny and was leaving him out there to broil, or he was totally clueless regarding manners and was waiting for his wife to ask him in. Though the sun was in his eyes, Rensburg could see the small, satisfied smile on Mr. Clark's face and came to understand that he was being left there as a test of wills.

"Oh, for heaven's sake, Sam, reel it in and invite the officer in out of the sun." Mrs. Clark stepped out the door and motioned Rensburg in. She turned and frowned at her husband, who had the grace to look slightly abashed, and sat down at the table in the shade. "I'm Maxi Clark, Maxime actually. And you are?" She held out her hand to shake the officer's smooth brown one and gestured for him to take a seat.

"I am Detective Inspector Joachim Rensburg of the Bonaire Police Department. As I told your husband, I am investigating how the body you discovered this morning came to be in the sea." He sat.

"May I offer you some lemonade? It's freshly made."

"I would enjoy some. Thank you." He made as if to rise. "Can I help you?"

"No, thank you. That's very kind of you." She sent a look to Sam. "I'll be right back."

The conversation on the porch was guarded and superficial while they drank Maxi's excellent lemonade.

She said, "My secret is to squeeze one orange into it and then toss the orange pieces, peels and all, in. I think the orange cuts the tartness of the lemons just enough."

Detective Inspector Rensburg nodded politely and said, "I will remember that the next time I make lemonade."

Finally, the deliciousness of the lemonade and the hot dry weather were no longer gripping subjects of conversation.

Sam was pleating his napkin, and Maxi was making a series of interlocking rings of moisture on the glass tabletop with her glass.

Rensburg cleared his throat, and they both looked at him. "I am interested in knowing exactly what occurred this morning at Thousand Steps." He stopped talking and left it up to the Clarks to fill the silence.

Sam and Maxi looked at each other for a time as if having a silent conversation. After a couple of minutes, Sam shrugged and nodded. Maxi cocked her head and then nodded, too.

She turned to face Detective Inspector Rensburg and took a deep breath. "Well, there's not much to tell, really. Sam and I got our gear together and suited up. We walked down the steps, and Sam was counting to prove to me there really aren't one thousand steps, and I turned to laugh at him at that landing place there in the middle."

Rensburg nodded to encourage her to keep going.

"When I turned, my eyes swept the shallows and saw that man. I thought he was snorkeling and said to Sam it was funny that he was wearing clothes. Then we looked harder and realized he was not wearing a mask, snorkel, or fins, and," she shuddered at the thought, "there were a lot of fish around him. Eating him." She turned pale, and her breath became shallow. "I turned right around and headed back up. I could tell there was no saving him, and I wasn't going down there to pull him out or let Sam do it. So, we went right back to the truck, took our gear off, and drove up to BOPEC to call the police." She reached out with a shaking hand and refilled everyone's glass, then picked hers up and drank half of it in one swallow. "Your officer, um, Hale, was it, Sam?"

He shrugged.

"Oh, your memory is a disgrace. I'm going to get you some ginkgo biloba when we get home." She patted his arm and then turned back to Rensburg. "Officer Hale didn't believe us when we said we didn't know the man. He made us look at the body when the paramedics brought it up on the stretcher. It was horrible. A crab crawled out of his eye socket."

Rensburg said, "It must have been terrible for you."

"Well, to be honest, it was more gruesome than terrible, but not something I want to see on my vacation. Anyway, I got a little woozy, Sam got mad, and we came home. That's all we know."

"It seems as if Mr. Jack Spencer fell or was pushed off the cliff on that part of the island," Rensburg said.

"Jack Spencer?" Maxi sat up straight. "Sam, wasn't that the name of the guy we picked up at the lighthouse last week? He had somehow gotten there without his truck, so we gave him a lift home."

Sam scratched his temple. "I think you're right. I asked him how he got there without wheels, but he was a little cagey, so I dropped it."

Rensburg leaned toward Sam. "What did he say exactly?"

"Not much. Just that a business partner played a trick on him and left him stranded at the lighthouse. When we got to his place not far up the road from here, his truck was parked at the gate. He shrugged, got out, and went through the gate. Now that I think of it, he didn't even say thank you."

It took another hour and another pitcher of lemonade before Rensburg was convinced that Sam and Maxi had nothing to do with the death, accidental or not.

"Thank you for your cooperation, and please do not leave the island without contacting me."

Sam blurted out, "Sgt. Hale told us that too. We aren't leaving. We have no intention of leaving until we're good and ready."

Maxi silenced him with a gentle hand on his thigh. "Thank you, Detective Inspector. We're happy to speak with you if you have further questions."

They watched Rensburg walk back to his car.

"Could you have been any smarmier?" Sam asked as Rensburg drove away.

"Smarmier? Is that even a word? And what, pray tell, does it mean?" she said, hands on hips, never a good sign.

"It means you practically licked his boots. It means you were so nice, I feel like I need an insulin shot." Sam stood up so fast he knocked his chair over.

"Oh, really?" Maxi stood too, her face pink and her teeth gritted. "Since when do we have anything to hide from the police? Is there something you are not telling me about your past? Hm?" She leaned closer to him and peered into his eyes until he flinched.

He backed off and stammered. "Well, no, not really. I guess I just... Well, I didn't like being grilled again about things we know nothing about."

"And you thought you would try on a movie tough guy role? Sam, I thought you were a better man." She looked at him and shook her head. Then she gathered the empty pitcher, glasses, and wet napkins onto her tray and carried it into the kitchen.

As he drove away, Rensburg mentally drew a line through the Clarks on his list of suspects. He was nearly convinced they had nothing to do with the killing of Jack Spencer. Neither Sam nor Maxi Clark had flinched when he told them the name of the deceased. The news surprised them, but he didn't think either of them, Sam especially, was that good at hiding things.

CHAPTER 32

Once Nora was back in the villa, she didn't know what to do. She called Amelia Eastman to tell her Jack was dead, and the local detective thought she had something to do with it. "I just know Detective Inspector Rensburg thinks I engineered Jack's fall off that cliff."

"Oh, I'm sure he doesn't." Then Amelia's voice developed a sharp edge. "What makes you think that?"

"Just the way he looks at me when he's asking questions. And he asks a lot of questions. Most of which I can't answer."

"Well, don't make up answers. That's a sure way to make him think you're lying." Amelia was quiet for a moment. "Nora, do you want to come over for a drink? Charles is out, and I've another woman friend here. We could sip a little wine and talk."

"I don't want to interrupt your visit with your friend. She won't want to sit listening to me agonize over what happened today."

"Nonsense. We women have to stick together. She's juggling the attentions of a few men, and I'm sure Lucia will be happy to meet another woman on the island."

Nora sighed. "All right. If you're sure, I'll be right over."

"I'm sure." Amelia put down the receiver and turned to Lucia. "Nora Davidson is on her way over. Her male friend, Jack Spencer, was found dead today, and she's just spent a horrific couple of hours being grilled by a police detective. I hope you don't mind."

"I don't mind." Lucia tipped her wine glass toward Amelia. "Then I'd better stop drinking. I'm not used to it, and when I have too much, I have trouble controlling my tongue. I met Jack Spencer only once, at your cocktail party, and I wasn't impressed."

"Neither was I. Jack was a bully and too full of himself. He thought he was smarter and richer than everyone else and didn't hesitate to let us all know." Amelia lifted her head at the sound of tires on the gravel parking area in front of the house. "That'll be Nora." She went to the door to let in her other guest.

"Oh, my dear, I'm so sorry you're having to go through this. Come in. We're on the patio. I'll get you a drink." She slid her arm around Nora's shoulders and squeezed.

At the friendly touch, Nora bowed her head and burst into tears. "I don't know what to do, Amelia. With Jack gone, I don't have any money and no place to go."

The older woman escorted her through the house and out onto the patio, where Lucia sat at the glass-topped table. "Here, sit down and let me pour you a glass of wine." She held up the open bottle. "Or would you rather just have the bottle and guzzle it down?"

The absurdity of the statement brought Nora's head up and dried the flow of tears. She giggled and then put her fingers over her mouth. "Oh, I shouldn't laugh. Jack died today, and I'm supposed to be sad."

Lucia looked at her. "Are you sad?"

Nora blinked away the tears that clung to her eyelashes. "Actually, I'm kind of relieved, but if you tell anyone I said that, I'll deny it. It was getting harder and harder to pretend to love Jack or even like him much. His obsession with the shipwreck hunt was driving both of us crazy." She looked startled and said, "You don't suppose Manning had anything to do with

Jack's death, do you?"

Amelia set a wineglass down in front of Nora. "Oh, I don't think so. Manning seems like a bit of a pirate, but commit murder? I'm sure he wouldn't." She resumed her seat at the table and picked up her own wineglass. "What are you planning to do next?"

"Well, the policeman told me not to leave the island, so I guess I'm stuck here for now. It's a good thing Jack paid the villa rent in advance, so I've got months before I have to come up with more money. I have some saved that Jack didn't know about so I can buy groceries and keep my little rental car, at least for a while."

"Will you look for a job?" Lucia asked. "What skills do you have?"

Nora gave a rueful laugh. "Believe it or not, I've got an associate's degree in accounting, so I can keep books. It's been a while since I've practiced, but I don't imagine entering debits and credits has changed all that much." She looked thoughtful. "Maybe I can find some small businesses on the island that need a bookkeeper or want help in that area. I don't really have anything to go back to the States for. Being with Jack cut me off from most of my friends, and I've been estranged from my folks for decades."

For all Nora's confident talk of being relieved instead of sad, Lucia suspected she was afraid the police would decide that she had done Jack in, and she wouldn't be able to prove that she hadn't.

Lucia told the two women about her troubles with Burke, Pietr, and now Manning. "I don't know what I've done to warrant the attention of all those men, but they couldn't be any more different if they tried."

Nora teased her about being a *femme fatale* and then caught the meaning of what she'd said and blanched. "I... I didn't mean that the way it sounded. Just that you seem to be attractive to a wide range of men."

"We know what you meant, dearie. No need to apologize," Amelia said, patting her hand. "Our Lucia seems to have very strong pheromones for available men on the island."

Lucia drained her wineglass and looked at the other two women. "It looks like I've driven Burke away, anyway. I told him I was tired of eating fish every day, and he hasn't been back since. Even Susanna is moping around." She twirled the stem of her glass between two fingers. "And every time I have supper with Pietr, he gets a gleam in his eye like he's sure I'm going to want to start a relationship. I just want his help with the estate. And I wish the darned government would get on the stick and come up with an offer to buy the place and get it over with. My boss won't tolerate my working remotely for much longer."

"How did Manning get into the mix?" Nora said.

"I'm not sure. Maybe he heard I'm an heiress and figured I'd be coming into bags of money, so he thought he'd see if he couldn't cut himself in. Not that there's going to be bags of money. I figure once the house and property are sold to the government, I'll be lucky to have a few thousand dollars left after estate taxes and things like that."

Amelia looked at her over the rim of her wineglass. "You be careful around Manning, Lucia. I hear he's got a violent streak. Especially where women are concerned."

****

On his way back to the station from questioning the Clarks in Belnem, Rensburg stopped at the Bananaquit Restaurant at the Flamingo resort to sit on the upper deck and have some supper.

He turned his chair around so that he was facing the sea and the setting sun, then allowed himself to sip a gin and tonic to unwind from his stressful day. It had been months, nearly a year since someone had died on the island under suspicious circumstances, so he had the feeling that he needed to gear down, or tool up, or somehow get up to speed to deal with the many different aspects of investigating the death. His visit with the coroner in his lab this morning had helped him to focus on a few of the things he needed to be thinking of while interviewing people who might have an interest in killing Jack Spencer.

That woman, Nora Davidson, for example, she seemed like she might have a motive if he could learn from Mr. Spencer's attorney if she would inherit his estate or was the beneficiary of a nice fat life insurance policy. He suspected her lack of emotion when he had gone to tell her that what he thought was her husband was dead. She had turned pale, yes, but that could have meant that she had committed the crime and thought he was there to arrest her. Even taking her down to the police station, removing her from her comfort zone, had not shaken her contention that she had nothing to do with his death. She shed few tears in Rensburg's presence, but he didn't think that meant she was guilty, at least not for certain, but he intended to speak to Ms. Davidson many times before being convinced of her guilt or innocence. While he was thinking, the sun had set, and he heard the people at the other tables talking, especially two women nearby who were talking about Jack Spencer's death.

"I didn't meet him, but David did at the casino," said a woman with an Eastern European accent.

"I only met him once at that climatologists' cocktail party Charles and Amelia had a couple of months ago when you were off-island, Verna," said the other woman. "Amelia had quite a bit to say about the way he treated his mistress or companion, or whatever they are calling them these days."

"Oh? What did she say?" asked Verna.

"Well, she saw him ordering her around at the party. He made her stand beside him all evening, even though he was wrapped up in Dax Manning's treasure hunter tales. Honestly, that Manning is some womanizer, isn't he?"

"I don't believe a word he says. He's too full of himself and can talk of nothing but his own narrow interests. I tried to engage him in a discussion of poetry, but all he did was recite a string of crude limericks having to do with bodily functions."

Detective Inspector Rensburg casually slid his chair so that he could see the women's table out of the corner of his eye.

The other woman laughed. "That sounds like Manning. But back to Amelia, she said that she witnessed Spencer grab Nora's arm so hard it had to have left marks and drag her over to his side. She said Nora had called her to meet for lunch the next day and was wearing short sleeves. Amelia could see bruises on her arm, but she didn't want to ask about them. Amelia said Nora was near tears the whole lunch."

"It sounds to me as if Mister Spencer was beating her up. That's despicable."

"Yes, it is."

Rensburg could see one woman look around for eavesdroppers and then motion the other nearer. It was quiet enough in the restaurant that Rensburg could still hear her lowered voice.

"It makes me wonder if Nora pushed him off a cliff to get him to stop beating her up. I wouldn't be surprised in the least."

Verna nodded her agreement. "I would push David off a cliff if he even dared to raise a hand to me, and he knows it. He would never think of it."

Rensburg slowly turned his head to glance their way. Looking at who he assumed was Verna, the Eastern European, he wasn't surprised. She looked formidable.

****

When she got back from Amelia's, it was dark, but Nora didn't turn on any lights as she walked through the villa. When the Detective Inspector escorted her out to his police car, he had held her arm as if she were an invalid or as if he thought she might collapse with emotion. He had lost some of his sympathetic tone once they had settled in his brightly lit office downtown, and it had taken what seemed like hours to convince him (if she had) that Jack hadn't told her where he was going or who he planned to meet.

It had been necessary for her to admit that Jack had kept her for years. That she was his arm candy, his sexual plaything, his brainless admiring mirror who reflected his egotistical preening, cleaned up and polished as flattery. The naked truth of the situation sickened her.

She sat long into the night outside on the patio with the clattering of the palm fronds overhead sounding like gossip.

****

Manning prowled around the dock outside Burke's apartment after midnight. He planned to disable Burke's fishing boat. Manning couldn't let him get away with accusing him of staging a wreck site as a scam. That public brawl was unforgivable, too. He'd fix it so that the boat took on water when Burke was out fishing and maybe it would sink out from under the guy, and he'd be out of Manning's way.

As soon as he got close to the boat, the outside light on the boathouse turned on and illuminated the entire area. Manning froze, waiting to see if Burke came down to see why the light was on. He waited a long five minutes until the light turned off, but no one came. Manning figured he was in the clear. As he reached to board the *Miss Ana,* a voice came out of the darkness.

"What do you think you're doing, Manning?" An iron hand grabbed his collar and nearly lifted him off his feet.

"Just admiring your boat."

"At one o'clock in the morning? I don't think so." Burke shoved him away from the boat, and Manning teetered on his heels before he regained his balance. "Go on," Burke said. "Get out of here before I call the cops. And remember, I'll be watching you."

Manning's fingers twitched on the wrench he was holding, gauging whether he would be fast enough to hit Burke with it.

Burke smiled at him. "I'll see your wrench and raise you one baseball bat." He pulled the Louisville Slugger out from behind his back. "I got pretty good with this thing in college. Do you want to risk it?"

Manning backed away, one hand raised as if to fend off a blow. "Not tonight. Tonight, you win, but I'm keeping my eye on you, and one of these days I'll catch you napping, and it'll be all over." He turned and walked up the gravel drive to his car parked in some scrub by the side of the road. He drove back home the short way, ignoring the one-way road.

CHAPTER 33

The sun was high when Nora finally awoke and squinted her way out to the patio. Yana was in the kitchen clattering pots around but took a moment to carry a mug of fresh-made coffee out and set it silently on a mat on the glass-topped table. Her fingers rested ever so fleetingly on Nora's shoulder as she turned to go back to her work.

Tears sprang to Nora's eyes at the simple gesture. The news of Jack's death must be all over the island, she thought. In the center of the table sat a clear glass bowl; three flowers floated on the surface, their yellow centers looking like a pin-wheel of yolk in a fried egg. The petals were so waxy she had to touch them to see if they were real. She had the feeling that nothing would seem real for a while until she could leave the island and begin building a new life without Jack.

****

There was a knock on the front door of the plantation house, and Susanna came through from the kitchen to answer it. Lucia hoped it wasn't Burke. She didn't want to have to deal with his frowns and sharp tongue today.

"Miss, it's the police," Susanna said from the study door. "He says he needs to talk to you."

"A policeman wants to talk to me? What about?"

Susanna shrugged. "I don't know, Miss. Should I let him in?"

Lucia got up from the desk, smoothing her hands over her hair and adjusting her shirt. "Yes, let him in."

A middle-aged man followed Susanna into the room. "Miss, this is Detective Inspector Rensburg. I'll leave you to talk." She scuttled out of the room as if she had something to hide, giving Lucia a frightened look.

Rensburg walked across the floor with his hand outstretched. "I am Detective Inspector Joachim Rensburg of the Bonaire Police Department."

"Yes, how do you do? What can I do for you?" Lucia shook his hand and gestured to a chair across from the desk.

The detective cleared his throat. "I don't know if you've heard, but an American, Mr. Jack Spencer, died yesterday in a fall from a cliff not far from here."

"I heard. I spent yesterday evening with Nora, his companion. What can I help you with?"

"We were just wondering if you had any dealings with Mr. Spencer, if you knew anything about his time on the island." He removed a notebook and pen from his shirt pocket.

"Aunt Anneke had gotten a few letters from him wanting to purchase the plantation house, boathouse, and the property. She'd willed it to the government, so that's what she wrote back to him." Lucia shook her head. "I'm sorry, but I only met him once, at a cocktail party. He tried again to convince me to sell him the estate, but I'm bound by the will and said that I couldn't. Jack gave up pretty easily, being enthralled with the tales of treasure hunting and derring-do that another party guest was telling."

Flipping to a blank page in his notebook, he said. "And who was that?"

"Dax Manning."

"What do you know about Mr. Manning?" Rensburg looked up at her from under his eyebrows.

"Not much," Lucia said. "He talked a lot about finding

treasure on shipwrecks and seemed like he was looking for investors. He's tried a couple of times to interest me in investing, but I'm afraid he's got an elevated view of my finances. Just because I'm inheriting Aunt Anneke's estate doesn't mean I'm a rich heiress."

"Is that all he's tried?"

Lucia rubbed her hands across the cover of the ledger on the desk. "Well, he's also tried to get something a little more personal started, but I thanked him for his attentions and sent him on his way. The swashbuckling adventurer guy isn't my type."

Detective Inspector Rensburg closed his notebook and put it and the pen back in his pocket. "I thank you for your time, Miss Vandersteeg. I hope you have a pleasant visit to Bonaire." He stood and started for the door but then turned back to her. "Are you happy with Susanna?"

His question surprised Lucia. "Yes, why wouldn't I be?"

"When she was a younger girl, she got into some trouble. I know Miss Anneke gave her a job when many others wouldn't. I was just wondering how she was doing."

"Susanna is an outstanding employee. She's always on time, and I trust her with the key to my house. Nothing she has done or said has given me any cause not to trust her."

Rensburg nodded. "Good. That's good to hear. I thank you for your time, Miss." He touched his forehead in salute and let himself out.

****

Nora stumbled down the irregular cement steps to stand clutching the obviously handmade wall with gaps carved in it. Her knuckles grew white and tight with the strength of her grip. One of her red-painted acrylic nails broke with a sharp crack and fell into the sea like a drop of frozen blood.

This is where they found him, the Detective Inspector

told her. This is where the couple of divers were climbing down, burdened by their scuba gear, to dive at the site they call Thousand Steps, resting in this very spot. From here, the wife saw Jack's body floating face down in the clear blue water. She said to her husband how odd it was for the man to be snorkeling in a shirt, shorts and sandals when the husband realized Jack wasn't snorkeling. Jack wasn't lucky to see Barracuda so close. Rensburg told Nora that the wife had run up the steps as if she weren't wearing fifty pounds of gear. They drove to the petroleum tank farm at the top of the island to call the police, not willing to stand in the stillness of Thousand Steps to keep what was left of Jack company.

****

Detective Inspector Rensburg spent the next day canvassing the local bars where he knew Manning or Bunny were frequent drinkers. Very few of the people leaning on the bars, mostly men, had anything to say to him. He knew that many of them had had run-ins with the police and were reluctant to rat on another barfly.

No one would admit to seeing either Manning or Bunny in Jack's company, and none of them had anything to say about Jack Spencer. Most of what he heard was a variation on, "I never met the guy." A few of the men said, "Bunny hangs with that guy Manning. I don't know what they do for each other."

It was a long, hot day of driving from bar to bar, asking questions, and getting few usable answers for his trouble.

****

Nora carried her woven beach mat and the tote holding her bottle of water and paperback novel far down the beach to avoid the happy families and napping tourists. Nora was overdressed. She had packed for one of the more cosmopolitan islands, where her six-hundred-dollar swimsuit and cover up worn with gold leather thong sandals and two-hundred-dollar sunglasses, would put her squarely in the middle of the female pack. Instead, she found herself alone on an island where the best dressed wore khaki cargo shorts, Polo shirts, and Teva sandals. She couldn't have stuck out more if she'd worn a sign. She would go home, except Detective Inspector Rensburg had asked her not to leave the island until he finished his investigation. That, and the unpleasant realization that she had no home, kept her there. She had spent the last five years with Jack in a series of apartments and hotels. All she had was the contents of her three suitcases—and a little emergency money stashed in a safe deposit box in Chicago. She was stuck.

****

The little black bird with the bright yellow breast stood on the glass-topped patio table, its delicate feet spread, its bright eye seeming to judge how far Nora could be trusted. It turned its head from side to side, long tongue flicking in and out of its curved narrow beak, working up the courage to scoop up the grains of sugar Nora had spilled when sweetening her tea.

"Come on, little bird," she said, "I won't hurt you."

She picked up her cup, which caused the bird to fly to the safety of a nearby palm, sitting on a frond and chattering its displeasure. But fear didn't keep the small Bananaquit from getting what it wanted. Nora decided to be more like it from then on.

****

It was another hot day, and Lucia was at her desk in the study sorting papers. At least there was a breeze. She'd read through the piles of ledger books and now was tackling more of the seemingly endless stacks of loose papers. Every once in a while, she'd find something interesting, maybe a letter from a friend or, best of all, one from old Mr. Burke. The oldest letters from old Mr. Burke to Aunt Anneke were charming and affectionate, but the couple must have had a falling out because his later letters were terse and businesslike. She'd been diligently studying the Rosetta Stone lessons, so reading the letters written in Dutch got easier by the day. What hadn't gotten much easier was deciphering the handwriting. Lucia put the letters aside so that if Burke ever came back to visit after her fish tirade, they'd be ready for him to look at.

Late in the afternoon, after Susanna left for the day, Lucia heard a car climbing the gravel drive. It didn't sound like Burke's truck or Pietr's car. Who else could it be? She hoped it wasn't another one of the Historical Society women come to press their suit to have Lucia donate all of the estate to them. There was the scuff of a shoe on the front porch before someone tried the knob. Then there came a knock. She went into the entryway and said, "Who's there?"

"It's a friend," said a male voice.

The fact that the person didn't identify themselves made her suspicious. She was glad that Burke had installed deadbolts on the doors after the break-in. "But who are you?" she said to the closed door.

"It's Manning." He sounded exasperated. "Come on, Lucia, let me in. I've got something to show you."

Not sure she wanted to see anything that Manning had to show her, she took the last step and reached for the locks. When she pulled the doorknob to open the door, Manning was leaning on it with his forearm, and his weight forced her back into the entryway. "What are you doing?" Lucia said.

He stepped over the threshold and was inside before she could shut the door in his face. "I wanted to see you, so I came out. I even brought your favorite drink." Manning held up a bottle of Coca-Cola. He lifted his other hand, holding a six-pack. "I brought beer for myself." He stepped around her and went into the study. "It's a hot day. I thought we could cool off together."

Lucia closed the door and followed him. "That's very thoughtful. I love a Coke on a hot day. I'll go get a glass of ice." She left the room and was back in a minute with a tall glass filled with cubes.

Manning held out the open bottle toward her. "Let me

pour for you." He filled the glass, careful not to let the foam overflow.

"Thanks."

He cracked open a beer and held it out toward her. "Cheers!"

She raised her glass to him. "Cheers."

Manning put the beer to his lips and chugged the whole thing. "Your turn."

When she took the first drink, she noticed something different about the taste, but she drank about half the glass. Lucia felt the unmistakable feeling of alcohol in her veins. "What did you put in there?"

He grinned at her. "Just a little vodka to make things easier."

"Make what things easier?"

"This." He swept his left arm around her waist and pulled her to him so hard that she bent back over his forearm. "And this." He stuck his right hand up her tee shirt and clamped down hard on her left breast. "You have nice tits. Just a handful, the way I like them. Anything more is a waste." He squeezed her breast as if it were a stress ball. "Next, you can tell me where your aunt hid the gold doubloon that I sent her when I tried to get her to invest in my treasure hunt."

"I found the letter and Pietr's reply, but I've never found a doubloon." She twisted in his grasp, but that only made him tighten his grip on her flesh.

Even though she felt the effects of the vodka coursing through her body, Lucia wasn't about to let him manhandle her like that. She screamed and fought, slapping him and punching his ears as hard as she could. Her cousin had boxed her ears when she was a kid, so she knew how painful that was.

"Let go of me!" she hollered as loud as she could. "Stop. I

don't like this."

Through gritted teeth, Manning said, "You should have drunk more. Then this would have been easier and more fun."

"This is not fun." Lucia groped for one of the full beer bottles standing on the desk. She raised it up and brought it down on Manning's head with all her might. He dropped like a rock.

Just then, the door burst open, and Burke rushed into the room. "What's going on? I saw Manning's Jeep out front and thought you might need some help." He looked at the man sprawled on the floor. "But I see you've got things taken care of. Want me to call the police?"

Catching her breath, Lucia said, "Yes, please. And stay here until they arrive in case he wakes up."

Burke looked up from dialing 9-1-1. "I'm not leaving."

Since Lucia lived so far out of town, it was a while before the police arrived. Manning had just begun to stir when they drove up, lights blazing and sirens wailing. The policeman quickly got him in handcuffs while the female officer took Lucia's statement.

Lucia handed over the half-empty bottle of vodka-laced Coca-Cola. "He must have doctored it before he arrived because I don't have any liquor in the house."

The officer looked skeptical. "You don't have any liquor?"

Lucia shook her head. "No. I'm not much of a drinker, so I don't keep it around."

"Do you want to press charges?"

Burke interjected. "You bet she does."

"I can answer for myself," Lucia said. "Yes, I want to press charges for home invasion, assault, and whatever it's called when someone tries to drug you."

The officer wrote furiously in her notebook. "I will need you to come to the station to give a statement. Tomorrow morning?"

"I'll be there."

"I'll drive her." Burke's gray eyes looked like the sky before a thunderstorm.

Once the police got the groggy and protesting Manning out into the patrol car, Burke turned to her. "Why'd you let him in? You know he's trouble."

"I didn't let him in. I opened the door, and he muscled his way in. Give me a little credit for bonking him on the head and knocking him out."

Burke laughed. "You get full marks for that maneuver."

Lucia looked at the desk and said, "Oh, no." Her glass of Coke had gotten knocked over in the struggle and soaked some papers. She hurried to get towels to mop up the mess while Burke lifted the wet papers and blotted them on his shirt.

He said, "I'm afraid some of these might be ruined. The ink's running on the letters."

She handed him a towel. "Use this instead of your shirt. See if you can save them. Most of them are from your grandfather. I was making a pile for you to have since they're not really part of the estate."

They worked side by side, sopping up the spilled liquid and drying old papers with a gentle hand. When the top of the desk was empty and dry, Burke turned to her. "I could really use a hamburger. How about you?"

"I would love one. Where can we get one around here?"

"Downtown there's a small burger joint tucked between two stores. It's called Wattaburger and they do a pretty good job of it. Their fries are outstanding. Want to go?"

Lucia looked up at his smiling face. "Let me put on a

clean shirt and grab my purse, and I'll be ready."

Burke drove his faded green pickup truck at a reasonable speed around the north end of the island, through Rincon, into Playa, and parked in the town lot. They walked two blocks to the restaurant, and he kept his hand protectively on the small of her back the whole way.

CHAPTER 34

The rain came down hard, slashing at the leaves of the oleander, swirling in the palm fronds. Nora stood, drink in hand, watching it pound the surface of the ocean. Absent-mindedly, she raised the glass and sipped, surprised when the ice cubes clattered into her teeth. Her inner voice kept repeating two words: "Jack's dead" over and over. The hour she had spent in the police station being bombarded by Detective Inspector Rensburg's insistent questions seemed unreal. Her hand shook as she lowered the empty glass, the pale dawn light glimmering on the curtain of raindrops that kept her off the patio.

****

The dawn cloudburst had just ended when Burke slowed his boat and coasted toward the dock. A man he didn't recognize got out of his car, walked over to the dock, and held out a hand for the bow line to tie up the boat. "Can I help you?" Burke said as he jumped onto the wet dock planks and secured the stern line.

"I'm Detective Inspector Joachim Rensburg with the Bonaire Police Department, and I'd like to ask you a few questions." He held out a leather wallet with a shiny gold badge pinned to it.

Burke straightened up and stood, dripping, with his hands on his hips. "What about?"

"Do you know Jack Spencer?"

"I've heard of him. Don't know him."

"Mr. Spencer died yesterday in a fall from the cliff along the north shore road. A tourist couple found his body at Thousand Steps. Have you heard anything about that?"

Burke rubbed his hand over his chin, stubble rasping. "No, I haven't been in town to pick up any gossip."

"How about Dax Manning? Do you know him?"

"Yeah, him I know. What of it?"

"I heard that you and Mr. Manning got into a fight at Bobo's a few weeks back. Someone overheard you accuse Mr. Manning of perpetrating a shipwreck scam. Is that correct?"

"That's correct." Burke stood up straight. "I saw Manning and Santiago, one of the Venezuelan fishermen, putting what I thought were pieces of wreckage underwater up north off Malmok before dawn one morning not too long ago."

"Really? And you confronted him about it? What did he have to say?"

Burke folded his arms across his chest. "Of course he denied it. Then he pushed me, I pushed him back, and we got into a fight. Bobo and a couple of other guys broke it up, and Bobo sent both of us home with a warning not to fight in his bar again. And I saw him and that Rasta Bunny driving into town from the northern sites in a white minivan the other day. It looked like a rental."

Rensburg was scribbling in his notebook. "And you have had no further dealings with Mr. Manning?"

"Actually, I have. A few nights ago, I caught him sneaking around my boat with a wrench at 1 o'clock in the morning. I threatened him with a baseball bat and ran him off. Then yesterday he tried to take advantage of Lucia Vandersteeg. When I saw his Jeep in her driveway, I ran up to see if she needed help, but she'd already knocked him out with a full beer bottle. I called 9-1-1 for her and stayed until the police arrived to cart him away."

"Mr. Manning seems to have quite an effect on people on our island," Rensburg said as he continued to write what Burke said. "Maybe I need to speak to him." The detective put his notebook away and stretched out his hand. "Thank you for your time, Mr. Burke."

Burke watched him walk back to his unmarked car and drive away. "Well, that was interesting."

****

They didn't look natural, like real birds, to Nora when they flew. They looked like cartoons, with their elongated necks in the lead and their spindly legs trailing behind. Even the sparse lump of the body spread out, making barely a hump. Only the wings slowly flapping changed the vision of them from an alien being to something possibly earthly and natural. The vivid pink of their feathers was lost in the deepening orange of the sunset, their silhouettes slicing across the sky, and their raucous honks sounding too much like Canada geese to be believed. Nora lay on the chaise on the patio facing the sunset. Her empty glass barely held by her fingertips above the tiles as she watched the skein of flamingos trail across the sky to their roost in Venezuela, sixty miles across the sea.

****

Rensburg got a report from the coroner the next day. It affirmed that the skin Sergeant Hale and Officer Royal had found on rocks at the base of the cliff near Oil Slick Leap dive site was Jack Spencer's skin. That meant that he had to have been pushed or fallen from the cliff top and hit the rocks on his way into the water. Rensburg knew it was possible to park at Witch's Hut, two sites away, and walk back along a narrow shelf of land from there to Oil Slick Leap. An experienced or determined climber could scale the cliff and lie in wait on a narrow ledge just below the top. He knew that was what had occurred because there were cigarette butts crushed in a niche a man's height above the ledge, as if someone had spent some time there. The coral rock was too rough and way too narrow to have served as a lover's trysting place. So Rensburg surmised the killer had waited there for Jack. How he lured him to the killing place was another matter, one he intended to look into.

****

The next morning, Burke drove Lucia to the police station, where she gave her statement about the events of the night before, waited while it was typed up in triplicate, and signed each copy. Retelling the incident didn't bring back the shakes of the previous night but made Lucia quiet on the ride back to Karpata.

"Will you be all right?" Burke asked when he stopped in front of her house.

She nodded. "I think so. Susanna is here too, so we'll keep the doors locked and bolted."

"Which you should have done last night."

"Don't criticize. How was I to know what Manning had on his mind? Now I know not to let him in." She clutched her purse in her lap with both hands. "I wish they'd kept him in jail instead of letting him out on bail this afternoon. How could the judge let him go like that?"

Burke shook his head, then reached across the seat and touched her hand. "I can stay here for a few nights if that would make you feel safer."

His touch sent a shiver up her arm. "Thanks. I'll think about it."

"Call me if you decide you want overnight protection. I'll be home all evening."

She leaned across and kissed his cheek. "Thanks for everything, Burke."

"Anytime."

For the rest of the day, Lucia kept going to the doors, front and back, making sure they were locked, and the deadbolts were thrown. Susanna was horrified when told about Manning's attack on Lucia, and she, too, offered to spend the night, but Lucia assured her it wouldn't be necessary.

In the afternoon, once Susanna had putt-putted away on her scooter, Lucia thought about all the dark hours between dusk and daylight. Maybe having Burke sleep in the second bedroom just for a few nights would help calm her nerves. She pulled the cellphone out of her back pocket and tapped out his number. He answered on the first ring.

"Are you all right?"

"I'm fine. Just a little scared to be alone. Did you mean it when you said you're willing to sleep here for a night or two?" Lucia heard him take a deep breath.

"I'll be right there."

"You don't have to hurry," she said. "You can come over around nine o'clock if that works."

"What will you do until then?" His voice was low and soothing.

"I don't know. Read a book? I brought a bunch of books on my e-reader. I'll pull up one of those and be just fine."

He cleared his throat. "I have an idea. Why don't we go for a swim? It's hot tonight and nearly windless again. Grab your towel and flashlight and come on down. I'll meet you on the shore."

Lucia's voice was small when she answered. "Would you come walk with me?"

In contrast, Burke's voice boomed. "Of course, I should have thought of that. I'll be right there."

"Don't hurry. It'll take me a few minutes to change."

It wasn't long before Burke tapped on the big wooden door. Lucia made sure it was him before opening it. Locking it behind them, they walked in silence down the driveway, across the one-lane road, and down to the beach next to the dock. Halfway there, Burke reached and took Lucia's hand. Neither of them said anything, but their hands felt natural together.

After they swam down the shore to the neighbor's sailboat and back, Burke surprised Lucia by building a little fire on the beach with wood scraps and dried cactus husks.

"This is great," Lucia said. "It's been years since I've sat by a campfire. Probably since Girl Scout camp when I was about twelve years old. Too bad we don't have any marshmallows to toast."

He pulled out the basket he had stashed earlier. "Who says we don't?" In his basket were two long metal forks with wooden handles and a bag of marshmallows. "Can't have a fire without marshmallows. Do you like yours toasted or burnt?"

"I like mine toasted." She reached for a fork. "I can do it myself. I suppose you're in the burnt category?"

He laughed. "I prefer mine toasted too but get impatient and usually end up burning about half of them."

After toasting and eating a few sugary puffs, Lucia shivered. "Even with the fire, I'm getting chilled. Maybe I'd better go in."

"I can fix that." Burke got up, sat down behind her, and pulled her back against his chest. "I'll share my warmth with you."

She felt his breath on the side of her face and shivered again, this time with anticipation.

Lucia gradually leaned her weight back onto Burke. His arms held her against his broad chest, and she reached her hands up to clasp his.

"This is nice," she said, turning her head around to look at him.

"It certainly is." And he dipped his lips down to brush

hers.

She inhaled, and then her lips softened and met his. She turned so that she was facing him and put her arms around his neck. "This is very nice," she said against his lips.

"Oh, yes."

While the untended fire died down, they sat entwined until they were both chilled.

Lucia spoke first. "It must be about time to turn in."

"Okay." Burke paused. "Do you still want me to sleep up at the plantation house tonight?"

Lucia could feel her cheeks burn. "In the second bedroom, yes, I would like that." As her words sank in, Lucia could feel him swallow.

"In the second bedroom, that's what I meant." Burke tightened his arms around her. "Let me throw a few things into a duffle and we can walk up together."

She sat on the steps to his apartment while he gathered his overnight things.

He was back in a few minutes. "All set." He reached down to pull her to her feet, then tucked her under his arm. "Don't worry, sweetheart, I'll keep you safe."

CHAPTER 35

Rensburg interviewed Amelia Eastman first thing in the morning. He had heard of her husband, Charles Eastman. Rumor held that he had been some sort of business tycoon and had tangled in boardrooms with David Flemming, whose wife he'd overheard in the restaurant. Rensburg had sympathy for David if his wife was as severe and humorless as she seemed.

The next morning, shortly after nine o'clock, he rang the bell at the gate of the Eastman's house just down the beach from where Nora Davidson was staying. Eastman himself came to the door.

"Yes? Can I help you?" he said, holding the door close to his side so Rensburg couldn't see in.

Rensburg handed him one of his cards. "I am Detective Inspector Joachim Rensburg of the Bonaire Police Department. I am investigating the suspicious death of Mr. Jack Spencer, and I wondered if I might speak to Mrs. Amelia Eastman?"

Charles frowned. "Why would you want to speak to Mrs. Eastman? She had very little to do with Mr. Spencer." He stood firm in the doorway, not budging an inch.

"I'm sure that you are correct, Mr. Eastman, but I have to get familiar with Mr. Spencer's life on the island. May I come in?" Rensburg didn't smile at Eastman. He understood Charles didn't consider this a smiling occasion and appreciated the seriousness Rensburg took in his work.

Charles thought for a moment, then stepped back, opening the door wider, and motioning the policeman in. Charles escorted the Detective Inspector through the house and out onto the shady patio that ran the width of the house. He showed Rensburg to a chair and inquired if he would like coffee or tea.

"Tea would be nice, thank you," he said with a small smile.

"Sugar, milk, or lemon?"

"No, thanks."

Charles went back into the house and returned quickly with a small tray bearing two mugs of tea and two spoons. He put the tray on the low table next to the police officer and sat down in the other chair. "Amelia is in the shower," he said. "I'll get her for you when she comes out. Now, tell me again why you need to speak to her."

Rensburg said, "I need to get a picture of Mr. Spencer's life on the island. I understand that Nora, Ms. Davidson, has formed a friendship with Mrs. Eastman. Perhaps she might have an insight into the relationship between Ms. Nora and the deceased." The detective looked at Charles. "You know, a woman's view."

Charles said, "We really don't know them well. I met Jack at the Plaza Casino a few months ago and invited him to a casual cocktail party we held for a group of visiting scientists whose work I am interested in." That night had been the first time he, Charles, had met Nora. He thought she was pretty enough and nice, but that she was also well under Jack's thumb. "I know Amelia was angry about how Jack treated Nora, and she attempted to encourage Nora to join her art group and to become more active on the island." Charles said he thought his wife hoped to lure her away from under Jack's domination.

Amelia emerged from their bedroom, surprised to find a policeman on her patio having tea with Charles. She teased Charles about having done something criminal but sobered up when she learned Rensburg wanted to speak with her about Jack and Nora's relationship. At first, she was reluctant to speak about something that was really none of her business. But Rensburg's delicate questioning eventually led her to denounce the way Jack used Nora as a decoration, denying her the chance to circulate at the party. She also talked eventually about the bruises on Nora's arm the next day and Nora's tears when quizzed about her life.

Rensburg asked about Manning. Could he have been after Nora?

"Of course he was after Nora," Amelia said. "He was sure that she'd inherit Jack's money when he died."

"What else do you know about Manning?"

That was when Amelia really let fly with her opinions about Manning. She disapproved of his womanizing and the way he treated women as if they were put on the earth for his entertainment and to support him. She said, "I know a few women who had affairs with him, and he was out only for his own enjoyment. It's too small an island for someone like Manning to operate in concealment. People know the shenanigans he gets up to."

Rensburg asked what sort of shenanigans. Amelia looked at Charles, who looked back, gave a small nod, and then Amelia turned back to Rensburg.

"Manning runs drugs," she said. "And he is a gold-plated scam artist. He will do anything he can do or get into that will make him easy money or help him squeeze money out of unsuspecting people. At our party, he wore a gold doubloon necklace and spent the whole evening monopolizing the attention of many of the guests, Jack Spencer included. He spun tall tales implying that he was an experienced and successful treasure hunter."

Charles chimed in, saying that he had done a little research, and no treasure ships went down in the waters around Bonaire. "I said as much to Manning that night, but Manning looked at me with pity. Said he was sure I meant well, but new information had come to light that a treasure ship might lie right offshore. My efforts to curb Manning's lies about treasure ships earned me disdainful looks from a group of my guests. So, I left to talk to the scientists and let Manning make chumps out of the listeners if he wanted to."

Rensburg thought hard about whether Amelia Eastman was angry enough at Jack Spencer's poor treatment of Nora for her to have met him in an out-of-the-way place and shoved him off the cliff. But he decided she was too much of a lady to have done it.

If he were a better judge of women, Rensburg would have known that Amelia would likely have pushed Jack eventually with very little remorse. But only after she had tried many times to get him to change his ways and reform.

Shortly after Rensburg got back to the police station, he received a call from Jack's attorney, who gave him the news that Nora was not mentioned in Jack's will, nor was she the beneficiary of his considerable life insurance. This information all but cleared her in his mind.

CHAPTER 36

Sam and Maxi were driving from the orange bungalow to a dive site just north of Playa and, as they passed through town, Maxi waved at someone walking along the street.

"Who are you waving at, honey?" Sam said.

"It was that nice Detective Inspector who visited us the other day."

Sam snorted. "What do you mean, nice? He might as well have accused us of murdering Jack Spencer."

"He did not," Maxi said. "He asked the questions he needed answered, we told the truth, and he drove away."

"Hmph." Sam drove on without responding.

****

Rensburg took a walk down to the Club Nautico marina, where the *Baca di Amor* water taxi docked, hoping to find Dax Manning at work. Clifford Oxford, who also drove the water taxi, was working instead. Rensburg asked him what Manning did besides driving the water taxi. Oxford told him that Manning used to divemaster for Lora Divers but got fired for flirting with an American woman whose husband didn't appreciate it. Manning had sported a big black eye and limped around as if he had broken ribs for a week after that. Now he spent a lot of time with one of the Venezuelans. Oxford didn't know the man's name, but his boat's name was the *Santa Marta*. It was blue and white and usually rafted to the red boat with the palm trees on its deck.

"Anyone else hang around with Manning?" Rensburg asked.

"Yeah," said Oxford. "That young Rasta guy, Bunny, runs

errands for him. He even borrowed my cousin Diego's skiff to do a little fishing off the windward side last month when the wind had first died down." Oxford wiped his brow and neck with a blue bandana. "Do you think the night wind will ever come back?"

Rensburg smiled and shook his head. He was a policeman and was still trying to figure out what made people do the things they did. He never thought he could figure out what made the weather do what it did or didn't do.

"How's the fishing?" Rensburg asked.

"Rotten," said Oxford, spitting over the side of his boat. "The water is so flat that all the fish are hiding in cracks underwater and not coming out to get sunburned. Just like people are staying in the shade or in their air-conditioned hotel rooms and not taking the water taxi out to the island for a little hoochie cootchie on the beach."

Oxford winked and nudged the policeman, figuring that even though he was with the police, he was still a man. And men understood that even when it was hot, a man was still a man and had his needs. Oxford had been trying to tell his wife that ever since the night breeze had stopped, but she just pushed him away. She said he could start being a man again when he brought home an air conditioner for their bedroom, as if he had enough money for such foolishness.

Although if it went on much longer, maybe he would find a small one in the window of an empty house and just borrow it for a week. It wouldn't be like stealing, and well, he was a man with needs.

Rensburg thanked Oxford for his help and walked over to the shady side of the street, returning Maxi Clark's wave as they drove by. He walked down to the Town Pier, where the Venezuelans had their boats tied. He didn't see the *Santa Marta,* but he saw Bunny sitting with the fruit and vegetable vendors under the awning. When he walked over to speak with him, Rensburg saw Bunny's pupils widen and the trapped look on his face.

"I am not looking to bust you for using a bit of sacramental ganja, Bunny," he said. "I need to know what you have been doing with and for Dax Manning."

All the Venezuelans looked from him to Bunny. The Detective Inspector knew most of them didn't speak English or Papiamentu, but they understood the tone of the question and the sudden tension that flooded the air.

"I been just driving him around. He need a driver, and I need the money."

"What were you doing over at Lac Bay with the skiff belonging to Diego Marquez?" Rensburg pulled out his notebook.

"We was just fishing. The water lay down so nice when the wind went away, we thought we might fish where no one fishes." Bunny squirmed, his hands knotted together.

The Detective Inspector wrote something down. "And you were driving a white rental minivan through town the day Jack Spencer died. I have a witness who saw you. Where were you going?"

"Just through town. Running an errand for Manning." Bunny stammered, "I... he... I had nothing to do with pulling that Jack off the cliff."

Rensburg stayed silent. He let Bunny incriminate himself and Manning, spilling out all the details of the treasure scam. Jack getting wise to it and wanting his money back. Nora's rejecting Manning's advances. Manning's determination not to give Jack his money back and also to clear Jack out of the way for him to hook up with Nora, thinking that she would inherit Jack's money.

The policeman let Bunny talk until he ran out of words, and then he helped Bunny to his feet and escorted him to jail, arresting him for being an accessory to murder.

****

Maxi was the first to reach the shore after their dive. She carefully navigated around piles of broken coral so that the pieces wouldn't roll under her feet and make her fall. She could hear Sam's breathing behind her.

"You okay, Sam?" she said.

"Fine. Just trying not to fall."

Maxi reached a hand back to him, and they walked the last few feet up above the waterline together. Getting to the tailgate of their rental pickup, Sam held Maxi's scuba unit while she slid out of it. He put it in the rack and turned so she could return the favor. Once they'd both taken off their wetsuits and dried off, Sam handed Maxi a bottle of water and set a zipper bag of trail mix on the tailgate for them to share.

Sam held up his water bottle as if he were toasting. "Here's to having the rest of our vacation be as uneventful as today was."

Maxi tapped her water bottle to his and said, "Amen."

****

Rensburg gathered up a few more officers and headed to Manning's place. It was easy to find him; he was sacked out sleeping in his filthy apartment, one arm thrown over an underage island girl. Rensburg had no trouble waking her and shooing her out the door with an admonition to think better of herself in the future. The policemen waited while she slipped into her dress, picked up the rest of her clothes, and scooted out the door, never saying a word.

He stationed one policeman at each door of the apartment. Then he roused Manning. Manning didn't go quietly. He stood with his legs spread apart, wearing only his briefs, arms flailing, laying blame on everyone but himself.

"It was the Venezuelan's idea to bring up pieces of an old wreck he found outside his home harbor. I tried to talk him out of it, but he was determined to use it to scam some rich guy out of his money. He's ruthless and conniving. Ask anybody."

"I don't think so," Rensburg said, arms folded across his chest, watching the American's antics. "Santiago isn't smart enough or mean enough to plan a con like that."

"Bunny! Bunny is the one who drove Jack out to the dive site where he fell off the cliff." Manning ran his fingers through his curly hair, making it stand out around his head like a halo.

"It was his idea to lure Jack up there, and he made me go along with it."

The Detective Inspector stood in the middle of the room shaking his head while Manning ranted. "You're trying to blame Bunny for this long con? Bunny isn't bad as a wheelman, but he is no long-range planner. And Mr. Spencer didn't fall off the cliff; you pulled him by the ankle. Who else are you going to blame?"

Manning shook his finger in Rensburg's face. "Jack Spencer made it too easy for me. He was so focused on treasure hunting that I just went along with it. It was his idea to find a shipwreck and loot it. Yeah, it was Spencer's idea all the time."

As he paced back and forth, his foot nudged the big wrench he kept under his bed. Manning's eyes lit up, and it was obvious he was wondering if he could use it to get away.

"Don't even think of it," the Detective Inspector said. "You will be shot before you can raise it over your head."

Manning's shoulders slumped, and Rensburg could see he was facing the inevitable.

Rensburg grasped Manning's wrist. "Dax Manning, I am putting you under arrest for premeditated murder, for running a confidence game, and for destroying protected underwater property. I will get to the home invasion and assault charges later." He pulled Manning's wrist up behind his back and nodded at Sergeant Hale to handcuff him.

"Wait! Can't you let me put some clothes on? I can't go out like this." He looked down at himself, clad only in a dingy pair of briefs. "This is police brutality."

"Be glad I let you pull on your underpants." Rensburg waved to the officers to escort the protesting prisoner out to the waiting squad car. "Get him out of here, please. I'm tired of listening to his lies."

CHAPTER 37

When Lucia rose in the morning, she hoped to hear the sounds of Burke making coffee. The house was quiet. She slipped into the bathroom to brush her teeth and comb her hair. She didn't want to walk into the kitchen looking like a hag if he was there. The door to the second bedroom was open, and the bed was made. She hurried into the kitchen, hoping to see Burke, but the kitchen was empty too. There was a note on the coffeemaker. She picked up the scrap of paper and read it.

Gone fishing. Burke.

Just two words. Lucia's heart sank. No sign that he'd come back when he was done fishing. Last night's kisses must have meant more to her than they did to Burke. She brewed a pot of coffee and made herself some toast. Lucia stared at Burke's handwriting, imagining his strong hands gripping the pencil. While she read and reread the note, her coffee went cold, and she took only a few bites of toast. Lucia left the table and went into the study. She sat down at the desk, uninterested in finishing the last of the estate work.

After their evening on the beach toasting marshmallows, Lucia couldn't get Burke out of her mind. The memory of his lips on hers and his muscular arms holding her tight left her gazing out of the window instead of organizing more estate papers. Even getting a phone call from Nora saying that Detective Inspector Rensburg had arrested Manning for Jack's murder didn't shift her thoughts away from last night's embrace.

Pietr stopped by to tell her he'd heard from the government that they were ready to close on the purchase of the property and house. "That means that Burke will have to move," he said.

"I'll have to move, too. I'm sure they won't let me stay in the house once they've bought it," said Lucia.

Pietr leaned over her shoulder as she sat at the desk. "Are you planning to stay on Bonaire? I would like it if you did. We could keep getting to know each other better."

Lucia shook her head. "I'm sorry if I've given you the wrong impression, Pietr. I consider you a friend, not a lover. I don't mean to hurt your feelings, but I have to be honest." She felt his body sag and saw his hand drop to his side.

"Is there anything I can do to change your mind?"

"No, there isn't."

Smit walked around the desk and slumped into the chair across from her. "It's Burke, isn't it? You're in love with Burke. It's always been him."

"You're right. I think I've been in love with Burke since the day I arrived. It's just taken me a while to realize it."

Pietr stood up and rubbed a hand down his face. "I'll get the papers ready and let you know when you can come to my office to sign them. The representative of the government will be there as well to lay out their expectations about when they can take over the property."

"I really appreciate all your hard work in this matter." Lucia stood and extended her hand across the desk. "I don't know what I'd have done without your counsel. You've been a real friend, Pietr. I couldn't have done this without you."

"I'll prepare my bill." He shook her hand softly and left, closing the front door quietly.

****

Lucia turned back to the stack of letters on her desk. She sat down and picked up the top one. They were love letters sent to Aunt Anneke from Burke's grandfather. She kept them aside, hoping that Burke would come back, and she could give them to him. Maybe she should write Burke a love letter. Could she tell him how much she had grown to love him? Tell him she had loved him from the day she arrived, and he was so eager to get rid of her? Would he laugh at her?

There was the sound of a step behind her. She thought Pietr had come back, but she turned around to see Burke standing in the doorway. His clothes were rumpled, and fish scales glittered on them. His hair was wet, like he'd just gotten off the boat. Her heart raced, and her breath got short. The desk chair rolled away as she stood up and turned to face him.

"I had to come," he said. "Last night on the beach was a dream. I'm in love with you, Lucia."

Something tight in Lucia's heart loosened, and she took a step nearer. "I'm in love with you, too, Burke."

Burke reached out to her. His hands shook slightly. Lucia moved toward him, and he pulled her to his chest. He said, "Don't leave. Stay in Bonaire. Stay with me."

"I want to, but where would I live? The government is finally ready to buy the estate." She burrowed into his chest, not for one minute minding the fishy smell, tears flowing down her cheeks.

"We can find a place together." He leaned back and looked into her eyes. "If you want to."

"Yes. Yes, I want to." She gripped his shoulders.

He dipped his head and pressed a kiss to her temple. She leaned into him and hummed with pleasure. The sound emboldened him to kiss down the side of her face. He relished the softness of her golden tanned skin as he worked his way to her lips. Lucia gripped his arms to keep him close. When he reached her lips, they parted in invitation. An invitation he eagerly accepted.

They drew even closer together as their lips met, and they held each other as if they'd never let go.

The End

If you enjoyed this book, please visit Amazon and leave a review. Reviews help others decide to read this book.

BOOKS BY THIS AUTHOR

The Seaview

She knew it would be hard work, but what she didn't plan on was the electrically charged subcontractor and the way he made her feel.

Despite her son's vehement objections, Rose buys the ramshackle Caribbean beachfront bed and breakfast. She's confident that she can oversee the work in time for the start of tourist season. That is until the Health Inspector locks them out of the building.

Desperate to get the crew back to work she pleads with the plumber to get the key and finish at least one bathroom. The plumber has his own agenda. Rose's confidence is nearly destroyed by this major setback.

Can Rose and her crew finish the job before the first guest arrives?

The Seaview is the first book of The Seaview Series. If you like engaging islanders, breathtaking scenery above and below water, and a little romance this book is for you.

Open For Business

It's opening day, and Rose eagerly awaits her first guest. Juggling excitement and nerves, she's determined to keep her new bed & breakfast afloat despite bad weather and a lecherous plumber.

Now that Seaview is refurbished and reopened Rose's dream seems to be coming true, but the arrival of Hurricane Alphonso might end her dream before it can really begin. Her first guests are in residence and one of them acts like the hurricane with its wind, rain, and power outages is a personal affront.

Her attempts to fit into the island community are thwarted by nasty rumors spread by a local woman who resents Rose's romance with Ignatius "Iggy" Solomon. And a lecherous plumber just won't take "No!" for an answer.

In Open For Business, the second book of The Seaview Series escape to the Caribbean island of Anguilla. Enjoy Seaview with its changing cast of guests and the ever-faithful Iggy for delectable homemade breakfasts, beachside dancing, and rum punch as you dive into a tropical women's fiction story.

Spies Don't Retire

Some secrets refuse to stay buried… even in paradise.

Rose is settling into being a newlywed and hosting guests at Seaview Bed & Breakfast on the Caribbean island of Anguilla. Whispers of spies on the island begin to circulate. Someone threatens to unmask them. Rose's peaceful retreat risks becoming a battleground.

At a lavish party, the hostess introduces a British couple to a Russian one, and the tension seethes. Recognition. Sizzling hostility. Delicious gossip makes the grapevine hum. Were the men spies on opposite sides? Or do the wives share a more dangerous past?

As rumors fly, Rose finds herself caught between keeping Seaview's reputation intact and navigating the conflict between feuding friends. In the meantime, she's fighting to clear her name from the lingering lies of her nemesis.

Can Rose mend fences with the local women who distrust her? Will the two warring couples declare a truce—or set the island ablaze with old rivalries?

Spies Don't Retire, the third book in The Seaview Series, takes you back to the tropical shores of Anguilla where intrigue, scandal, and delectable island fare await. Escape to paradise

Horizon

Gail Logan, a widow in her mid-fifties, has lived her life by what other people think. That has to change.

Signing up for a watercolor class and thrifting a new wardrobe with a young classmate makes a good start. Replanting her regimented flower garden is another idea, but at the garden center, Abel Baker dismisses her plan and tells her what to buy. Gail doesn't appreciate his interference.

Widower Abel turns up in Gail's path again and again, but she buried one bossy man, and she's not interested in another. Should she give Abel a chance?

Her sons and her best friend feel threatened by all of Gail's changes. Should she go back to her dull existence or keep moving forward?

Immerse yourself in Gail's journey for a fresh perspective on life in Horizon. Enjoy her adventures learning to paint with watercolor, making new friends, and changing her life to please herself in this mature love after loss women's fiction story.

Better Than Mom's

Better Than Mom's is a neighborhood diner in a small city in Wisconsin where good food and interesting people come together.

Meet Brady, the warm-hearted owner who takes pride in making homemade food for his customers, Fay, the sassy morning waitress who cares for people more than she lets on, Naomi, the welfare mom who cooks like an angel and needs a job, Steve, who sits in the back booth and won't let anyone see what he's writing, and Officer Bates, who comes to investigate a crime but ends up sweeping Fay off her feet.

Stop in at Better Than Mom's for a bowl of homemade soup, a lighter-than-air biscuit, and a visit with people who could be your neighbors.

Island Dreams

He found his dream job. She's reduced to cleaning vacation rental homes.

Ella Thomas and Dan Martinson are excited to leave their families and friends behind in Green Bay and move to the island of Bonaire in the Caribbean to pursue their dream of owning a dive shop.

Dan finds a job as a diving instructor immediately, but Ella can't get a work permit. The excitement and beauty of the coral reefs fill Dan's days. Ella's stuck cleaning up other people's messes for cash under the table.

They're dedicated to saving as much as they can so that when a dive shop becomes available, they can act fast. An unexpected opportunity threatens to drive a wedge between them.

A frustrated Ella comes up with a plan to maximize their savings by chasing that once-in-a-lifetime opportunity. Will Dan go along or stubbornly insist that they stick to their original plan?

Follow the ups and downs of life with Ella and Dan as they chase their Island Dreams.

ACKNOWLEDGEMENT

I'd like to thank my critique partner, Connie Anderson, for her patient reading of this manuscript and her insightful comments. And thanks to the women of the Women's Writing Retreat at The Clearing for all of their help and support.

ABOUT THE AUTHOR

Barbara Angermeier Malcolm

Barbara Angermeier Malcolm, a Green Bay native, is an avid traveler and former retail SCUBA sales professional.

She has journeyed to countless islands with her family on diving vacations, collecting inspiration and stories along the way. A passionate storyteller, Barbara has been crafting tales for years.

When she's not writing, you'll find her sketching, painting with watercolors, knitting, cooking, or doting on her grandchildren. She is an active member of the Green Bay writing community and a proud member of the Green Bay Area Writers Guild and Wisconsin Writers Association.